INSTA-PROPHECY HOTLINE

B.V. Kingsley

Sleepless Decoy Publishing

INSTA-PROPHECY HOTLINE

Copyright © 2016 by B.V. Kingsley
www.BVKingsley.com

ISBN (trade paperback): 978-0-9983627-0-0
ISBN (ebook): 978-0-9983627-1-7

Library of Congress Control Number: 2016918836

This is a work of fiction. Names, characters, businesses, places, events and incidents are either the products of the author's imagination or used in a fictitious manner. Any resemblance to actual persons, living or dead, or actual events is purely coincidental.

Sleepless Decoy Publishing
www.SleeplessDecoyPublishing.com

All rights reserved. No part of this publication may be reproduced, distributed, or transmitted in any form or by any means, including photocopying, recording, or other electronic or mechanical methods, without the prior written permission of the publisher, except in the case of brief quotations embodied in critical reviews and certain other non-commercial uses permitted by copyright law.

Printed in the United States of America.

To Vicki,

You're my best friend, my editor, my cheerleader
and my arch nemesis.

I am damn lucky and even more grateful
to have you in my life.

This is for you.

This is because of you.

Thank you.

THE PROPHECY

Fear not what came before,
but what has yet to come.

Thirteen skulls will gather
amongst the setting sun.

The innocent will lose the fight,
the Red Cross falls to the Eye.

The skulls call to their gods
in their home up in the sky.

The Eye then falls to a skull,
which bears the innocent's face.

She becomes a god herself
and, unlike man, falls not from grace.

The Phoenicians will bear witness
as man makes their final stand.

Yet the war was lost
when they were gathered upon the rocky land.

INSTA-PROPHECY HOTLINE

Insta-Prophecy Series
Book 1

PROLOGUE
NOVEMBER 24, 1971
SOMEWHERE OVER WASHINGTON STATE

Darius Benedict Cooper sat on the Boeing 727 and stared at the half-open briefcase on his lap. It contained road flares and cannibalized radio parts he had passed off as a bomb when he hijacked the plane.

In hindsight, he may have been a little rash.

"How amusing." An elderly woman, the only other passenger, slipped into the seat across the aisle from him. She plopped a floppy purse onto her lap and rested her gnarled, arthritic hands on top of it. "Desperation does not look good on you, Darius."

Her voice exuded the familiar, exotic lilt that had always reminded him of sand and ancient civilizations. It did not, however, match this woman's pale skin, frail body and white hair.

She glanced down in the aisle at four parachutes and a bag containing FBI ransom money. "Jonathan would never have resorted to such dramatics."

"But Jonathan's dead thanks to you." Darius kept his voice flat and emotionless as he buried the pain over the death of his friend and mentor.

The woman leaned towards him and a metallic glint in her eyes flashed in the dim overhead lights. "How long will you last before I break you, too?"

He refused to answer. It took only one look around to conclude he was closer to the precipice than he cared to admit.

"What are you planning, L.G. Man?"

She merely smiled, pulled back the zipper of her purse and caressed the polished obsidian skull inside. It was the very skull he had spent so many years hunting and it was suddenly within reach.

He lunged across the aisle to grab it, but L.G.'s hand shot up out of nowhere and punched him in the throat, hurtling him backwards. She flung her purse over her shoulder and sprang out of her seat with an agility he didn't think possible for the feeble, possessed body.

She snatched a parachute from the aisle and turned towards the back of the plane. Just before she was out of reach, Darius pulled the rip cord and grabbed the unfurling nylon chute. Then he whipped out a knife from the sheath on his ankle and severed the cords.

She hissed and threw down the now useless pack of strings.

Darius took a steady step towards her, confident he had finally trapped L.G. Man. He had finally won.

Her mischievous smirk was his only warning that he was wrong.

She pulled a palm-sized, black metal box from her purse and pointed it at him. The box crackled and two darts with trailing wires shot out of it towards him. They imbedded in his chest and instantly coursed high-voltage electricity throughout his system. Every muscle in his body seized and he slammed to the floor, nearly braining himself on a metal armrest on the way down.

Darius could only watch as L.G. Man dropped the device, zipped up her purse and shuffled the half dozen steps to the back of the plane.

She gripped the handle on the exit door and looked back at him. "I do hope they do not replace you, Darius, because of *this*." She waived her hand around the plane.

"Don't," he said through clenched teeth. "You won't survive the fall."

She shrugged. "Plans change, can you adapt?"

She opened the door and lowered the stairway. Freezing wind screamed into the cabin and the plane pitched violently.

"Bloody hell." Darius ripped the darts from his chest and pulled himself to his feet.

But L.G. Man had already disappeared into the dark.

CHAPTER 1

PRESENT DAY

The sun crested over the hills, lighting up the sky in a soothing blend of oranges, reds and pinks. The birds trilled their morning song and the air was heavy with the smell of ocean brine.

Darius stood in black, silk boxers with one arm braced against the window frame in his bedroom and tried to appreciate the view from the house he no doubt paid good money for. How much, he didn't know since his sister-in-law, Allyanora, took it upon herself to purchase the home for him. It was the result of a one-sided conversation on her part about the downside of living out of a suitcase and hotel rooms. That was two years ago.

Instead of appreciating the peaceful panorama from his home nestled amongst the rolling hills of the exclusive enclave of Carmel, California, he only saw the view for what it was, a restrictive cage meant to lull him into a sense of quiet acquiescence. A punishment for one rash decision made over forty years ago.

He turned away from the view to face his master bedroom. Thanks again to Allyanora, the room was furnished with the bare essentials – a bed, a chair and a dresser with matching nightstands, the surfaces of which remained barren of any photos or mementos he might have acquired during his long, long life.

The only item of his was the battered, black leather suitcase on top of the dresser, its lid haphazardly flipped open to reveal an assortment of his clothes, all in black like his perpetual mood.

He strode towards the bathroom and grabbed a pair of jogging shorts, socks and a t-shirt from the suitcase as he passed. He quickly ran a razor over the night's worth of stubble on his chin and pulled a comb through his dark brown, wavy hair that fell in a tousle over his forehead.

In less than two minutes he was dressed and pulling on his black running shoes that had been neatly placed on the floor next to his California king-sized bed, its comforter thrown back on only one side. He had already complained to Allyanora the bed was too large to be of any convenient use. He invited no one over.

He locked the front door, jogged down the winding driveway, then turned onto the narrow road that led to the summit of the hill on which his estate-like home was situated.

He steadied his breathing and focused his attention on the monotonous labor of his morning ritual. Maybe this day he would manage to exhaust his energy to the point his brain would stop replaying the events that cost him damn near everything.

Why did he have to hijack that plane?

Had he followed protocol and just shadowed L.G. Man, allowing the plane to land in Seattle as scheduled, he might have caught her and her obsidian skull without drawing the undivided attention of the entire nation.

He knew all too well the hazards of being the center of attention. He was a Templar Knight seven hundred years ago during the height of their power when they were forced to hide their existence in order to survive. Since then, they had one rule above all, 'Drift through the world, causing no ripple, drawing no notice.'

And he had to go and bugger it all up.

The Templar hierarchy was able to step in and cover up the truth about 'D.B. Cooper,' but he was benched as punishment for his actions. They told him it was just until the notoriety died down. More than forty years later though, he was still damaged goods in their eyes, volatile and unpredictable.

And with L.G. Man lying low since then, they had no need to put him back in the field.

He ran for two hours, long enough to mentally list every person who had died at L.G. Man's hand since he joined the cause. The list might have grown by now, he didn't know. He tried not to dwell, but he had nothing else to occupy his time.

As the cool, crisp air of dawn burned away, he sprinted back up his sloping driveway lined with Cypress trees. He slowed down to a walk as the driveway flared out to his four-car garage, wiped his brow of sweat and peered at his watch. It was just past nine in the morning.

Christ.

He stepped onto the flagstone walkway that curved around the garage to the front door, then stopped short when he spotted a lone, brown cardboard box on the front stoop.

Double Christ.

If he was a normal man, the innocuous box wouldn't

have been cause for concern. As it was, he didn't get packages, especially delivered to his front door. He had a post office box in town for that.

He surveyed the towering trees, driveway and manicured bushes that surrounded his home. It was no surprise when he found no one lurking.

His heartbeat sped up a notch from the excitement of danger. It was like being out in the field again and he missed the rush.

He crept up to the package and studied it, looking for any trip wires or sensors that would set off something nasty. When he found nothing, he crouched down and with a feather-light touch ran his fingers over the top of the box. His address was printed across it in bold letters, but there was no return address, company logo or even the telltale markings it had been sent through the mail.

He eased the box off the ground. It weighed almost nothing. He raised it to his ear and listened. No ticking, a good, if outdated, marker of a bomb. Still, old habits die hard.

Holding the box in one hand, he pulled out the knife from the sheath always strapped to his ankle and slit the masking tape. The box flaps perked open. He waited for his face to disintegrate from the deployment of some aerosol acid, but again, nothing ominous was triggered.

He peered inside and saw a folded piece of paper. Beneath the paper was a gaudy, silver cuff bracelet with ancient cuneiform writing etched heavily into the flat surface.

He opened the folded piece of paper and froze.

Printed across the stationary was the most recent logo for Insta-Prophecy Hotline. But it wasn't the logo that caught his attention, it was the neat, cursive handwriting below it.

D.B. Cooper,
The wait is over. Do you still think you have it in you to stop me?
L.G. Man

Bloody hell. He wasn't sure what made him more livid, the fact that L.G. was back or that she had used Insta-Prophecy Hotline stationary.

He took the box inside and kicked the door shut behind him. With the note still clutched in his hand, he snatched his phone off the kitchen counter and hit the speed dial.

"Insta-Prophecy Hotline warehouse, how may I direct your call?" A pleasant female voice lilted over the phone.

"Are you now storing or have you ever stored an obsidian skull?"

"Excuse me?"

"An obsidian skull, do you have one?"

"I cannot divulge any objects that may pertain to a current or future prophecy." Her voice took on a guarded edge. "If you have an issue, you can take it up with one of the Seers."

"I'm with the Templar Knights, you will answer the question."

"Oh, well, the Knights. That means absolutely nothing."

"One of your warehouse clerks may already be dead."

Silence met his words. He wanted to punch something out of sheer frustration. So he did. The drywall crumpled around his fist.

"Hold please." There was a perceptible click and then canned, crackly and annoying waiting music blasted over the line.

The music cut off and a breathy voice spoke. "Samantha's dead."

He didn't know Samantha, but that didn't stop her death

from weighing down on him as if he had murdered her himself. He might as well have for all his failures.

He mentally added her name to the list of L.G.'s victims he couldn't save.

Resisting the urge to punch another hole in the wall, he hung up and dialed another number.

"I'm a bit busy." The deep, British-accented voice of his twin brother, Bastian, burst out without so much as a hello.

"Where are you?"

"San Francisco, remember? My wife's attending her Seer's conference. I called you about it last week, informing you we were going to visit you when it was over and, as I recall, you told me to sod off."

"Which hotel?"

"The Sir Francis Drake, why?"

"Because," Darius forced the words out through his tightened jaw, "I'm coming there to throttle your wife."

CHAPTER 2

"I'm sorry, could you repeat that?" Mackenzie almost reached up to clean out her ear with her finger.

"Your services are no longer needed." Mr. Reynard reclined in his throne of a desk chair, with its high-winged back and garish brass embellishments, and steepled his fingers in front of his protruding stomach.

The nickname she gave him behind his back was Mr. Rotund, which she thought of now as she tried to process his words. "You're firing me?"

"That would be the layman's term for it, yes."

"But I'm your personal secretary."

His leering gaze flicked to her crisp white, button-down blouse. Clearly, she wasn't showing enough cleavage if the slight tightening of his lips was any indication. But the cretin was too smart to say it out loud.

"Economic downturn and all that, have to let a few

people go. HR has your severance check and a letter of recommendation for your future endeavors." Mr. Rotund motioned with his sausage fingers towards the door of his office. "Leave your security card at the front desk as you leave."

Five years she had dealt with his subtle sexual harassment shtick, but without tangible proof and with everyone else in the building vying for her job, she put up with it. The pay was just too damn good.

Key word, was.

She pushed herself to her feet and peeled her lips back in what she hoped was a semblance of a smile. "Mr." *Rotund.* "Reynard."

His gaze once again flicked to the front of her blouse.

Yeah, you take one last look you perverted asshat... Her internal lambasting of her former boss continued as she left his office.

Her desk, situated just outside his door, now had the addition of a large, empty box sitting on top of the lacquered wood. It announced her fired status to the rest of the minions working there better than a flickering neon sign.

She could feel the curious gazes of her coworkers and hear their hushed murmurs. She moved the box to her chair and started the process of cleaning out her desk. It drove home the fact that her steady paycheck was now a thing of the past.

Oh, God, she would have to find another job. She wasn't good at interviews. She tended to speak first and think second.

She brushed her copper-colored hair behind her ear and held back the tears that threatened to fall. The vultures wouldn't get any further gossip from her, she had some dignity left.

It didn't take long to pack her things, five long years and

they barely filled the box. She stuffed a stapler, a three-hole puncher and a tape dispenser in for good measure. Not that she needed them, but it eased her indignation at being canned over some downsizing cock-and-bull story.

She flicked off the desk lamp and gave her space one last thorough look-over to make sure she hadn't left anything behind. In reality, she was stalling.

She hoped some of her curious ex-coworkers would go back to their work. Unfortunately, the thirty seconds it took to check and double check her desk drawers didn't do much to lessen their interest.

She heaved the box into her arms, raised her head high and started the walk of shame towards the front of the building.

"I'm sad to see you go," mumbled a pensive coworker from the cubicle closest to her desk. He gave her a look of pity, but she knew all too well what he was thinking, 'I'm glad it's you and not me.'

She didn't answer him, the constriction in her throat prevented that.

"Good luck." A soft-spoken encouragement came from a woman Mackenzie had nicknamed Mrs. Quiet, who barely ever spoke above a whisper and flinched whenever anyone talked too loud.

Mackenzie acknowledged the older woman and picked up her pace. There was one person she hoped to avoid, Queen B, a curvaceous harpy with a superiority complex that would make Napoleon Bonaparte jealous. She had been there for only three months and had managed to spend more time inside her boss's office than out.

Mackenzie had just made it halfway out of the office when the bleach-blonde bombshell blocked her path.

"Such a shame you were fired."

The 'B' in Queen B stood for 'Bitch,' and while that may

sound spiteful and mean, the woman lived up to her nickname in spades.

Mackenzie tried to step around her, but the infuriating woman stepped with her.

"I'm not surprised though." She leaned forward, showing an ample amount of cleavage no push-up bra could ever achieve on Mackenzie. "You were just dead weight around here. Now the job can be filled by someone more qualified."

Mackenzie's fingers curled around the cardboard box as she envisioned pegging the woman in the head with it. Instead, she shoved her way past. "I wonder how long it'll take before you're doing the job on your back."

Two weeks tops.

Queen B sneered.

Scratch that, make it one week.

Mackenzie was a dozen steps away from the main reception area, and her escape, when one of her high-heel shoes decided this was a good time to become a flat and down she went.

The box flew out of her arms. She threw one hand out in front of her falling body and pawed at the water cooler next to her with the other. She grabbed the spigot, but her downward momentum was too much and she snapped it right off.

She swung her other foot out to catch herself and felt, more than heard, the seam at the back of her tight pencil skirt give way. Her epic fall ended with her on her hands and knees.

Mackenzie cringed when the quarter-full water cooler emptied out on top of her from the broken spigot with a glug, glug, glug. She heard a few gasps and one snicker at what she could only assume at this point was her soaking-wet, see-through blouse and exposed panty-clad backside. The only solace she could find in the mortifying event was at least she had worn her good underwear that day.

She hesitated one second, then two, her eyes closed, hoping the universe would take mercy on her and swallow her whole. When nothing happened, she let out a sigh of defeat. Blast her luck.

She grabbed her sweater from the box, wrapped it around her waist and stood. With her back end covered, she turned her attention to her top. There wasn't anything she could do to make her blouse less see-through, but she was relieved by the fact her padded bra hadn't gone transparent as well. With an indignant flip of her now soaked copper hair, she pulled off her traitorous shoes and did her best to make it seem as if none of this was a big deal.

Mrs. Quiet held out Mackenzie's box to her with a faint smile.

What was her name? Mary. "Thank you, Mary."

The woman smiled a little wider, maybe with a smidgen of surprise at the recognition. Mackenzie felt a pang of regret. Why hadn't she ever gone out to lunch with this woman? She seemed nice enough. Mackenzie gave Mary a final nod, tossed her ruined pumps into the box and made a hasty exit, trying her best not to shiver in the air-conditioning.

The HR lady was waiting for her in the lobby reception area. She held out her hand. "Security card."

Mackenzie unclipped the wet plastic card from the waist of her skirt and handed it over.

"Your severance package and letter of recommendation."

Mackenzie took the offered manila envelope and the woman disappeared into the bowels of the building.

"What happened to you?" The dark-skinned, even darker-eyed receptionist gave her soggy appearance a once over.

"Got into a fight with the water cooler."

"Huh." The woman's interest didn't go much further than that. She shoved a clipboard with some papers on it at

Mackenzie. "A package came for you. A personal package. Sign."

Mackenzie took the clipboard and stared at the paper with her name on it.

"I didn't order anything."

"Clearly, you did." She pulled out a plain brown box from underneath the counter.

It was a perfect cube, about a foot all around. Mackenzie's name and work address were scrawled across the top in black felt pen. Other than that, there were no other markings showing where it came from or how it got there. Mackenzie signed the paper and placed the box on top of everything else.

She took one last look around at the place where she had spent the last five years of her life, from the whitewash walls to the soul-sucking gray cubical panels. The stark ambience killed the creative mind and dulled the senses into mindless complacency. Even so, it was hard not to feel a little sad at never seeing it again.

And she would sure miss that paycheck.

CHAPTER 3

Darius barged into the hotel suite at the Sir Francis Drake Hotel using a keycard the front desk clerk had given him without question. Sometimes it paid to be a twin. He stormed into the spacious, richly decorated sitting room that brought back memories of Rococo-era France and found the target of his ire curled up on the couch flipping through a magazine.

"Honey..." Allyanora looked up with a smile. Her light blue eyes were bright and her black curls tumbled around her shoulders in wild abandon. Her smile faded. "Oh, it's you."

He wasn't sure what he wanted more, to strangle her slender neck or shake some sense into her. His hands clenched and unclenched at his sides as he settled for glaring at her in a way that would have made any war-hardened Templar Knight snap to attention.

"Over forty years," he burst out, "and you didn't think I

should know?"

"Whatever are you talking about, Darius?" Her British accent flowed lazily over him as she flicked her magazine shut.

"You know exactly what I'm talking about, L.G. Man's obsidian skull, the entity I've been hunting for the last seven hundred years. Oh, and this." He pulled out the gaudy, silver bracelet from his back pocket and shook it in front of her. "What does this have to do with anything?"

Allyanora tossed the magazine aside, plucked the bracelet from his hand and examined it closer. "Where in the world did you get this?"

The door to the suite opened and Bastian walked in carrying some groceries in a cloth bag and two steaming paper cups in a cardboard drink carrier. "Darling, sometimes I think you like sending me on fruitless errands because I know you knew I wouldn't find— oh, Darius, you're here already."

Bastian and Darius were almost exact copies of each other. Six feet in height, dark brown eyes, wavy dark brown hair, lean muscular build and naturally olive-colored skin from their Roman ancestry. Aside from Allyanora, no one could tell them apart. Their only differences were cosmetic. Darius kept his hair long and a bit unkempt, and preferred to be clean shaven. Bastian tended to have shorter hair and a day's worth of stubble on his chin.

Bastian set the bag down on the counter in the little kitchenette and scrutinized his brother's appearance. "You're wearing black. Still? You're not living in Victorian-era England anymore."

"It's better than khakis and a striped shirt." Darius gave him the once over. "When did you become Charlie Sheen?"

"Honey, I needs me some coffee, otherwise I might just die." Allyanora tossed the bracelet at Darius and skipped towards her husband. Her black curls bounced down her back over her white, ruffled blouse and her many layered skirts flounced about reminding Darius of a gypsy.

Allyanora leaned up on her tip toes, kissed her husband on the cheek and took the paper cup he offered her. She moaned in sheer joy when she sipped the steaming drink. "Perfect. Hey!"

Darius snatched the cup from her hand and held up the bracelet again. "Explain. This. Now."

"Give my wife her coffee back." Bastian moved towards Darius but stopped when Allyanora placed her petite palm on his chest.

"You fight him for it and no one gets coffee, and a cranky Seer means bad news all around. Now, you." She turned on Darius. "How did you get that bracelet?"

"How do you think?"

Realization lit her face and a frown wrinkled her delicate brow. "That's impossible, her skull was locked away. No one should have been exposed to it, except the one to whom it would have been sent. I took precautions."

Darius set the coffee down on an end table and crossed his arms over his chest. "Try explaining it to me again. And this time, don't sound so naïve, it's not becoming."

And there was the bane of the relationship between Insta-Prophecy Hotline and the Templar Knights. Because of their close relationship, the Seers didn't know if their world-ending prophecy included the Knights' meddling beforehand. So, they kept the Templars out of the loop until the last conceivable moment.

Darius called it madness.

Allyanora believed it a necessity.

"I found the skull in the woods. She was supposed to come to me, that was our arrangement. But the plans changed and we adapted."

Darius flinched. "L.G. jumped out of that plane without a parachute at night over a national forest, how in the hell did you find the skull?"

Allyanora tapped her temple. "Sometimes being a Seer has its upside."

"You had no right to keep this from me."

"I had every right," Allyanora snapped.

"No, you didn't." He grabbed her arm and shook her. "It's my job to end this."

"Let her go." Bastian pried Darius's fingers off her.

Allyanora stilled and her eyes unfocused as if she were having a vision.

Which, in fact, she was.

Bastian led his unresponsive wife to the couch and gently eased her down to sit, and she acquiesced. It was a rare sight to see because Darius knew Allyanora did nothing with obedience.

But today was not a day for patience. If need be, he was willing to slap her out of her trance to get the information he wanted.

Bastian straightened and blocked his path as if reading his mind. "Brother or not, you lay another hand on her, so help me..."

Darius grabbed the front of Bastian's shirt. "Because you're my brother, I've shown restraint."

"This is restraint?"

"She should've given me the skull when she found it. And this bracelet—"

"Was discovered by the very Seer who witnessed the prophecy." Allyanora's gaze now focused on Darius, but her eyes held the weary, aged look of someone who'd seen far too much. "The bracelet was supposed to have been sent along with the skull to protect the Chosen from possession."

"Protect?" Darius let go of Bastian and turned the bracelet over in his hands. He didn't think anything could protect a victim from being possessed once targeted by L.G. Man. It felt no different from any other benign, silver object. Aside from the cuneiform writing scrolled across its surface, there wasn't anything that made the bangle stand out, no feeling of power emanating from it, no subtle drawing of awareness. Nothing.

"The girl won't receive the skull until tomorrow, so you needn't worry," said Allyanora.

"Don't tell me what I need to worry about. If I'd known about this sooner, your warehouse clerk would still be alive."

Her face crumbled as if she had lost a close friend. For all Darius knew, she had. She bowed her head in silence, but when the moment passed her head shot up. "Do you know how hard it is to replace warehouse clerks? Most of the ones who apply are spies for Interpol, the Mossad, FBI, CIA, the KGB–"

"The KGB doesn't exist anymore."

"Tell that to them, they're looking to make a comeback. Now, give me the bracelet." She held out her hand.

"Why?"

"Because I think it's time you passed the torch of hunting the skulls to someone else. Maybe Finley should take over for a while."

"I wouldn't wish this burden on him."

"I don't think it wise–" Bastian gave him a pained look of pity.

"Wise?" Darius couldn't stand that look in his twin's eyes. "The skulls have been my responsibility since I joined the damn Templars. They were the reason Jonathan recruited me. I should've been informed the moment the Seers got involved." He looked at Allyanora. "How long has the prophecy existed?"

"Since Nostradamus."

Insta-Prophecy Hotline

"Nostradamus?" Bastian looked at his wife.

Allyanora absently patted him on his arm and stood. "Don't be jealous, honey, I knew him long before our paths crossed." Bastian raised an eyebrow, but she had already turned her attention back to Darius. "Jonathan and I were friends. I watched as his mission tore him apart. By the time Nostradamus had his vision, Jonathan was already gone and you were slowly spiraling down the same self-destructive path."

"I'm not Jonathan."

"Of course you're not, that man was a Spartan, an entirely different creature from the men of your Middle Ages. Yet, the end is always the same. L.G. Man and the hunt for the obsidian skulls have eaten away at you. It's why I took control of the prophecy and kept you out of the loop. Now give me the bracelet."

"If you had just given me her skull, I could have locked her away where no one would have found her. I could have beaten her."

"There's no beating L.G. Man," she scoffed. "Locking her away is the equivalent of putting a band-aid on a festering wound. Eventually she'd break loose. Let me do you a favor, I'll call the Grand Master and request he put another Templar Knight on the task."

The Grand Master was the head of the Knights Templar, his word was law. To disobey, well, it never ended well for the one foolish enough to do so.

Allyanora pulled out her cell phone from a pocket in the fold of her skirt.

"Don't you dare." Darius grabbed her wrist and squeezed until she squeaked in protest.

Bastian fisted his hands in the front of Darius's shirt. "Let go of my wife."

"Down, honey," said Allyanora.

"No, dear."

"Men and their egos." She glared at Darius. "How do you think this will end? You can't destroy the skulls, they're indestructible. You of all people know this."

"I'll stand sentinel over them."

"Forever?"

"Yes."

"Who's the naïve one now?"

Allyanora turned back to her cell phone and tapped away on the touch screen. Darius was tempted to tighten his grip and break her wrist but refrained, even if she deserved it. When she finished, she looked up at him and waited. His cell phone in his pocket beeped, signaling an incoming text.

"I just texted you an address and a name. Consider yourself in the loop. Now be gone before I drop a house on you, too."

He frowned and looked at Bastian who just shrugged. "She's going through a Wizard of Oz phase."

"Right." Darius let go of her, and his brother let go of him. He slid the bracelet into his pocket and headed for the door.

"I know you've counted them." Allyanora's voice made him pause in the doorway. "Everyone who's died since you took over the hunt. The ones you felt you could have saved had you stopped L.G. sooner. Know that counting was the beginning of the end for Jonathan. And his mentor before him."

Darius pulled the door closed behind him, but her words echoed in his mind.

CHAPTER 4

The door shut behind the damned Darius Cooper. Allyanora could see the darkness eating away at his soul, an erosion he cleverly hid beneath a layer of feigned anger. It was the same black aura that surrounded Jonathan at the end.

She knew Darius would never deviate from his chosen path. He was going to die, it was in the prophecy.

Bastian rubbed the small of her back, his calloused fingers trailed goose bumps along her skin as his worried gaze studied her. "My dear?"

She knew without a doubt losing Darius would devastate her husband.

"I'm fine."

"You sure?"

"Bah, stop giving me those puppy dog eyes or I'll rip off your clothes and we'll never make it to the conference." She took a sip of her now lukewarm coffee and set it aside. "You know I'm so very popular at these things. American officials will want to know if the Chinese will call in their exorbitant debt, the Chinese will want to know if the Americans will start a war to avoid paying it back. The North Koreans will demand to know when the world will start to take them seriously. And the Russians always ask when global warming will heat up their sodding country. Busy day ahead."

Bastian let out an exaggerated sigh. "Then take note of the sacrifice I'm making."

"Noted. And later you'll be greatly rewarded." She stood on the tips of her toes and gave him a quick kiss, then danced out of his grasp when he tried to pull her closer. She turned her attention to her cell phone still clutched in her hand. Her fingers danced across the screen as she quickly typed out the obsidian skull prophecy for Darius.

Bastian gave another harried sigh as he walked over to the kitchenette and put the food in the mini-fridge.

Allyanora was almost finished when Bastian spoke. "Um, dear?"

"Hmmm?" She pressed 'send' on the screen and then saw Bastian staring at the small stack of papers she had left on the counter.

Damn.

"You told Darius that L.G.'s skull was being delivered tomorrow?" Bastian already had his phone out.

"That's what I said."

"This paperwork says a courier delivered a package today and you wrote here 'the skull has left the building.'"

She sidled up to him and planted feather-light kisses along his stubbly jaw to distract him. Then she trailed her fingers down his arm and snatched the phone from his hand. With a pirouette she threw the phone against the wall like a professional cricket player.

Bastian glared at his broken phone on the floor and clenched his jaw. "You could have just asked me for it."

"You would have interfered." Allyanora wrapped her arms around his waist and rested her head against his chest. "He's part of the prophecy and there's nothing you can do to spare him from what's to come. He made his choice and now must bear witness to the consequences."

Bastian's muscles stiffened beneath her cheek and she didn't need to see his face to know he was in pain. She wished she could offer him some comfort. The downside for a Seer was they couldn't envision the prophecies divined by other Seers. The magic didn't work that way and she had no idea why.

Allyanora only hoped that maybe, just maybe, Darius would manage to save himself when Jonathan couldn't.

All she and Bastian could do now was wait.

Allyanora wove her fingers through Bastian's and gave him the warmest smile she could manage in hopes of taking even the slightest edge off his worry.

She tugged him towards the door. "Come, love. Before we meet the ambassadors, we must first see a man about an Olmec chicken."

CHAPTER 5

Mackenzie dropped the box from her office just inside her apartment. It landed with a loud 'womp' and teetered onto its side, spilling its contents onto the floor.

Lauren, Mackenzie's best friend and roommate, walked out of her bedroom holding an eyebrow pencil and wearing a scowl.

"Hey, you know how Mr. Morganstein gets when we get too stomp happy." She took one look at the box and her finely shaped eyebrows shot up, her blue eyes wide. "That doesn't look good."

"I got fired." Mackenzie sagged against the front door.

"Girl. That sucks." Lauren disappeared back into her room, but her muffled voice carried out to Mackenzie. "You can't say this isn't a good thing."

"It isn't."

"You really didn't like working there."

"Doesn't mean I wanted to get sacked." Mackenzie nudged the box aside with her toe, crossed the apartment and leaned on the doorway to Lauren's room.

At the moment, Lauren's room of mismatched furniture was a disaster zone containing piles of brightly colored clothes, countless pairs of shoes, fingernail polish bottles and magazines. Lauren stood in front of the mirror that hung over her dresser and applied the finishing touches to her eyes with dark eyeliner.

With her ample bust, tan skin and long, natural-blonde hair, Lauren was a striking contrast to Mackenzie, who, though taller than her friend, had boobs she always felt were on the small side, skin she gave up trying to tan, concluding it just wasn't in her ginger genes, and a build that leaned more on the athletic side than Lauren's slender, waif-like form.

It wasn't that Mackenzie was jealous of her best friend, okay maybe a little, but sometimes life just wasn't fair.

"Come on, 'Kenzie, cheer up. Now you can look for a job you don't hate."

"Like yours?"

"Hey, I like working at the Mystery Spot. I get to be outdoors and watch people make fools of themselves. It's a grand ole time."

It also paid pennies compared to Mackenzie's paycheck. Well, ex-paycheck.

But showing tourists around a vortex in the forest where the laws of gravity wavered made her best friend happy. Mackenzie couldn't help but wonder if her own life wasn't so focused on material goods, she could be happy too.

"Are they hiring?"

Lauren snorted. "You hate the outdoors. The last time you saw a spider, you cowered in the corner of the bathroom with your pants around your ankles and screamed for help."

"That's an over-exaggeration and you know it." An all-out lie on Mackenzie's part. In her defense, the spider was the size of her fist.

"I think the spider was the size of my thumbnail," Lauren added.

"Fine, don't help your friend in need." Then again, Mackenzie was rather fond of her smartphone, laptop, and HD television. She needed a job that paid well enough she could keep her unlimited data plan, high-speed internet and premium cable service, which was a huge step up from Lauren's pay-as-you-go flip phone, no computer, and no TV.

"Don't worry, I have plans for us tonight. Since it's Friday, we're going out. And while guys buy us drinks, you'll forget about losing that stupid job of yours." Lauren put down her eyeliner, picked up a bottle of perfume and sprayed the underside of her wrists. "But first I have to run an errand."

She made it sound like she was going to the dentist for a root canal. Yet, her short skirt and low-cut top said she wanted to turn heads while she was at it.

"Where are you going?"

"Eric's." Lauren fluffed her hair and gave herself one last look over. "We broke up—"

"Again?" How many times did it make this month alone? Mackenzie lost count.

"For good." Lauren huffed and walked out of her room. "I'm just going to pick up my things and this outfit is gonna make him regret being such a tool."

She snatched her purse and keys from the battered dining room table they used more as a junk dump than for actual eating. "I should be back in an hour, so get yourself ready because you and I are gonna have some fun."

"I don't think I'm in the mood to go out and have fun." Mackenzie eyed the refrigerator as a different idea of fun came to mind.

"Oh, no. You're not heating up that chicken pot pie. I don't even know why it's in there." Lauren ran into the kitchen and pulled out the pot pie from the freezer. "I'm taking this with me, and do something with that." She motioned at all of Mackenzie's work stuff, then to Mackenzie's less than pristine form. "Do I even want to know what happened?"

"It'd take too long to explain."

"Right. Talk when I get back. Byes." She waved the chicken pot pie, stepped over the toppled box and walked out the front door.

Mackenzie shook her head. Dancing and drinking wouldn't be enough to dull the full-on anxiety attack she knew was coming. The only thing capable of fighting that off was comfort food.

Like chocolate.

She did have a bag of chocolate hidden in her room, unless Lauren had ferreted it out during one of her many break-ups with Eric. That girl had a nose for chocolate.

Mackenzie went to her toppled box and shoveled the stapler, hole puncher and manila envelope back inside. When she got to the mystery package, she hesitated. She still had no idea what was in it, but that sort of lent it a small tendril of excitement.

She took the box into the kitchen. It weighed a good five pounds and there were no identifying features on any of the sides of the package to hint where it came from.

"Maybe Mr. Rotund got me some chocolate truffles to cry into." She set the box on the counter, pulled scissors from a drawer and cut open the tape. "It would be the only nice thing he ever did, unless he did it to get laid. In that case he's a pig, but I'm still keeping the chocolate. Pervy asshat."

The flaps popped up and she peered inside. White tissue

paper concealed the contents. On top of the tissue paper was a business card. Printed across it was:

Insta-Prophecy Hotline
We see the end of the world, so you don't have to.
1-800-555-7337
(Flip Over to Other Side)

She flipped the card over and squinted at the finest print she had ever seen.

Prophecies dictated do not reflect the views of IPH. Injuries sustained up to, during and in the aftermath of said prophecy are by no means IPH's liability. Side effects upon having your prophecy revealed to you may include nausea, dizziness, severe bouts of anxiety, debilitating laughter, incontinence, denial, fainting, falling into a suddenly forming volcano, spontaneous combustion, snakes on a plane, disappearing into the Bermuda or Dragon's triangle and/or sudden death. This is not a complete list of all side effects that may occur. Please contact your physician before seeking out your prophecy. If you're still reading this, then you've been warned. If you aren't, well, we tried.
Namaste.

"What in the world?" Mackenzie set the card aside and pulled back the tissue paper to reveal what looked like a skull made entirely of polished, black stone.

It seemed to grin up at her as if laughing at a punch line to a joke she couldn't hear. One thing was for certain, Mackenzie hadn't ordered the thing. She didn't much care for skulls, they were far too macabre for her taste.

"Queen B must have sent it for some last idiotic crack

at me."

She went back to the box by the door, dug her phone out of her purse and called the number on the card. Maybe she could return it and get something less ugly.

She re-read the warning label as the phone rang.

"Insta-Prophecy Hotline, we see the end of the world, so you don't have to. Hello Mackenzie, I've been waiting for your call." A soft British voice chimed over the line.

Mackenzie looked over her shoulder towards the living room window of her third-story walk-up. She saw no one, not even the creepy guy who lived on the same level in the apartment across the street. "How—"

"Did I know you were calling?" The woman's voice was the perfect British tone of oh-so-annoying chipper. "Our service is called Insta-Prophecy Hotline, established in three thousand B.C. We've obviously been doing something right."

"Well wooptie freakin' do." The remark tumbled from Mackenzie's mouth before she could stop herself. "I'm sorry, I didn't mean that. It's been a long day."

"Understandable, losing your job and all. So, what can I do for you?"

Mackenzie ignored the tingly feeling that ran down her spine and peered more closely out the window to see if anyone was spying on her with binoculars. She again saw no one and shut the curtains.

"You know that I'm calling, like some sort of stalker, but you don't know why I'm calling? Aren't you supposed to be a psychic or something?

"You're not my case, otherwise I'd have an idea. The Seer responsible for you was busy, so I'm filling in. I do know you have a prophecy that technically hasn't started yet, that's why I have the ability to *see* you. But no, I can't read your mind, I'm not a god."

"You did send a package to my workplace."

"Former work place."

"Stop it. That's really—"

"Freaking you out? You think I'm sitting outside your window using binoculars to spy on you from the building across the street where that creepy guy lives, the one who always seems to be clad in only his knickers. I imagine you want to know if you should hang up and call the coppers, or perhaps invest in some sort of alarm system because you feel violated to the very core of your being, because you're hearing things from me that I could only know if I were actually there. How am I doing so far?"

Mackenzie locked the dead bolt on the front door and proceeded to check all the nooks and crannies that could serve as hiding places. "Surprisingly, spot on."

"I know. Anyway, first off, I'm currently on the east coast, Salem, Massachusetts to be exact, nowhere near Santa Cruz in sunny Nor-Cal. You do call it Nor-Cal, right?"

"Not really." Mackenzie searched Lauren's room for the interloper and found a nice, sharp-looking hunting knife under the bed, which she happily commandeered. She checked her own room, then moved onto the kitchen and living room.

"You can stop searching your apartment. Rest assured I have better things to do than stalk someone who'd rather eat a chicken pot pie than go out dancing in a nightclub with her best friend."

"That's it. Listen here, creeper, I've had just about enough. It's not funny. So, if Lauren put you up to this, know I'm not in the mood. And when I find you—"

"Which you won't."

"You've installed cameras, haven't you?" Mackenzie glared at the closest air vent high on the wall in the dining area. She saw it in a movie once. The bad guy had bugged an entire home by hiding web cams in the vents. She grabbed a

Insta-Prophecy Hotline 33

screwdriver from the junk drawer in the kitchen and dragged a dining chair over to the wall underneath the vent.

The woman on the other side of the line sighed. "Again, if I don't care about your boring, little life, why would I feel the need to watch it?"

"You tell me." Mackenzie started unscrewing the vent cover. "Question, is this phone call coming from inside the house?"

"This is why I never do phone duty. Allyanora owes me so much for covering for her."

"Who?" Mackenzie removed the vent cover and found the air shaft completely empty, except for a surprising amount of dust. She put the cover back on and dragged the chair to the vent in the living room.

Another heavy sigh carried over the line, followed by a clack of something being moved and then the quieter pitter patter of typing. "What was sent to you?"

"Again, you know my name before I even tell you, but you don't know what you weirdoes sent me?"

"What was sent to you?" The woman just repeated.

Mackenzie stomped back into the kitchen where the skull was still grinning in its box. "A skull."

"Skull… An obsidian skull?" The typing got more fervent. "Wooden skull? Or an actual demon's skull?"

"Is obsidian black and look like polished stone?"

"Yes."

"Obsidian it is then."

"Oh yes, Prophecy Number 1553N13." The woman actually tee-heed in delight. "Oh, Allyanora gets all the fun ones."

"Care to read it out loud or am I supposed to guess? Because right now I'm guessing this ugly thing is going to take one long header out the window."

The woman tsked. "Your prophecy was divined by

Nostradamus himself in November of 1553. This was one of the first prophecies he ever wrote. You're quite lucky."

"Right, lucky." The entire situation took a turn from really creepy to downright surreal. "Who's Nostradamus?"

"Do you not have history books in school?"

"America wasn't around in the fifteen hundreds."

"Oh, Americans." She said it like it was a curse. "So self-centered. I wouldn't be surprised if your scientists are trying to figure out a way to make the entire universe revolve around you. I'm talking about world history. You know what, it doesn't matter. Nostradamus was one of the more famous Seers, and a man, which is unusual. It's such a shame he refused to drink from the fountain. Nonetheless, he was one of the best."

"Yaay." Mackenzie really couldn't put much enthusiasm into it. "So, what does it say?"

"Right, let me see, let me see." She cleared her throat and the voice that came over the line next was deep and bone chilling. If Mackenzie believed in such nonsense, she would have thought the voice sounded downright ominous.

> "Fear not what came before,
> but what has yet to come.
>
> Thirteen skulls will gather
> amongst the setting sun.
>
> The innocent will lose the fight,
> the Red Cross falls to the Eye.
>
> The skulls call to their gods
> in their home up in the sky.
>
> The Eye then falls to a skull,

which bears the innocent's face.
She becomes a god herself
and, unlike man, falls not from grace.

The Phoenicians will bear witness
as man makes their final stand.

Yet the war was lost
when they were gathered upon the rocky land."

Silence hung heavy in the air as Mackenzie waited for the punch line. Skulls? Crosses? Eyes? All she needed was some eerie violin music and a cheesy horror-movie villain to make the moment complete.

She glanced around hoping to spot a hidden camera crew.

The woman on the other side of the line cleared her throat and spoke as if she hadn't just thoroughly creeped Mackenzie out. "Nostradamus was particularly troubled by this prophecy because he makes a notation here that says he took special precautions to prevent this vision from coming to pass. He entrusted the Seers with an ancient, silver bracelet he procured while on a trip to Italy. It will protect you against possession, which will happen should you touch the skull without the bracelet securely affixed to your wrist. That being said, Insta-Prophecy Hotline sent you one business card, one obsidian skull capable of possession and one ancient silver bracelet engraved with a cuneiform inscription."

The skull glinted in the artificial overhead lights of the kitchen. Just the skull, nothing else. She pulled the tissue paper free from the box, careful to avoid touching the polished obsidian. There was no bracelet hidden underneath.

"I only have a skull. And the card, obviously."

"I see. Well, I'm sure there's a reason for it. We don't make mistakes. Is there anything else I can do for you?"

Mackenzie found herself nodding as if she understood what the hell was going on. Then she gripped the kitchen counter with a firm hand and refused to go along with this nonsense. "How can I return it? Do I just wish really hard and fairies come and take it away?"

"Oh, you can't return it. Once a prophecy has been delivered to its Chosen One, it cannot be undone. It's on you to prevent this apocalypse."

"Apocalypse?"

"Why yes, what part of 'as man makes their final stand' in the prophecy did you not get?"

"Apocalypse." Somehow she thought if she said it again the word would take on a new definition. It didn't.

"You are at the heart of your very own apocalyptic prophecy. You have my congratulations and condolences."

"But you sent me one skull, not thirteen."

"Then you have nothing to worry about."

"Crackpots," Mackenzie mumbled under her breath because it was the only explanation for this nonsense.

And it was nonsense, she had no doubt.

One question lingered in her mind. "How exactly do you know I'm this Chosen One?"

"Because Nostradamus also wrote down your name, work and home address and a little note in the margin. Hmmm, my medieval French is rusty, but I think it says, 'Eat the chicken pie and you will head down a path of morbid obesity and thirteen cats… who'll murder you one night because you'll decide to switch to a different brand of cat food, which they will whole-heartedly dislike.'"

"What kind of food do I switch them to, cardboard?" Mackenzie made a face of disgust, she wasn't a cat person. At all. "Wait, don't tell me, I don't care. This is mad."

"If that's all then, I'll let you go. Have fun tonight, dance the night away. Jump into the arms of the first man who catches your eye, he'll take you on an adventure of a lifetime. Cheerio."

The line went dead.

"Hello?" Nothing.

She looked at her phone. Did that call just happen? The call log on the illuminated screen said yes, but she hoped no.

She set her phone aside and peered down at the obsidian skull. "A stone skull in a box leads to the apocalypse, with gods, crosses and eyes, oh my." She shoved the box down the kitchen counter until it fell off into the waiting trash bin and then headed towards her bedroom, pulling at her ruined outfit along the way. "Prank call. Elaborate, freaky, prank call."

One garbage run and she could forget the last twenty minutes ever happened. She could stop being freaked out.

A shiver ran through her body and she shook herself. She couldn't believe she was afraid of some nut-job on the phone and a skull-shaped paperweight in the kitchen. She spun around and marched back to the trash bin.

"Touch the skull and get possessed, my ass." She wanted the creepy feeling to go away and the best way to do that was to prove the nutter wrong.

She pulled the box out of the trash, slammed it down on the counter and reached inside.

The black stone was cool to the touch.

CHAPTER 6

"Well that took longer than expected." Lauren slammed the front door and dropped something heavy on the hardwood floor.

The noise yanked Mackenzie out of whatever daze she was in.

She blinked a few times until she was able to focus on a hand holding up the creepy obsidian skull right in front of her face like some Gothic Christmas ornament.

To make things worse, the hand that held the skull was hers. Her issue with that was she had no memory of pulling the skull from the box.

Lauren's clicking, high-heeled footfalls stopped in the kitchen. "Um, should I be worried you're reenacting Hamlet?"

"That is the question." Mackenzie dropped the skull back into the box and shoved it to the corner of the kitchen

Insta-Prophecy Hotline 39

counter. "So, how's Eric?"

"He wanted some post break-up slap and tickle." With a huff, she rested a hand on her hip and examined the nails of her other hand. "And I had the satisfaction of saying 'oh, hell no.' But I stayed a while because it boosts my ego to hear a grown man beg."

"What really happened?"

Lauren dropped her hand. "He thought I was coming back for some make-up sex and made some half-assed attempt at fondling my boobs. It took two good smacks upside his head to make him to realize I wasn't there for that."

"Men."

"What can I do? Douche-bag guys with gorgeous bodies are my weakness. I'm not proud of it, it just happens. Why can't I fall for the boy-next-door type?"

"Because, and I quote, 'they're too nice.'"

Lauren let out a groan. "There's something so sexy about a man who can grab you and just... Well, you wouldn't know. You always go for the sweet ones." With a dismissive wave of her hand, Lauren walked through the kitchen and headed towards her room. "Give me a few minutes and I'll be ready to go out, too."

"Too?" Mackenzie looked down.

Gone was her rumpled work shirt and torn black skirt. In their place was a corset top made of faux leather and a tight, fitted skirt that molded to her assets like a second skin. She bought the thing two years ago on a dare and shoved it so far back in her closet she half-expected it to be in Narnia by now. She even had on her favorite pair of high-heeled, black-leather ankle boots she saved for special occasions.

Mackenzie half-ran, half-staggered to the mirror that hung on the wall next to the front door and discovered her hair and make-up were done, too, and quite impressively at that. She had a green, smokey-eyed look that complimented her hazel eyes. Her red hair no longer hung lifeless and limp, but cascaded over her shoulders in a sexy, tousled look she could never manage on her own. All in all, she looked hot, except for the disturbed expression on her face.

"Um, Lauren? How long were you gone?" Mackenzie yelled over her shoulder.

"About two hours."

"Well, that's not good." If it were possible, her already pale skin looked a shade whiter. "It has to be stress."

💀

Mackenzie and Lauren filled the ten-minute drive to downtown Santa Cruz with blaring music and off-key singing, which to Mackenzie's relief distracted her best friend from asking questions about the skull she left sitting on their kitchen counter.

Mackenzie parked her small, fifteen-year-old Subaru in a two-story parking garage smack dab in the center of downtown.

It was already nine o'clock when they sauntered down the main drag. The shops were all closed, but that didn't deaden the thrumming pulse of life that congregated there. It just meant the more eclectic side of Santa Cruz had come out to play.

Hipsters, hippies, Goths, surfers, preppies and the idiosyncratic few who blended all the looks together in one confusing mess mingled together in effortless abandon. That they were able to do so without conflict was probably due to the copious amounts of marijuana ingested one way or another. Either way, Mackenzie's hometown was one of a kind.

She and Lauren walked a handful of blocks towards a

local club called the Maroon Room. Lauren droned on about... well, something, Mackenzie wasn't sure. She was preoccupied with telling herself everything was okay, normal even.

"I mean, come on, like I'd believe that?" Lauren looked at her in question.

Mackenzie trained her features into what she hoped was a scoff and bluffed. "No, of course not."

"Exactly." Lauren wrapped an arm around her. "You know, once we get some liquor in you, things will look up."

They turned the corner and Mackenzie felt an acute awareness that someone was watching her. The small hairs all over her body stood on end and she looked over her shoulder.

Down the street to her left, an impromptu street party was taking place next to an old, silver van with techno music blasting out of large speakers on its roof. More than a few people were jumping around and slamming metal trash can lids together. Some even wore animal masks and gyrated to the music. To her right, two street performers sat cross-legged and played their guitars while a couple made out on the street corner.

There was nothing out of the ordinary and yet she couldn't shake the paranoid feeling she was being watched.

Lauren opened the red painted door of the club. "What's wrong?"

"Nothing." A lie. Mackenzie feared she was losing her sanity.

CHAPTER 7

Darius kept to the shadows and did his best to avoid the swinging metal trash can lids. He was tempted to snatch the flailing metal disks from the dancers before they bludgeoned each other to death. Instead, he stayed on task and continued to tail his target.

He had yet to determine which of the two girls was Mackenzie, so he made an educated guess and chose the shorter, blonde woman. Darius could count on both hands the times L.G. Man had chosen victims that weren't blonde, but those, of course, were only the times when he had gotten close enough to see the poor innocent she had possessed.

So, he tried to focus on the blonde, but his attention kept drifting to the taller redhead, whose outfit, he thought, was just like a present waiting to be unwrapped. Her skirt revealed just enough of her pale legs to tease his senses, and it hugged the roundness of her backside in a way that left him imagining how her curves would hug him.

He lost sight of them when they disappeared through the red double doors of the Maroon Room, its sign overhead lit by a single, exposed red light. He dashed across the street, slipped through the doors and up the carpeted staircase, following the bass-heavy dance music that permeated the air around him. When he reached the archway leading to the main room of the club, he was forced to stop.

The room was packed. He couldn't stand, let alone move, without getting up close and personal with about five strangers at once. The lighting accentuated the shadows, instead of illuminating them, and distorted people's faces, making it almost impossible to find the blonde and her delectable friend.

No, not delectable, she was just another woman. One he would never meet or even touch. His only job that evening was to secure the bracelet around Mackenzie's wrist, thereby saving her life, and leave. Sometime tomorrow, L.G.'s skull would be delivered and he'd intercept it. He would redeem himself and at long last move on. The plan did not include indulging his desire in getting to know the redhead. Intimately.

There was a flash of blonde to his left. Nope, not the right one. Another blonde bumped into his side. Still not his target.

He ran his thumb over the cool metal of the bracelet in his pocket. No matter how long he held it, it never got warm.

A streak of red caught his eye, he honed in on it like a heat-seeking missile. She was exactly whom he was looking for. No, he corrected himself, the one he was looking for was the blonde who stood next to her. His attention, however, refused to deviate as he pushed his way through the pulsing sea of bodies.

'Red,' that's what he would call her because 'the blonde's

friend' didn't quite fit.

The two women downed two shots each at the bar before he could get within reach. He had the bracelet in his hand, ready to attach the thing to the blonde's wrist.

But Red stopped him.

Not with anything she did, she didn't even know he stood there getting jostled by the crowd. She just looked distracted, frowning as she tried to appear somewhat interested in what the man on her right was yelling to her over the booming music.

Darius's self-imposed exile from civilization must have had some ill effect, because right then he changed his plan from get in and get out, to stay and linger a bit. The blonde looked like she would be occupied for a while with the guy she was flirting with anyway, so he moved Red to the top of his to-do list.

He closed the distance to the bar and stepped between Red and her uninteresting suitor. He could have pretended to order a drink, faked a polite conversation with her like anyone would do when they bumped into a stranger at a bar, but when her gaze rose to meet his, whatever ploy he devised to break the proverbial ice died.

CHAPTER 8

He had piercing brown eyes, like chocolate, Mackenzie thought. One thing was for certain, he was out of place in the Maroon Room.

As eclectic as her hometown crowd was, there was something about the tall, lean, dark-haired man that set him apart from everyone else. Yeah, there were a few others matching his physical description, but he had an aura about him that wrapped around her and drew her in.

She was gawking and judging by the smirk that pulled at his lips, he had caught her at it.

Still she gawked on, unabashed.

"Mackenzie," Lauren shouted over the blaring music.

The spell broken, Mr. Choco-Eyes looked over at Lauren with a jolt and Mackenzie heaved an internal sigh. It had been fun the whole three seconds when all he noticed was her. She would look back on it fondly as she added him to the list of Lauren's admirers.

"Mackenzie." Lauren pushed another shot glass into her hand with a teeth-flashing smile that should have lit up the dark room. "Shawn and Zack here bought us drinks. They're surfers." She giggled as if that was a huge plus.

'Surfer,' in Mackenzie's dictionary meant broke and self-involved. Neither of them held a candle to Mr. Choco-Eyes, who in the end would easily win the 'who gets to go home with Lauren' challenge.

Mackenzie offered a wan smile to the two bleach-blonde-headed men, who were at that moment trying to look down her friend's low-cut top.

"Screw it." Mackenzie tossed back the vodka shot, bit back the bitter taste of defeat and slammed the shot glass on the bar.

First she got fired, next she had a weird-ass phone call from a crazy-ass woman who claimed to foresee the apocalypse and then two whole hours vanished from her memories. Now, the hottest guy in the room had given her a grand total of three seconds of his attention before moving on to her hotter and sexier best friend. She was done, she had enough.

Screw men, screw life, she was just going to dance.

Which was exactly what the psychic predicted.

Screw psychics too, what did they know?

She pushed away from the bar and made a beeline for the postage-stamp-sized dance floor. With every shove and weave she made through the crowd, the bass of the music flowed through her. The tension that had been building up, the stress, the worry and disappointment, ebbed away. By the time she reached the center of the room, her muscles had relaxed and she started to move with the beat.

Her hips swayed, her head bobbed. It didn't matter she danced like a white girl, all that mattered was she felt good

Insta-Prophecy Hotline

doing it.

The song changed and she opened her eyes that had drifted shut to find that Lauren had joined her on the dance floor with someone other than Mr. Choco-Eyes.

She did a double take. Who in their right mind would pass up a chance with him?

Before she could yell the outrageous question to her friend, the crowd surged like a tidal wave. Lauren was pushed into her and Mackenzie was jettisoned off the dance floor. Her ankle rolled, her arms flung out, accidently smacking someone in the back, and down she went for the second time that day.

She barely had a chance to envision getting trampled by the crowd when a strong arm caught her around her waist and pulled her up against the brick wall of his chest. A chest that felt absolutely fabulous under her splayed fingers.

She looked up to find Mr. Choco-Eyes staring down at her with an intensity that should have disintegrated her bra, or at the very least unsnapped it. Blame it on the alcohol, but she was damn well tempted to stay in his arms and let him 'take her on an adventure of a lifetime.'

"You okay?" Lauren yelled and was barely heard.

He easily righted her and his gaze bored into hers as if he searched for something in them, but what, she had no idea.

"I'm fine." She pushed off his chest, but then flinched when her ankle flared in protest.

"You're hurt." It wasn't Lauren who spoke this time, it was the gravelly, low voice of Mr. Choco-Eyes, right in her ear. She felt the stubble that darkened his chin brush against her cheek and it sent the most pleasurable tingle down her spine.

"You twisted your ankle, Mackenzie," Lauren said with obvious mock concern as she studied Mr. Choco Eyes from head to toe. "Could you help her find a seat? I would, but

I'm... busy?"

Subtle, Lauren, really subtle.

Mackenzie wanted to be embarrassed that her friend just voluntold a random stranger to help her. But, the temptation of holding Mr. Choco-Eyes's attention for a little while longer was too much to pass up. Luckily for her, he wasn't against it, either.

His arm locked around her waist again, easing some of the weight off her ankle, and they ventured away from the crowd to look for a seat.

Unfortunately, what seats they could find were already overflowing, literally. People were sitting on each other's laps or balanced on the arms of chairs and sofas, filling every available flat surface.

They ended up in a dark corner away from the dance floor. She leaned against the wall and he stood in front of her like a bodyguard against the intoxicated crowd. It was kind of nice and chivalrous of him.

"So, you're Mackenzie?"

Wait, was that a hint of a British accent she heard over the music? Drool.

She nodded. "What's your name?"

He was silent as he studied her, measuring her up, probably against Lauren.

He leaned in and his lips brushed the shell of her ear. "Darius."

Such a sexy name.

"How's your ankle?"

"Feachy." Mackenzie winced. Fine, or peachy, would have worked, but no, she had to combine the two like an idiot.

Her self-reprimand was cut short when she felt Darius nibble on her earlobe.

His hand trailed lightly down her left arm and every nerve

Insta-Prophecy Hotline

in her body came alive and cheered, like Super Bowl Sunday when the crowd favorite scored the winning touchdown.

He nibbled her ear again and she stopped breathing.

She turned her head towards him, determined to kiss the man. No, not just any man, Darius.

She was a mere hair's breadth away from a touchdown of her own when something cold and hard locked around her left wrist.

She looked down to find an ugly-looking cuff bracelet with triangular, blocky symbols etched across the surface. A bracelet decorated like the one the psychic described, the one that was supposed to have been sent with the obsidian skull.

"No, no, no." Her chest constricted, her vision tunneled and in a span of a single second Darius went from possible endurance-testing one-night stand to predator.

It felt like someone turned the volume up on the booming speakers, sucked the air out of the room and added a few hundred more people to the already overflowing club.

"Macken—"

"Take it off."

He was quiet for a second. "No."

"I'm not asking."

"It's still no."

Her fingers tugged at the cold metal, but it didn't budge.

Darius stood too close. Her fight or flight instincts warred with each other as he blocked her in, trapping her in the dark, unseen corner of the club.

She slammed her knee into his groin and air left his lungs with a grunt. She shoved past him and limped into the crowd towards Lauren, who was back at the bar talking to some new guy.

She grabbed her best friend's arm and tugged her towards the door. "We're leaving. Now."

Whatever expression Mackenzie had on her face was

enough for Lauren to abandon her current conquest, take the lead and sucker punch any poor soul who dared block their escape. Mackenzie burst out the double doors onto the street and gasped for much needed air.

"What happened?" Lauren yelled in the calm, near silence of the street.

"This." Mackenzie raised her left wrist and flashed the bracelet.

"He gave you that?" Lauren squinted at it. "I didn't know he was a weirdo."

It wasn't like Mackenzie did either. She was just lucky she found out the truth before she did anything too stupid, like take him home with her, or worse, go home with him.

They power walked in their heels back to the car. Darius, to her relief, didn't follow, but the night was already ruined and she wished she had just settled for the chicken pot pie. While it may have led down a path to a thousand cats, it wouldn't have destroyed her sense of reality.

They had just entered the parking garage when Mackenzie's equilibrium tilted on its axis and she stumbled into a concrete pillar.

"You all right?" Lauren sounded worried.

Mackenzie couldn't answer because her world spun again and then it all went black.

CHAPTER 9

Mackenzie woke up slumped over her dining room table with her head pillowed in her arms. She had no idea how she got home last night, but she knew she owed Lauren a very big thank you for saving her sorry ass.

Mackenzie's back popped as she stretched and massaged the mother of all kinks from her neck. Next time, she would have to insist Lauren drop her off on her bed or at the very least on the couch.

Her mouth was dry and her eyelids heavy, though they weren't too heavy to miss the small, black velvet drawstring bag on the table in front of her. The finery of the bag was out of place amongst the sloppy piles of mail and old magazines, and she had no idea where it came from.

She reached out to pick it up when she noticed the flat, silver cuff bracelet shackled to her left wrist and the events of the previous night came rushing back in panoramic, high-def clarity.

"Crap-ola." The crazy psychic and the all too good-looking Darius weren't figments of her imagination.

She tried to wrench the thing off her wrist. She could see the delicate-looking hinges where the bracelet would normally open, yet no matter how many times she yanked and pulled, it simply wouldn't come off. Her wrist started to ache from the abuse and she was forced to stop.

"This isn't happening," she whispered to herself and ran her fingers through her hair.

She felt something slide down her scalp, then heard a rustle as all her hair slipped off her head and fell to the floor. She froze and her focus stayed on the velvet bag as an image of her bald head filled her still sleep-fogged mind.

She took two, long, calming breaths before she dared look down. Instead of a pile of her long red hair on the floor, she saw what looked like a shoulder-length, blonde-haired wig.

"What the hell?"

Mackenzie didn't own a wig and Lauren already had blonde hair, so she didn't borrow it from her. And just like when she had changed clothes and done her make-up to go to the club, she tried to think back, but found that her memories ended when she stumbled in the parking garage. A gap of time where she was out and about doing God knows what in a blonde wig.

She slumped back into her seat and looked down at the black velvet bag on the table. It sat on top of a flat, black piece of felt. She lifted the bag and uncovered a small pile of what looked like finely cut rubies, sapphires and emeralds.

"What the double hell?" She picked up what she assumed was an emerald and held it up to the light.

It looked real enough, but what did she know? Someone could have handed her a piece of green glass and she would have thought it was an emerald, which was obviously what she was looking at now. Glass, nothing more.

She dropped it back onto the pile of stones and flipped the velvet bag over. Printed in neat gold letters across it was 'Tucker's Jewelry.'

She knew that store. It was a few blocks down from the Maroon Room. A quiet, ritzy boutique with a price tag to match their exclusive, one-of-a-kind baubles.

A shiver ran down her spine. Not at all like the shiver she felt with Darius before he turned into a lunatic. No, this was much like a shiver a person gets when they find themselves waist deep in sludge.

This had to be some sort of mistake. Her smart phone lay next to the pile of apparent stolen gems, key word stolen, because hello, she was jobless and broke. Of course, that had to be wrong, too. She wasn't a thief.

The problem was she didn't own a velvet bag from Tucker's Jewelry or a pile of glass rocks.

"This is crazy." She could settle this nonsense with one internet search.

Mackenzie grabbed her phone, turned on the screen and needed to go no further. Her new lock-screen photo had been changed from a picture of a baby turtle trying to eat a strawberry twice its size to a selfie of a blonde-wigged version of herself holding up the Tucker's Jewelry bag next to an open safe. What made things worse, if that was possible, was the coy little smile on her blonde self

"What the frak?" The phone slipped through her fingers and clattered onto the table.

There had to be a reasonable explanation. It was a prank, that was it.

With shaking hands, she pushed the gems into the velvet bag as if hiding them from sight would make this moment less horrific. She left the bag next to her phone and backed away from the table.

Something moved in the corner of her eye. She jumped to the side and raised her fists to attack whoever it was head on. It took her a second to realize the movement was Lauren, who was currently hog-tied and gagged with a scarf in the middle of the living room with her back to her. Lauren grunted something through the gag as she struggled against the scarves binding her feet and wrists.

Mackenzie grabbed the scissors from the kitchen and then froze. Her heart pounded as she held her breath and listened for anything to indicate there might be someone else in the apartment.

Even though she heard nothing, her muscles tightened further. She and Lauren needed to get out of there and figure out what was going on and who was responsible.

She rushed to her friend's side and cut through the scarves.

Freed, Lauren yanked the gag out of her mouth and let out a battle cry. The next thing Mackenzie knew the scissors were slapped out of her hands and she was pinned on her back with Lauren on top glaring down at her.

"Who are you and what have you done with Mackenzie?"

"What kind of question is that?"

"You look like her, but whoever you are—"

"I'm Mackenzie, your best friend." She struggled to get free, but Lauren had the advantage of being on top and the rage to back it up.

"You're not Mackenzie. She would never attack me and tie me up."

"Clearly, I was drunk."

"Well, when I'm drunk, I don't tie up my best friend, throw her in the back seat of the car and then go rob a jewelry store. Answer me this, am I your best friend?"

"Get off me you fat cow."

Lauren glared. "Am I or am I not talking to the thing that possessed Mackenzie?"

"If I was possessed, do you think I'd tell you?"

Lauren paused and mulled that over for a minute.

Mackenzie thrashed about, trying to get free and failing. "Seriously, if you don't get off me, I'm going to shove my foot so far up your ass, you're going to be spitting out my toenails for a week."

"Mackenzie, so good of you to show up. I'm sorry, but I'm going to have to tie you up now."

"Like hell." Mackenzie bucked Lauren off her and crab-walked backwards until she bumped into the couch. "Getting possessed isn't a thing, you know."

"No?" Lauren grabbed the laptop from the coffee table and turned it on. "Do you remember what happened after we reached your car?"

"Sort of."

Lauren glared at her.

"No, I don't. Happy?"

"Well, you got weird. You spoke in this strange accent and your eyes were all... glint-y. I thought the alcohol had just hit you until..." Lauren started typing, casting Mackenzie looks every other key stroke as if to make sure Mackenzie stayed Mackenzie. "... you robbed Tucker's Jewelry store."

"Impossible." Mackenzie hoped.

Lauren turned the laptop around and plastered across the screen was a news article with the headline "Burglary at Tucker's Jewelry. $5 Million in Jewels Stolen. Possible Satanic Symbol Left Behind."

Taking up half the screen was a single, pixilated, black-and-white photo that looked like it had been pulled directly from an old security camera. It was of a woman clad in a corset top and a tight skirt, Mackenzie's outfit she wore to the Maroon Room. Even pixilated she could tell that. The woman also wore big, bug-eyed sunglasses that hid most of her face, the very sunglasses Mackenzie kept in her car, and shoulder-length, blonde hair, the same as the wig she woke up in.

"I didn't do this. I couldn't. I don't rob jewelry stores nor do I know any satanic symbols."

A loud banging on the front door made them both jump.

"Mackenzie." Darius's British-accented voice carried through the door, followed by more pounding.

"It's the weirdo." When Lauren looked confused, Mackenzie raised up her wrist with the bracelet attached.

"How does he know where we live? I'm calling the cops."

"No!" Mackenzie scrambled to her feet and threw herself at the cordless phone on the kitchen counter before Lauren could reach it. "We're currently holding five million dollars in stolen gems and you want to call the cops, are you insane?"

"Mackenzie, open the door!" Darius yelled.

She dashed to the entryway and flung the front door open. "What do you—"

Darius was on her and kicking the door shut behind him before she could finish the sentence.

She tried to shove him off, regretting her idiotic mistake to open the door in the first place. He grabbed her wrists and trapped them in one hand above her head.

He grabbed her chin with his other hand and angled her head so he could peer directly into her eyes. She still hadn't the foggiest idea what he was looking for.

His eyes widened as if surprised by what he found. "You're clear."

"Stay away from my best friend!" Lauren came out of nowhere, swinging a frying pan at his head.

Darius ducked and missed being clocked by the Teflon-coated weapon. He grabbed Lauren's wrist as she made another swing, pulled her to him and peered into her eyes.

"You're clear, too." He pried the pan from her fingers and let her go. "But the symbol at the jewelry store had to have been done by L.G. Man."

"Well our initials aren't L or G, nor are we men." Mackenzie moved next to Lauren, hoping a combined front would even the odds against him. Lauren sidestepped away from her with a frown.

"Have you already received an obsidian skull?" Darius demanded.

"You mean this?" Lauren dashed into the kitchen and came out holding the box containing the skull. "I came home yesterday and found her holding it."

"You had to touch it, didn't you?"

"Well." Mackenzie crossed her arms over her chest. "You would too, if a screwball claiming to be a psychic goes off on a tangent about prophecies and the end of the world."

"And your opinion now?"

"I may have under-appreciated the warning." Not that she was willing to admit the psychic was right.

"It still doesn't make sense. Neither of you show signs of being possessed." Darius frowned as he took the box from Lauren.

"I don't?" Mackenzie let stupid hope pepper her fear.

Lauren snorted. "She has five million dollars in stolen jewels that say you're wrong."

That got his attention. "Show me."

CHAPTER 10

Darius hung onto the box with the obsidian skull and made sure to keep both girls in his sights as Lauren led the way through the kitchen to the dining area.

Neither girl displayed L.G. Man's telltale sign of possession, a metallic glint in their eyes, nor did they have L.G. Man's exotic accent or homicidal tendencies. All those traits were present in every possessed victim he had encountered during his seven hundred years of hunting the entity and her skulls.

Something wasn't right.

The dining area off the kitchen was small and homey. There were family pictures hanging on the walls and knick-knacks picked up over time adorning a tall, red display cabinet that stood next to a large window with closed blinds.

His attention was drawn, however, to the cluttered table Lauren motioned towards. A small area was cleared off and in the center was a small bag with Tucker's Jewelry embossed on it. It just didn't make sense. Their eyes were clear, so why was it there?

He reached out towards the velvet bag when a knife sank through his hand and into the wood table underneath.

He barked out a yell more out of surprise than pain as a pale, freckled hand snatched the bag of gems off the table mere inches from his fingertips. He saw Mackenzie wave another, bigger knife at him as she backed away.

"Darius," said L.G. Man from Mackenzie's lips, her hazel eyes now glinting in that inhuman way and her accent weighing heavily on Mackenzie's vocal cords, making her voice deep and sultry.

"That's the voice I heard last night." Lauren yelled from where she was pressed against the wall next to the red cabinet.

Darius set the box with L.G.'s skull on the table out of her reach. "But your eyes."

"These?" She pointed towards her eyes. They shimmered and faded until they were just plain hazel, not a glint of silver metallic in them whatsoever. "Human bodies are so malleable. I can control them at will."

"And your acting."

"Acting?" L.G. smiled. "Do not insult me. This is the first time in a long while where I have let the host's soul linger."

"If you kill her, I'll kill you," Lauren yelled.

L.G. ignored her.

All these years and the host had never survived L.G.'s initial possession. Darius just assumed it was because the human body couldn't hold its soul and L.G.'s at the same time. He should have known L.G. had the ability to save the host if she wanted to.

Darius grabbed the handle of the knife embedded in his hand then stilled when L.G. stepped forward and pressed her larger knife against his throat.

"Ah, ah, ah, not yet. I have plans for you, so be a good boy and stay."

"If I don't?"

"You have had seven skulls for so long, now you have eight." She looked over at her skull nestled in the cardboard box. "How would you like to finally have them all?"

"You're just going to give them to me?" He couldn't keep the sarcasm at bay.

L.G. shrugged. "It is better than the Illuminati having them. And as long as there is one skull unaccounted for, they will always be a threat. There is also that prophecy guaranteeing a complete set."

She had him there. He eased his fingers from the knife embedded in his hand and the knife at his throat was removed.

L.G. backed away with the black velvet bag of gems clutched in her hand. "Good boy."

"Don't patronize me, L.G., I can end this here." He had a gun under his jacket.

A coy smile played at her lips. "Ah, but the temptation of acquiring the whole set is far too tempting for you, and all you have to do is keep up." She tossed the bag in the air and caught it. "Aside from my skull, another skull is about to come straight to you."

"That would be a first."

"I know." She winked. "I am almost making it too easy."

"I feel like I'm stuck in a Stephen King novel," Lauren mumbled to no one in particular.

"The symbol I left in the jewelry store will get the Illuminati's attention. It is also a cipher that will lead them right here. I am surprised they are not here already. They are not as sharp as they used to be."

The symbol she left on the wall next to the safe was a

lesser known symbol for the Illuminati, one Darius was quite familiar with. The cipher, however, he didn't catch, though admittedly he wasn't really looking.

"Why would the Illuminati bring a skull here?"

"Because they have one and they are as impatient as I am to find the rest. They are also the reason I need you."

L.G. Man asking for help? Something was going on and Darius needed to think.

He took a deep breath and focused past the pain in his hand. He shouldn't get greedy. He had the skull he wanted, the one that really posed a threat to the world. L.G.'s skull was the only one that could possess anyone who touched it, except for the Templar Knights and the Seers, who seemed immune to the invasion. Everyone else was fair game.

With her skull he could end it there, walk away and disappear, making sure L.G. would never surface again, because without her, the other twelve skulls were just indestructible stone that looked like obsidian.

His free hand twitched to grab his gun. It would be one more life on the list, but it would be the last.

He could handle one more, couldn't he?

As if reading his thoughts, L.G. gave him a smile that didn't reach her eyes and the temperature in the room plummeted ten degrees. "Kill me and this host dies."

"She's already dead." While Mackenzie may have survived the initial possession, he had no idea how to get L.G. out. What he did know was that whenever L.G. left her victim, the host body always died.

"Oh, she will not survive me, that is not what I meant. I will not merely kill her as I have all the others. If you do not help me, Darius, I will shred this soul apart, piece by piece."

The false smile fell away. Left behind was a look of pure evil with no ounce of human compassion. "Unlike all the others before her, there will be nothing left of her soul to go to the afterlife, she will cease to exist. Can you bear the weight of her permanent demise on your shoulders? They are drooping so low already. And just because you have my skull does not mean the Illuminati will stop coming after it and the others."

She was playing him somehow.

He felt blood trail down his hand to the table. He could play her too, and he would win because he now had eight of the thirteen skulls. The prophecy was over before it had begun.

Darius moved his free hand and placed it on the table. He grit his teeth and didn't speak. Anything coming out of his mouth at this point would be nothing but a strong and steady stream of profanities.

"Will you fail her like you did Jonathan?" she asked.

"I didn't fail Jonathan."

"You did fail him. I broke him and you failed to see it." L.G. gave him a knowing grin and Darius looked away.

He didn't want to see the victory on her face. She hadn't won. Not yet.

Suddenly, L.G.'s playful smirk was back. "How about we make a game of it? It can last seconds or months, it is up to you. I will start at ten and count down. Should I get to the point where I eviscerate her soul, our cooperation ends."

A faint sound of sirens interrupted his response. They were quiet but grew louder as they neared.

"Good, they have figured it out."

By 'they,' he assumed she meant the Illuminati. Like the Templars, they had infiltrated governments all over the world. Unlike the Templars, their motives were self-serving, to the extreme detriment of mankind.

"Ten, Darius, ten." L.G. spun around, walked through the kitchen and disappeared out the front door.

"Wait." Lauren snapped out of her stunned silence and

ran after her. "No one is destroying anyone's soul."

"Lauren, stop." Darius pulled the knife from his hand, biting back the pain.

Lauren stopped in the open doorway and looked back at him, her eyes white-rimmed in fear. She looked lost and angry, like any normal person would when faced with overwhelming circumstances. He had seen that expression a thousand times before.

He liked letting L.G. leave about as much as she did, but this time it was different. She couldn't jump bodies, he had her skull. And for now that had to be enough.

CHAPTER 11

Darius stared at his phone and read the most recent text from L.G. Man. 'Do not make me stab you in the hand again, Darius.'

In the day that had passed since he last saw her, he had managed to steal the obsidian skull from the Illuminati, spirit Lauren away from her apartment just before the Illuminati blew it up in retaliation, and read a copy of a hacked Illuminati email that not only sanctioned the manhunt for Mackenzie for obvious reasons, but for Lauren too, by association.

"You know, staring at the phone won't make it ring." Lauren sat next to him in the back of a town car as they made their way through the rural roads outside Salem, Massachusetts.

Lauren, unlike most women, had an indefinable character that made him want to reach out and steady her soul before she drifted away. She was a literal free spirit and on some spiritual level Lauren called to him, yet it was Mackenzie he couldn't get out of his mind.

Darius clutched the phone tighter in his hand. "For a friend, you should be more concerned."

"I am." Lauren turned to face him. "And if I thought it would help, I'd raze the entire world to the ground to get my best friend back."

Lauren's calm serenity vanished and a well of untapped anger kindled just beneath the surface of her blue eyes.

"But that won't help, will it?" Her voice calmed, belying the storm that brewed. "I can't do anything, but I know you can."

His phone rang and seeing who it was, he answered it with a sigh.

"The Grand Master wants your head for letting her go." Bastian's voice carried over the line.

"Put your wife on."

"You know as well as I, she couldn't have interfered."

"She interfered quite enough."

"Please tell me you at least have L.G.'s skull."

"Of course."

"Then why let L.G. walk away?"

"The victim, Mackenzie, is alive."

"You're mistaken."

"I can assure you I'm not." Darius couldn't forget the fire of pure outrage that damn near made her glow in the shadows of the nightclub when he gave her the bracelet, or her fear that followed in her apartment. L.G. was good, but she wasn't capable of faking human emotions. She wouldn't demean herself that way.

"That's impossible, Darius." Bastian's tone sounded like pity. "She's a lost cause and the longer you let L.G. stay in that body, the more likely this prophecy will happen."

"Who is it?" Lauren nudged his side.

"Why did you call?" Darius watched out the window as the town car pulled up to an ornate, swirling, wrought iron gate. A woman dressed in jeans and a t-shirt stood there waiting for them.

Lauren didn't acknowledge they had arrived. A few hours earlier she had been bubbling with excitement and anticipation, but now she didn't move.

"I have a location where L.G. might be headed." Bastian's words were loud and clear and full of contempt.

"Hold on." Darius lowered the phone and motioned towards the gates of the Insta-Prophecy Hotline estate that housed the warehouse in the vaults underneath it. "Go ahead. I'll let you know when I'm finished," he said to Lauren.

She hesitated, then opened the door and stepped out into the brisk morning air.

When the door shut, Darius put the phone back to his ear. "Tell me."

"I've already informed Finley, he's closer and can handle it."

A polite way of saying Finley was going to kill Mackenzie.

"Unacceptable. Tell me where she's headed."

"Bastian, I swear to the gods!" Allyanora's piercing shriek made Darius wince. "I turn my back for one bloody second and you steal my phone? I thought our relationship was built on trust, understanding—"

"And destroying my phone so I can't warn my brother what you've planned."

"That, too. Well, now you can tell him what you know."

"No."

"So help me, my love, tell him or you won't like the consequences."

"Let me speak to her." Darius tried his best not to

pulverize the cell phone in his hands, but his frustration was growing. If he had to go rogue to save one life he would.

"Darius, I implore you, let this go. For your sake, for mine. I cannot lose you, brother." Bastian never begged, never implored. Much like Darius, he ordered and expected to be obeyed.

"I can change the outcome, Bastian, give me that chance. Let me save this one." Darius wasn't sure if he had spoken out loud. He wasn't even sure how he could save her, but the fact there was time to ponder the probability made all the difference.

"I'm sorry, Darius."

"Give me this." Allyanora's voice snapped over the line. "Bastian received news a girl matching her description bought a plane ticket under the nom de plume, Mackenzie Antoinette. I'll have the jet fueled and waiting on the airstrip for you."

"Allyanora." Bastian sounded censuring.

"I'm choosing to ignore your brother and the Grand Master. I give you full clearance to continue this mission. Every resource will be made available to you. I trust you'll do everything in your power to prevent the prophecy and if it comes down to it, you'll make the right call."

As Allyanora spoke, Darius watched Lauren say something to the woman at the gate, then saw her laugh at whatever comment the woman made in return.

Jonathan would have been disappointed in him. His mentor had dauntlessly pursued L.G. three times as long as he had, yet he couldn't bring himself to care. If this was the last mission of his life, he was going to save at least one.

"Darius, will you be able to make that call?"

Would he?

CHAPTER 12

Mackenzie drifted into consciousness. She didn't have to open her eyes to know she was sitting on a stiff, upholstered seat with her head propped up against a headrest.

The last thing she remembered was following Darius through her kitchen and, considering her track record on blacking out, that didn't bode too well. She was afraid to open her eyes to see what her possessed self had done this time. Then her ears popped and she noticed how the air hummed in a way that reminded her of when she flew to Orlando with her parents as a kid. Although, she somehow doubted this nightmare was going to end at the 'Happiest Place on Earth.'

Already she dreaded what she was about to see but opened her eyes anyway. There was a tray table in a fully upright position attached to the back of a dull, gray seat in

Insta-Prophecy Hotline

front of her. An overhead compartment loomed above and a seatbelt was strapped around her waist.

"Damnit, I'm on a plane." She said it out loud, but her voice was drowned out by the drone of the engines.

Belatedly, it dawned on her she was seated in first class. How nice.

The airplane tires hit the tarmac with a stuttering jolt as the screeching of the brakes filled the air. Her fingers gripped the armrests of her chair so hard her already pale knuckles turned stark white.

She looked out the window to take in her surroundings. She had no idea where she was, but one thing was for certain, she was not in Orlando.

When the roaring engines tapered off, a pleasant ding filled the cabin and an all too chipper flight attendant spoke over the intercom. "Welcome to Edinburgh. It's four in the afternoon and the temperature outside is a crisp twelve degrees Celsius, about fifty-four degrees Fahrenheit. We wish you an enjoyable stay and hope you fly with us again."

Mackenzie stopped listening at the mention of Edinburgh. She was broke, had no passport and most likely had been identified as the thief who robbed Tucker's Jewelry store. And somehow she was now in Scotland?

Her attention drifted to her clothes. Gone were her corset and tight skirt and in their place were black slacks, a cream-colored, short-sleeved, silky blouse and a gorgeous pair of matte, aquamarine heels. She pulled one off and looked at the brand. Louis Vuitton.

She didn't bother to look at the labels of the rest of her clothes to know they were expensive brand names, too. And they felt, amazing.

She slid her shoe back on and her other foot bumped into something under the seat in front of her. She pulled out a black leather bag and set it on her lap. The black leather felt buttery to the touch and like her clothes she knew that it, too, was expensive.

She should be freaking out, but she was rather calm.

Her fingers tugged the little silver lock on the lofty purse. She turned the silver embellishment and read the stamp on the bottom.

Hermes.

"No." She had read enough fashion magazines to know what that stamp on a high-end purse meant. She tugged on the leather zipper pull and it also read Hermes. "It's a Birkin."

Those bags came with ten-thousand-dollar-and-up price tags and were impossible to get. Images of how she might have obtained one flashed in her mind's eye, each one worse than the one before.

Mackenzie opened the purse a sliver and instantly snapped it shut. She stared blankly at the seat in front of her and her mind raced. Her eyes had to be playing tricks on her. She dared another peek just to make sure.

The purse was filled with bound stacks of very colorful one-hundred-dollar bills. They were most likely British Pounds, but she wasn't sure because she had never seen any before. She also didn't think it wise to start pulling out wads of cash to examine them at that particular moment.

"Shit." While she was filled with dread at seeing all that money, she couldn't help but feel a little gleeful at the same time. It was a confusing combination of emotions.

Keeping the flaps closed as best she could so no one could see she was loaded, Mackenzie reached into the purse. She hoped to find a cell phone or something that could be helpful, other than the wads of cash. In a side pocket she not only found a cell phone, but also some folded pieces of paper and a passport. She opened the passport and almost cried. While the photo was all her, the information was not.

For starters, her last name wasn't Antoinette.

When the plane docked at the gate, she kept her head down, clutched her purse to her chest and tried to will herself to be invisible.

She got two feet from her seat when the same chipper voice from the intercom called out her fake name. "Ms. Antoinette."

Oh shit, oh shit. She could already feel the cold metal handcuffs closing around her wrists just before being dragged off to Guantanamo Bay as a suspected terrorist.

"Ms. Antoinette."

Yup, they knew.

Three passengers blocked her escape to the exit, not that she would get far. She could see it now, border control dogs chasing her down the terminal. She would go down in a flurry of teeth, dog fur and chewed Louis Vuitton, all the while screaming, 'It wasn't me, my other personality made me do it!'

A hand touched her shoulder and all her muscles clenched. She had to push down her instantaneous need to fight her way to freedom.

"Ms. Antoinette." Her name now sounded forced and patronizing.

Assuming what she hoped was a pleasant smile, Mackenzie turned around and faced the woman. "Yes?"

"Your coat." The flight attendant held up a dark blue wool coat.

"I could kiss you," Mackenzie blurted, letting the tension leave her shoulders at the site of fabric and not handcuffs.

The flight attendant gave her a knowing look. "Louis Vuitton coats are nothing to joke about. I'd hate to lose mine if I had one."

"Yes, Luis Vuitton." She grabbed the coat and dashed out of the airplane before the woman could change her mind.

Mackenzie followed the crowd through the terminal to a large room with a sign overhead that read 'U.K. Border Control.' Hundreds of people with passports and hand-carry luggage inched through the zigzagged queues as they were herded towards the waiting officers.

She gripped her passport and joined the line as a moral dilemma waged within her. Should she just go along with whatever her possessed self had planned and lie? Or admit the truth and pray the entire situation would sort itself out without psychiatric incarceration?

She tried not to fidget when she stepped up to a booth and handed her forged passport to the waiting officer.

"What's the purpose of your trip?" He swiped the passport through the scanner and then scrutinized the little booklet.

"Vacation?"

The officer paused at the identification page and his brows furrowed.

Was the room getting hotter?

"Mackenzie Antoinette." His Scottish brogue held an edge and he looked up at her.

"That's me." She tried playing it coy, but had to clear her throat because it felt like the neckline of her shirt was strangling her.

The officer's trained gaze stayed on her, glued to every twitch and hesitation. "Where will you be staying?"

Oh, good question.

She offered him a shaky smile and slid her hand into her purse, careful not to flash her cash. She pulled out the folded papers from the side pocket and let out a mental cheer when one turned out to be a printed reservation for the George Hotel, which she prayed was somewhere in or near Edinburgh.

Her entire body trembled as she handed the paper to

him. He studied every word of the reservation and then stared at his computer screen. By the frown forming on his face, he didn't like what he was seeing. Was that a good or bad thing?

Seconds felt like hours and she almost broke under the mounting pressure. Suddenly, he stamped her passport and thrust it at her.

"Welcome to Scotland," he said flatly.

She didn't linger, didn't dare test her luck. She didn't know why he let her go and she didn't care. She was just exhausted from the emotional roller coaster ride. How career criminals managed to handle the stress, she didn't know. She needed a drink, make that half a dozen drinks.

Mackenzie tried to look inconspicuous as she made her way towards the airport's exit, and freedom. The hum of people walking on the hard, white-tiled floors and talking to each other acted as white noise for her nerves. It soothed to the point of numbness.

Truth be told, she wasn't sure how she should react. Should she freak out to find herself halfway across the world with no memory of how she got there? Be scared? Happy? She'd never been to Europe, didn't have the time or money. On a positive note, now she did.

She contemplated the appropriate reaction when a tall, skinny man wearing a black suit and holding a sign with her fake name scrawled across it caught her eye. She stopped in front of him and stared at the name.

"Are you Mackenzie Antoinette?" said the man with mild disinterest.

"Yes."

"This way to your car." He offered to take her bag and she all but slapped his hand away. Miffed, he guided her to a sleek-looking town car idling next to the busy curb.

He opened the back door for her and she slid onto the

supple leather seat, taking a moment to revel in the fact that for the time being she was safe. Well, relatively safe. Okay, possibly headed to her death by her serial-killer driver who would end up wearing her skin as a suit. But until she reached her destination, at least she didn't have to think about how she would get there.

"Ms. Antoinette." The man held out a note. "The person who reserved the car wanted me to give you this."

She opened the folded piece of paper. 'Relax. The apocalypse is still a few days away.'

"Is this a threat?" She looked up at the waiting chauffeur.

"I don't know what's on the note, lassie, only that I was supposed to give it to you." His expression twinkled in curiosity, exposing him as a liar.

"Thank you?"

He inclined his head and shut the door.

As they drove away from the airport, Mackenzie pulled the cell phone from the Birkin and turned it on. She had fifteen voicemails and a hundred and forty-seven text messages all from the same number, a number she didn't recognize.

"I've been out three days?" she whispered to herself when she read the date. "I'm going crazy."

The first text message from the unknown number read 'You'll pay for that, L.G.'

Her possessed self had responded in kind, 'Your people heal fast. Why must you insist on complaining?'

Dear God, she hurt someone. She felt a wave of guilt. What if the texter had to go to the hospital?

'Those gems weren't yours to pawn.'

And the answer to how she got rich became apparent.

'Did you acquire the other skull?' Her possessed self texted back.

'Where are you running to?'

Insta-Prophecy Hotline

'Do not make me stab you in the hand again, Darius.'

Her guilt ebbed a bit as she glared at the ugly, silver bracelet still shackled to her wrist. Then, flashes of Darius pressing her against the wall and nibbling on her ear played in her mind and deflated her anger like a punctured water balloon.

The text messages devolved into curses and insults being flung back and forth. She didn't have time to listen to the voicemails because the car arrived at the George Hotel. One thing was for certain, her possessed self... what did Darius call her again? L.G., that was it. Apparently, L.G was neither friends with Darius nor working with him. That was somewhat of a relief.

The driver opened the door and she got out of the car. She thanked him and handed him a hundred-pound note in gratitude for not skinning her alive.

She stared up at the well-kept, stately manor. The George Hotel was a gorgeous throwback to when buildings were works of art and monuments to power and, in this particular case, an emblem of intimidation because she had no idea what to expect once she went inside. Police? Interpol?

Whatever her possessed self had planned, it couldn't be anything good. But it wasn't like she could go anywhere else, aside from the loony bin.

So, she gathered her courage and walked inside.

The lobby was stunning, decorated with white marble floors, taupe-colored pillars and gold chandeliers. Mackenzie stepped up to the ornate, polished, mahogany front desk which was a contrast to the otherwise light and airy room. She checked in under her assumed name and no one called her out on it.

The clerk handed her a key card. "Your account has already been settled. You're in suite four-oh-six."

When she found her room, she stood outside the pristine

white door and formed a list in her head of things she was going to do.

First, she was going to have a relaxing soak in the tub and contemplate how to get de-possessed. Maybe she should use some of the money in her purse and book a plane ticket to the Vatican. They did exorcisms, right?

Next, would be to return the rest of the stolen money to Tucker's Jewelry store, because that was the right thing to do and when they arrested her, she could plead insanity. It wasn't the best plan, but she'd rather be tried for crimes her body did than live in paranoia the rest of her life.

Plan in mind, she opened her door and stepped inside the darkened room.

Strong hands yanked her forward, spun her around and pinned her to the wall, none too gently. She dropped her purse, curled her hands into fists and swung at her attacker, who by muscle mass alone she could tell was a man.

He grabbed her swinging wrists and pinned them above her head.

"Hello, L.G., weren't expecting me so soon, were you?" The familiar British accent rumbled in her ear, stilling her futile efforts to break free.

CHAPTER 13

"Honestly? Nothing would surprise me at this point," Mackenzie tried not to sound upset by the confession, but getting jumped by this man didn't even make her shock meter spike.

She also tried very hard not to contemplate how well Darius's entire body molded against hers as he tried to keep her from thrashing and wriggling away.

"Mackenzie?" His penetrating gaze searched hers.

This time she knew what he was looking for and she hated it.

"Do you mind?" She glared at her wrists and splayed her fingers in a gesture indicating she had had enough.

"Not particularly." He backed off an inch, but no more.

So, she did what any normal, twenty-first-century woman on the brink of insanity would do. She enthusiastically greeted his balls with her knee. Again. And if her point hadn't come across strong enough, she slammed her heel down on his instep for good measure.

Darius grunted, his grip on her wrist slackened and she slipped out of reach.

"What in the hell are you doing here?" She snatched her purse from the floor and held it out in front of her like a shield. "No, better yet, how in the hell did you find me? And get into this room? And, where's Lauren?"

Instead of answering her, he rested his hands on his knees and took deep breaths. Had he not been blocking the door with his body, she would have made a run for it. Instead, she inched back further into the room and searched for her missing friend. Lauren was nowhere to be found and she had seen enough of these types of movies to know this wasn't going to end well.

"Answer me, damn it." She raised her purse higher. "If you've hurt her, I swear—"

In a blur of motion, Darius snatched the purse from her hands and flung it across the room as if it weighed nothing.

She squeaked in outrage.

He tossed her over his broad shoulder and clamped his large hands around her thighs to keep her in place.

"Put me down," she yelled, as her stomach crushed against his collar bone with every long stride he took.

He didn't answer.

She huffed and smacked his back, not willing to do more than that, since falling face first onto the floor wasn't on her bucket list.

She pulled her hand back to smack him again when he flung her backwards off his shoulder. The world flew by in a blur just before her backside landed on an uncomfortable sofa cushion. She lunged forward and tried to get to her feet, only to be shoved back and bracketed in by Darius's arms as he pressed his hands against the back of the sofa.

"I find it disconcerting that your first instinctive reaction to every situation is instantaneous violence."

"Well, I find it disconcerting that every time I see you, you act like a douche, so we're even. Now tell me where Lauren is." She swung her foot up between his legs, but this time he caught her ankle right before she hit the sweet spot.

He pulled his cell phone out of his pocket with his free hand and put it to his ear.

Mackenzie struggled to free her ankle, but she might as well have been trying to stop the insane train to crazy town, because it just wasn't happening. "Let me go."

"No more kicking."

"Ass hat."

"That's mature."

"Knuckle-dragging oaf."

"Are you quite done?"

"No... Bastard." Petty? Possibly. Childish? Definitely. She crossed her arms over her chest, glared at him and imagined his hair catching on fire. "Now, I'm done."

"Put her on." Darius said to someone over the line and immediately Mackenzie's heart started pounding in her chest.

Were they holding Lauren hostage? What for? They were both broke, the money in her purse notwithstanding.

Then it hit her. Sex trafficking. Or worse... Although she couldn't imagine what could possibly be worse.

Wait, being turned into a human skin suit. Her brain was happy to supply a mental image of what that would look like.

He held the phone out to her and she eyed it, half expecting it to blow up in his hand.

"Take the phone, Mackenzie. It's Lauren."

She snatched the phone from his hand and he let go of her ankle. "Lauren?"

"Hey, girl, how's Scotland?" She sounded downright perky.

Darius loomed over her, so she turned sideways on the couch for some semblance of privacy. "That's not the question you're really asking me, right?"

"Well, no, I was concerned whether Darius would find you at all, but since you're talking on his phone, I assume all is good?"

"No, all is not good. He jumped me in my own hotel room."

"Go you! You have my approval if that's what you're worried about."

Mackenzie wished she could reach through the phone and smack some sense into her friend. "Not that kind of jumped me, more along the lines of frisking and pinning me against the wall."

"Again, go for it."

"You're joking, right?"

"No, why?"

She heard more than saw Darius walk away from her and the lights in the hotel suite turned on. She blinked a few times to adjust. "Please tell me you're okay," she whispered over the line. "They're not holding you against your will, are they?"

"What? The Seers? Not hardly. They gave me a once-in-a-lifetime job."

"Seriously?" Mackenzie glared at Darius over her shoulder. At least he had the decency not to look amused as he leaned against the wall and watched her. "They're telling you to say that, aren't they? Remember our SOS phrase? 'Something about a duck,' Lauren, 'something about a duck.'"

"Mackenzie, I'm fine. Of course, the job they offered me was only open because one of their clerks died, but you won't believe the stuff I get to work with. It's amazing. There's magic, Mackenzie. Magic!"

"Lauren, focus."

"What I'm trying to say is I'm all right. You need to be more worried about yourself."

"Oh, God, Darius is going to kill me, isn't he? And you're okay with that?"

"Noooo." Lauren stretched the word out for a few syllables. "He's there to help you. This Seer, Allyanora, showed me your prophecy and gave me the low down on what they do. Darius is a frickin' Templar Knight. It's in his job description to do whatever it takes to keep your prophecy from happening. And that means while you're possessed by whatever it is you're possessed by, he'll be attached to you at the hip. Lucky girl."

"Like he's doing a good job so far."

"Just listen to him. I'm safe and if it wasn't for him, I would've been in our apartment when it exploded."

"What exploded?" Mackenzie jumped to her feet. Her home, her belongings, her entire life was in her apartment.

"Everything's okay... Well, our stuff's totally torched, but—"

Darius snatched the phone from Mackenzie's ear and raised it to his. "Thank you for your assistance, I shall take it from here."

He ended the call and slid the phone back into the front pocket of his black slacks.

"How am I supposed to trust you when you blew up my apartment? Should I be grateful you bothered to save Lauren before it all went boom?"

"I didn't blow up your apartment."

"Oh?" She over acted a visual search of the otherwise empty hotel room. "I don't see anyone else here."

Darius looked at her as if she were the crazy one in this conversation. "It was the Illuminati."

"Who?"

"They're a secret organization of powerful people with

only one goal, to control the world for their gain."

"Like super-villains?"

"If you want to oversimplify things, yes, like super-villains."

"Seriously?"

His gaze was firm, his face emotionless. "Yes."

Laughter bubbled in her chest and erupted out of her mouth. She couldn't have stopped it if she tried.

"I'm sorry," she said between giggles, "but that would make you like, what, a super-hero? Do you have a spandex suit?"

She hoped so, because he had the body for one.

Darius's jaw clenched and when he didn't answer, her curiosity got the better of her. "Well?"

"No, I don't have a spandex suit. But in your general oversimplification of the situation, yes, I am in fact, a super-hero."

Her hysterical laughter quieted. The serious glare of Darius turned something so ridiculous as super-villains and super-heroes into something real and devastating.

"It may seem ludicrous," Darius said as he closed the distance between them, once again invading her personal space, "but you can't deny something's going on and it scares you. You want it to be a mental snap or some form of insanity because that's in the realm of possibility, because that's the only thing that makes sense."

He paused as if to study her. Or he just waited for her reaction. But she had none, nothing in her life had prepared her to accept something like this as a reality. She took a step away from him, then another.

"There are things in this world, Mackenzie, of which you're not aware. Things that are real, like myth and legend, and humans not being the only life forms in the universe. And it's the Templar Knights and the Seers who do their

Insta-Prophecy Hotline

damndest to keep this world exactly how everyone expects it to be, normal, boring and predictable."

Mackenzie focused on the wall over his shoulder, the normal, boring, beige wall, and wished she could go back to the night before the Maroon Room and choose that damn chicken pot pie. This was not the adventure of a lifetime she wanted. She shook her head, ready to say those words out loud.

Darius wouldn't relent. "Fear not what came before, but what has yet to come. Thirteen skulls will gather amongst the setting sun. The innocent will lose the fight, the Red Cross falls to the Eye. The Skulls call to their gods in their home up in the sky. The Eye then falls to a skull which bears the innocent's face. She becomes a god herself, and unlike man, falls not from grace. The Phoenicians will bear witness as man makes their final stand. Yet the war was lost when they gathered upon the rocky land."

He gently gripped her shoulders, lowered her down on the sofa and sat next to her. "I'm a Templar Knight, the Cross in the prophecy, and the Illuminati are the Eye. You're the innocent."

And the innocent would lose.

No, she wasn't going to lose because this wasn't real. It couldn't be.

"I've heard of the crystal skull myth, not an obsidian one."

"They're not actually obsidian, they're obsidian-like. But since we've never found anything close to the substance they're made out of, we call them obsidian. My predecessor was responsible for spreading the disinformation about there being crystal skulls. Couldn't have the whole world interfering with our search for something so apocalyptic, now could we?"

He acted like this was normal, like they were talking

about the weather. People didn't search out apocalypses, did they? The end of the world was just for blockbuster movies and doomsday preppers.

"Let's just blow the skull up," she blurted. Best idea she had all day if she said so herself.

In her mind she was already at the Vatican getting an exorcism. She'd be back in Santa Cruz by Friday, in jail by Monday and committed to an insane asylum by Wednesday.

Damn, her future looked bleak any way she looked at it.

"We've tried. We have some of the skulls from the prophecy in our possession already and we've done everything we can think of. I put a skull in the casing of the Hiroshima bomb before it left for Japan. I found it later in the rubble, unscathed and not irradiated at all. An American astronaut left one on the moon for us in the seventies. It found its way back to earth. We can't explain it. They're made from an indestructible substance found nowhere on this planet, and they somehow draw to each other, preventing them from getting irrevocably lost."

"Wait." Mackenzie frowned. "You put one inside the bomb that was dropped on Japan?"

"Yes."

"From World War Two?"

"I think you're missing the point."

Mackenzie checked him out again, but with a more discerning eye, from his intense brown eyes and strong broad shoulders to his muscular chest and big hands. You know what they say about big hands.

She smiled. "You look really good for an old dude."

"And I lost you."

"You didn't lose me, you just failed to mention you're geriatric, that's all. What plastic surgeon are you using? They've done a superb job."

She leaned in and touched his face, his five o'clock shadow tickled her palm, but his skin didn't have the papery-thin, brittle feel of an old man. It felt warm and sent pleasurable tingles up her arm.

Down, Mackenzie.

His hand wrapped around hers and pulled it from his cheek, but instead of letting her go, he held it on the couch between them.

A frown line marred the smooth, tanned skin between his eyebrows. "A perk of being a Templar Knight is that we don't age and we heal inhumanly fast. I'm seven hundred and forty-three years old to be exact. And I've been a Knight for seven hundred and eleven of them."

She wanted to laugh and brush off his words, which would be easy because his words were ridiculous. But his eyes kept her laughter at bay. They looked so haunted, like they had seen far too much.

She felt the warmth of his hand, felt the skin that was far too young for the age he claimed.

She took a breath, then another, afraid of her next words. "Prove it."

CHAPTER 14

How did one prove his age? Darius didn't know, but Mackenzie looked like she was about to accept what was going on and he loathed to lose her now.

"The healing thing, not the 'I don't age' thing," Mackenzie said with a roll of her eyes as if reading his mind.

That made things easier. Back when Jonathan told him about the agelessness and quick healing, Darius remembered he had focused on the ageless part. Even after joining the Templar Knights, it took another fifteen years to believe that he could live, in theory, forever.

Darius pulled his knife from the sheath strapped to his ankle. She eyed the weapon and shifted away from him on the couch. He said nothing to reassure her she was safe.

He pressed the sharp blade to the palm of his hand and with a clenched jaw he sliced his skin. Mackenzie's eyes widened and she inhaled with a hiss. Her fingers rubbed her palms as she was transfixed by his self-inflicted wound.

His pain was minimal compared to her morbid fascination as blood pooled in his palm.

One second turned into half a dozen and then he felt the heat build on his skin as it started to knit itself together.

Mackenzie shot forward and pulled his healing hand closer to her. Her fingers were soft against his calloused skin. Soft and warm. Just like the rest of her.

"Impossible," she mumbled as she pulled and stretched his hand, careful to avoid the drying blood.

No matter how she pulled his skin, the wound got smaller and smaller until nothing of it was left. Still, he didn't dare move and break her newfound fearless interest because that would result in hysterics.

She had to come to the conclusion that she needed him on her own. Well, he could just announce the reality that she had no choice, but for the sake of his groin he would make that his last resort.

She licked her lips, giving them a sheen that drew his attention.

He tensed, waiting for the tears, the accusations.

The violence.

"So, um." Her voice came out as a whisper as she looked up at him. "You're positively ancient."

Darius let out a bark of laughter.

A withering flower she was not, but he wasn't blind. He could see the whites of her eyes and her hands that gripped his quivered.

She, too, noticed her hands and shoved them in her lap, knotting her fingers together. "So how does this work? We go to the Vatican, get a priest or the Pope or someone to depossess me and I frolic into the sunset like in the movies?"

"What exorcism movies have you watched?"

She shrugged and stared down at her hands.

"I'm afraid it's not going to be that easy." He pulled a black handkerchief from his pocket and wiped his bloodied hand clean. "Or, as immediate."

"Why not? This prophecy needs me to be possessed to work. So, if we get L.G. out of me, *shabam*, no more end of the world."

The real issue was time. He needed time to figure out how to cast L.G. out before Mackenzie's soul was ripped to shreds. And there was the matter of needing L.G. to find the rest of the skulls, so he could finally be able to protect the world from L.G. destroying it.

"Casting L.G. out of you may be a priority, but there's still four skulls unaccounted for and the entity possessing you is the only one who knows how to find them. That makes you my obsidian skull radar for the time being."

"Fine then, I quit," she said.

"Unacceptable."

"No more unacceptable than what you're saying."

"You're oversimplifying the problem."

"How? Is the devil too strong?"

He cracked his neck, an annoying tick he picked up during the crusades that he never managed to quit.

"Darius."

"L.G. isn't a normal entity. Usual means of..." He trailed off searching for the right word.

"De-possession," she filled in as if he were a slow child.

"-wouldn't work in this instance."

"Vague much? Come on, old man, what aren't you telling me?"

So much. "I'm telling you, normal means of exorcizing the entity from you won't work. As in, she won't leave your body unless she wants to."

Mackenzie's cuff bracelet glinted in the artificial lamplight and he traced the cuneiform writing that marred the other-

Insta-Prophecy Hotline

wise smooth surface.

He'd been told the cuff was supposed to rebuff all kinds of energy from reaching the wearer. It would have protected Mackenzie and had she received it before touching L.G.'s skull, she wouldn't have gotten possessed in the first place.

In theory anyway...

"Well, you have to come up with something," Mackenzie said.

For all his years chasing after L.G., he never once had to think about how to save the victim.

Against his better judgment, he let a sliver of hope rise to the surface. It was something he thought he'd lost when he watched L.G. break Jonathan. Darius had even accepted that one day he would follow in his mentor's footsteps, but now to have a chance at success...

"There is a way to force her out of you," he said when the beginnings of an idea formed in his head. "There's an artifact we once used on another difficult entity."

Mackenzie lit up like a firework and jumped off the couch. "Let's go get it."

"My people don't actually have possession of the artifact at this moment."

"Then call your people and send a retrieval team to wherever it is." She clapped her hands at him as if that would speed everything along.

He smirked and slid his phone from his pocket. "It's going to take time, even for my people."

"Where the hell is it?"

"The Vatican."

"Well, goodie, that's where I planned to go anyway. So up-up, let's be off." She grabbed her purse and went for the door. He wrapped his arm around her waist and stopped her from skipping out of the room. He made a call with his free hand.

It rang once.

"I'm kinda busy," the heavy Scottish accent of his good friend, Finley, grunted over the line.

"I need a favor."

"Will you unhand me?" Mackenzie struggled, but she only managed in distracting him as her body wiggled against his.

"Will you stop?" He glared down at the top of her ginger head.

"You're the one who called me." There was a bang over the phone line and Finley cursed.

"I was talking to her, not you."

"You're with a lassie? Och, this is a new predicament for you. Should I give you some pointers? You may have forgotten how to be with a woman over the... how long has it been now, centuries?"

Mackenzie continued to struggle, and her pert ass rubbed against his groin in the most tantalizing of ways. "I'm not amused, Finley."

Darius spun Mackenzie around, pushed her back up against the wall and caged her there with his body and his free arm. Her face blushed and it was almost a relief to know she wasn't as unaffected by him as she acted. It made his lust for her feel a little less untoward. Not that he would act on it, since she was now, more or less, his charge.

His violent, unpredictable and sexy-as-sin charge.

"What do ya need?" Finley got to the point, before a loud noise of a body, not Finley's, crashed into something.

"Remember the Mixtec stone we used on Pope John Paul the First? I need you to get it."

Finley cursed again, but this time at Darius. "You're out of your damn mind. They're not gonna give it to us, not after we failed to save him with it."

"What's he saying?" Mackenzie whispered.

"I'm not saying we ask, I'm saying get it by any means necessary."

"What did he say?" Mackenzie said a little louder.

"Good God man, I'm a Templar Knight, not Houdini." Finley also had a soft spot for anything Star Trek.

"What's he saying?" Mackenzie stomped on his instep.

Darius winced but refused to move. He rather enjoyed where he currently stood, pain in the foot aside.

"Does this have to do with L.G.'s prophecy?" Finley said. "You think you can save the girl? Jonathan said that was impossible."

"I think it's worth a try."

Mackenzie huffed and tapped her foot against the hardwood floor. Tap tap tap tap.

God, this girl was infuriating.

"I'll see what I can do." Finley's voice broke up the tip-tapping noise just before Darius did something drastic to still Mackenzie into acquiescence, like kiss her. "But I'm going to need some time. Breaking into the Vatican's regular vaults is no easy task and you want me to break into the ones that are beneath the bowels of that damned fortress."

"Call me when it's done."

"And try to keep your distance, laddie. Whatever L.G.'s planning this time 'round, she's not gonna let it fail without taking out as many of us as she can."

Darius ended the call.

"Well?"

"My people are on the task. While we wait, you and L.G. can find the remaining skulls for me."

Mackenzie's lips thinned and he saw the fear creep back into her face. He understood why, he didn't like it, but understood.

"Until the moment we get L.G. out, I won't leave your side. I promise you that."

She nodded and shifted to the tips of her toes so she was eye level with him. Images of the Maroon Room drifted across his mind and this time he wouldn't stop her from kissing him.

She was a hair's breadth away when her eyes flashed metallic. "Nine."

He let her go like she had electrocuted him. "What did you just say?"

She backed away and blinked her eyes back to normal. "I didn't say anything." Her brows furrowed in confusion.

Darius had just learned something, L.G. was aware of what was going on even when she wasn't controlling the body. An annoying little tidbit best remembered.

The room phone rang and Mackenzie jumped.

"Answer the phone." He stepped back from her, he needed the distance.

Mackenzie looked like she wanted to say something, but he gave her his stern look, the one that always sent his 'people' scuttling off to do whatever he had ordered. It worked on her, too, sort of.

She strolled to the phone but at a damnable slow pace and gave him one last questionable look before she answered it.

"Hello?" She listened and her focus drifted towards the window.

He tried not to look at her, but her profile reminded him of a medieval noblewoman with her shoulders back and head high. Even with everything that had been thrown at her, she didn't cower. That kind of strength was sexy on a woman, but it also made her difficult to control and because of that he was tempted to have a hands-on approach with her.

He forced himself to look away and put his mind back on the task at hand. He wouldn't get attached, he couldn't afford to give in to that weakness, so he shoved his need and guilt to the dark recesses of his mind.

He had to get the skulls and stop the prophecy at any cost. Even if that cost meant sacrificing her life. A life he wasn't sure he could save anyway.

Mackenzie hung up the phone. "It would seem L.G. ordered a driver for us and he's waiting downstairs. We're going to Edinburgh Castle."

CHAPTER 15

"Wow." It was the only word Mackenzie could think of as she stood just inside the outer walls of Edinburgh Castle and gawked up at the medieval structure towering over her.

This castle wasn't your run-of-the-mill, stereotypical castle she had grown up reading about in fairy tales. Built on top of a dormant volcano, the castle's awesome beauty came from the fact there were no delicate designs, no whimsical features and nothing to give you the warm, fuzzy feeling that Cinderella would be traipsing around the grounds in search of her Prince Charming. This place was built in a time when wars were fought with knights, swords and interminable sieges. And it was that cold, war-like beauty that stole her breath.

It also made her realize her high school history class would have been far more interesting if the books had been filled with castles, palaces and monarchies. Maybe then she wouldn't have used that class time as her nap hour.

Darius walked up behind her and rumbled in her ear. "Ready?"

"How in the hell are we going to find a tiny obsidian skull in all of this?" She nearly smacked him in the face with the clunky bracelet as she waved her hand forward, around and overhead at the enormous castle that surrounded them.

He handed her a visitor's map, which she opened as if to prove her point. Scrolled across the tri-fold page was the layout of the castle grounds with its numerous buildings.

"It could be inside the stone walls for all we know." She flipped the map over and scoffed. "Oh look, not only are there, God knows, how many rooms above ground, but there are underground tunnels, as well. We're so screwed."

"Would you mind keeping your voice down?" Darius rumbled in her ear again.

"No, I get loud when I'm angry." She looked at him. "And annoyed."

"You're forgetting you also get violent."

She was tempted to prove his point right then. "Oh, I'm sorry if your obsidian skull radar doesn't have the stone cold, emotionless mask you've apparently mastered." She flipped the map over again in her hands and jabbed it with her pointer finger. "But if I were you, I'd get a little overwhelmed right about now."

"You're not my radar. You're the unfortunate soul whose body is harboring my radar."

"That's even worse. If you think I'm going to stay quiet while you order my other half to come out and play, you better think again."

"What if I ask nicely?" He held her elbow and escorted her up the sloping walkway towards the castle summit.

Yes, the castle had a frickin' summit.

No longer awed by the monument, more like daunted by it, she scowled at him. He pretended not to notice.

Darius didn't look around at the scenery like she was, he was focused straight ahead, only deviating his attention long enough to scrutinize the passing tourists meandering around them.

Then she had to remind herself he was over seven hundred years old and castles were nothing new to him. "Have you been here before?"

"No."

"Stayed in castles before?"

He nodded. "Many."

"Opinions?" Like any girl who dreamed of being a princess, she always wondered what it would be like to live in a castle.

"Dark, dank and drafty. And they're riddled with so many hidden rooms and spaces from which to eavesdrop it's hard to believe any secrets uttered within their walls remained so."

"You fill me with such optimism. Fine, how about this? When did L.G. come here to stash the thing? I mean, that could help narrow down the search to specific buildings. Wait, what if some archeologist already stumbled across it and put it in a museum? I'm not stealing it, I'm not a thief."

He cocked an eyebrow as if to say, 'really?'.

"That wasn't me and you know it."

"I don't know when L.G. visited this castle, but I can assure you an obsidian skull has never been found here."

How did Darius ever get her to agree to tag along? Oh, wait, he didn't.

Mackenzie stopped underneath the portcullis. The wide, stone archway had two drawn wrought iron gates, just in case one wasn't enough. It separated the outer part of the castle from the inner and served as a second line of defense from invaders. Darius showed no interest in the stone walls of the

Insta-Prophecy Hotline

portcullis as a possible hiding spot. She looked back at the map. "Where are we going to start looking then? I vote the palace."

Darius snorted. "If you want to hide something, the last place you hide it is in the palace. It's the first place anyone would look."

"Well then, Mr. I've-Stayed-In-So-Many-Castles-Before, where should we start?"

Darius paused. "I don't know. I know this castle has changed a lot over the centuries. We'll start high and work our way down. If we find nothing, we'll come back after hours and check out the cemetery."

She looked on the map. "The dog cemetery? Because that's the only cemetery on the grounds and you can't make me."

She crinkled the map in her fists. At that moment she hoped L.G. would surface and save her from becoming a canine grave robber.

"Fine, we'll start at the palace because that's at the top anyway, and avoid the graveyard." Darius pulled her towards him and out of the way of a backwards-walking tour guide as she narrated the history of the castle to a large group of red-shirt-wearing tourists.

Her stomach did happy little flip-flops as her body touched his, but instead of leaning into him more, she pulled free and focused on folding her map back into its tri-folded state and then rolled it in her hands.

"Maybe there's no skull here at all and L.G. just wanted to do some sightseeing." She was willing to believe anything to prevent digging up graves.

"Trust me, L.G. doesn't give a damn about castles, civilizations or the human race."

"Sorry, forgot, she's a super-villain."

"An over–"

"–simplification, I know." Mackenzie led the way through the portcullis, more than aware of Darius as he walked next to her. "You know, it seems counterproductive for super-villains to destroy the planet they live on. Especially, if they plan on surviving their victory."

"Not when this planet isn't L.G.'s."

"Not her planet?" That made Mackenzie pause, as she scrounged for some sort of explanation that would make sense. Then it hit her. "Oh yeah, she's going to call her gods from like, hell, or whatever magical world they live in." Mackenzie pondered that for a second. "What kind of magic does it take to possess someone?"

Darius looked at her, his expression unreadable. "Dark magic."

"Oh." How she wished her life was normal again because that should never be an answer to any question. "Doesn't dark magic involve, like, sacrifices and blood?"

"L.G. always has sacrifices."

"Fantastic," Mackenzie mumbled. Try as she might, she couldn't think of anything that could counter dark magic. Not that she ever believed magic was real, but a wand would probably help, it always helped wizards. "What does L.G. stand for? Loser Ghost?"

"L.G. Man. Little Green Man."

Mackenzie smirked, "Who came up with that, you or her?"

"Me, after Roswell. I was helping to mitigate the fallout there. I was bored and a little drunk."

"So, the true side of you comes out. A selfless knight with a sense of humor. And here I thought Roswell had something to do with aliens, instead of the paranormal, and that you were all 'bark out orders and expect to be obeyed.'"

Darius gave her a darkened look. "I'm not selfless, but I do always expect to be obeyed."

He veered them off the main path that sloped upwards and around the castle grounds towards the summit, and instead headed towards a foreboding stone staircase that served as a shortcut to the top.

Funny, Mackenzie missed that on the map.

"Wait." She jogged after him.

Darius stopped at the base of the stairs.

"Why doesn't she just magic her way home, why call her gods?"

"Just focus on finding the skulls. I order you." Any redeeming qualities she thought he had vanished.

He was an ass, plain and simple, with brief stints of non-asshole-ish-ness.

"Go to hell and answer the question."

He motioned for her to go up the stairs first, but when she refused to move, he cracked his neck and she got the feeling he wished the prophecy foresaw anyone but her as the bringer of the apocalypse.

"As the prophecy puts it, bringing those thirteen skulls together is the only thing powerful enough to reach her gods. I would explain it in more detail, but you wouldn't understand and we need to keep moving."

Yup, he was definitely an ass.

Mackenzie stomped up the stairs and could feel Darius's brooding superiority as he followed right behind her. She wanted to say something to him, knock him off his high horse, but every time she opened her mouth to retort something over her shoulder or demand detailed answers, she stopped short. What if the answers destroyed her safe little world of ignorance further? Could she handle it? Already her insides hummed with nervous tension from what she had learned so far.

Hell, she wasn't sure she believed all of it. For all she knew, Darius could have some nano technology to give him his healing capabilities. She could be blacking out due to some drug concoction his people keep slipping her. Her best friend could have been brainwashed into working with him.

That was far more believable than a demon possessing her, black magic and the apocalypse.

She needed to think. Alone. Without him pushing her into his crazy beliefs and his handsome proximity messing with her common sense.

By the time she reached a landing halfway up the staircase, she had formed a plot to run away. If she could get to her bag of cash, she could buy some time alone and think everything through.

Her world shifted and she stumbled into the stone handrail. Like being caught in a riptide, she struggled against the current that led to unconsciousness.

She took a breath, steadying herself, and just when she thought she might reach the shore, the next wave pulled her under.

CHAPTER 16

Mackenzie was thrust back into consciousness and found herself crouched over a glowing, skeletal face of an obsidian skull.

She screamed and jerked backwards. Her ankle rolled on the uneven ground and down she went, landing on her backside with a grunt. Her phone, which was clutched in her hand and her only source of light, skittered face-up across the floor.

She glanced around the shadows of the small, cave-like space she found herself in. Her heart pounded, her lungs seized and she searched for Darius.

He wasn't there.

She took a couple of controlled breaths and tried to get a grip on the fear that was threatening to overwhelm her.

Just a second ago, she had convinced herself Darius was the one responsible for all this. She had also wished she could be alone so she could think logically.

Now that she was alone, thinking logically was the last thing on her mind.

The light of her phone glinted off the polished, black surface of the skull, which sat atop a short stone pedestal. The skull would have been far less ominous looking if it wasn't back-dropped by shadows, like a silent gatekeeper to the pits of hell.

She rethought both her stance on Darius and her theory that this was all an elaborate hoax.

"Holy hell, magic is real." She looked around the shadowed room. "And this is so not the time to be realizing that."

Her breathing echoed around her, which didn't help the feeling of being buried alive.

"Okay, Mackenzie. Don't. Freak. Out." She got to her feet and wiped off the dust from her backside. "I can do that later, preferably with the sun on my face. After I've killed Darius."

She rushed to her phone, hoping she could call for help. The zero bars said she could not.

"Freaking skull, dumb castle, moronic prophecy and stupid L.G. for doing God knows what whenever she frakin' well pleases."

Using the light from her phone, she took a closer look around the claustrophobic space. The stone ceiling hovered close enough she could reach up and touch it with her fingertips. The wall closest to her looked like a typical medieval stone wall, reinforced, thick and impenetrable. The Hulk would have a hard time knocking it down.

She steadied her breath and listened in the darkness around her. She heard... nothing.

No sounds of the city. No sounds of tourists milling around the castle. It was like someone had put noise-cancelling headphones over her ears and the silence had never been more unwelcome. It meant she was truly alone.

Her thoughts went to an Edgar Allen Poe story she barely remembered reading in high school. Now every gruesome detail about a man forever entombed in a cellar flooded her memory in spectacular clarity.

"I'm dead."

Good lord, even her mind was against her. She tried not to think of her odds of survival without Darius. He had promised to stay by her side, told her she could trust him. He would have had a plan to escape had he been there.

"Nope." She shook her head. "I'm not dying here. If L.G. can get in, I can get out."

She felt her way along one wall, looking for an exit. There wasn't one. She moved on to another.

Her fear and panic subsided a bit when she contemplated retribution on her knight. Funny how anger kept her from of curling up into the fetal position and giving up.

"My knee and his balls are going to be fast friends." She was determined to see him again, even if it meant haunting the man.

She finished examining the second wall. Nothing there.

A faint sound of wood scraping against stone carried through the room.

She took in a breath to yell for help, then slowly let the air out in silence. It crossed her mind that whoever was making the noise could be the same a-holes who blew up her apartment.

That made this entire situation go from a horrific, surreal dream to actual reality. This was happening, right then and right there, and made death an all too real possibility.

With the goal of staying alive in mind, she looked for a weapon. There was nothing except for a few stone pebbles, the squat stone pedestal that was far too heavy for her pick up and the obsidian skull. She slipped her phone into the pocket of her slacks, grabbed the skull from the pedestal and clutched it to her chest.

If the skull broke in the process of saving her ass, well she would no longer have to worry about ending the world.

There were more scraping sounds and she looked around for the source. On the far side of the room, a single, weak beam of light fell to the ground from an opening in the ceiling.

She inched towards it, careful to be silent and not trip on the shadowed, uneven ground. A body dropped through the opening into the room. The darkness prevented her from seeing who it was, other than that it was a big man. As he straightened, she chucked the skull as hard as she could into his chest.

The man grunted as the skull dropped to the ground and rolled away.

She swung her fists, but unfortunately the skull didn't shock him like she hoped it would and he grabbed her wrists, stopping her attack with ease.

"Mackenzie." Darius's British accent lilted over her, but she didn't stop trying to hit him, in fact her rage doubled.

"Where the hell were you?" The fear and terror she had been holding back dripped with every word. "You said you'd stay by my side, you ass."

"I'm sorry."

Two simple words with no explanation, delivered with the same ease as when he ripped the reality as she knew it apart. She looked him in the eyes, searching for any warmth or comfort. She found cold, hard strength.

She pulled her hands free. "Sorry isn't good enough. I need to trust you."

"You don't."

Right, she was just a job to him and whether she liked it or not he was all she had.

She needed her best friend, a security blanket and a gallon of ice cream. She had none of those things, so she bundled her emotions into a tiny ball and cast it aside. She could handle this. Maybe.

She pulled her phone out of her pocket for more light. Darius did the same with his phone.

"How'd you find me?" She saw the damned skull a few feet away, unmarred and unbroken, which was unfortunate.

"L.G. said something about King David the First just before she pushed me down the stairway." Darius turned back to the opening in the ceiling. "Saint Margaret's Chapel is the only building still standing from his reign nine hundred years ago. We're currently standing in its cellar."

"More like a tomb." She looked around the foreboding place and then picked up the skull. "But go back to the part about how I was able to push a seven-hundred-year-old war-hardened knight down a flight of stairs."

He didn't answer, not that she expected him to.

"So, after you picked yourself up from your fall, you found out about this building and..." Mackenzie trailed off.

"Went to find you."

"By blindly jumping through a hole in the floor into a pitch-black room with the possibility of a homicidal demon waiting to off you the moment you landed?"

"Are you implying something?"

"I'm not implying anything." She marched right up to him, rested the skull against her hip and poked him in the chest. "I'm saying that you, Mr. Knight, are an idiot."

Darius raised a dark eyebrow as if to say in that silent he-man sort of way, 'care to say that again?'

"Maybe idiot is the wrong word. Sadly, there isn't a single word in the human language that means 'a person who has no self-preservation instincts.' Well, that's a lie, there's suicidal, but that doesn't apply here."

"Are you giving the person who's trying to rescue you a hard time?" He would have sounded harsh if his lips didn't quirk around the corners.

"If the idiot crown fits."

And their conversation continued in silence. He smirked, she smirked. It was a rather enjoyable smirk fest and Mackenzie almost got lost in his stormy brown eyes, warm with mirth and amusement. It looked good on him. Too good.

She didn't realize she'd moved closer towards him until her feet bumped into his. Warmth spread across her cheeks, which made his eyes darken with something similar to what she saw at the Maroon Room. She cleared her throat and punched him in the shoulder as hard as she could.

"Ouch?" His voice was a seductive rumble.

"That's for letting L.G. get the better of you." She walked past him and stood under the opening in the ceiling, her only viable exit.

The ceiling was a good six and a half feet above the floor and she was five foot seven at best. Even though she could touch the ceiling, it would require a certain amount of upper body strength to pull herself up through the opening.

She frowned down at her aquamarine high-heeled shoes. "L.G. seems to be pretty adept at jumping in these heels. Should I be annoyed that she can control my body better than I can?"

"Your control over your body is fine."

The look he gave her sent an excited tingle down her spine and she almost shivered. Almost. And she wouldn't have been able to blame it on the chill wafting off the stones.

Instead of satisfying her growing curiosity about what it would feel like to kiss the man, she shoved the skull and her phone into his chest and turned back to the task at hand.

"Of course I have perfect control over my body."

Mackenzie grabbed the edge of the opening. "Almost sent you to your knees. Twice."

She tried to pull herself upwards and got halfway before her strength failed her and she dropped back to her toes.

"My ability comes from years of playing soccer, you know." She attempted to lift herself again and failed. "Strong kicks and awesome reaction skills."

She pulled herself up once again, with a grunt this time. When the muscles in her arms weakened, she gave a few propelling kicks for added boost, but only succeeded in feeling ridiculous. She dropped back down to the floor and glared up at the opening that taunted her.

"All right, that does it. When this is over I'm going on a diet and hitting the gym." She kicked a loose rock near her foot with a frustrated huff, wiped her hands on her slacks and grabbed the rim again.

She got halfway when her arms started to shake violently from the exertion. Just when she was ready to accept the fact she was never going to leave what she now considered her final resting place, Darius's firm hand cupped her buttocks and his other hand wrapped around her upper thigh.

"That's, um, my ass." She felt the need to point out the obvious, just in case he missed it.

"And what a fine ass it is." She could have sworn she felt his fingers squeeze a little. "One that would be a shame to see get all bony should you diet."

He easily pushed her upwards and she pulled herself out with a minimal amount of swearing.

Mackenzie twisted until she sat on the ridge of the opening. She found herself in a closet-like room with a very low ceiling. There was a steel grate propped up against the wall across from her that was the perfect size to cover the hole in the floor. An old wooden door was ajar on her right and a weak light filtered in through the crack between the door and the wall.

"Take the skull." His stern order made her jump a little and she looked back down into the shadows. The skull smiled up at her.

"And to expand on my earlier comment," Darius gave her a smug look, "your ass also feels as good as it looks."

She should have felt outrage at his copping a feel and sounding so smug about it. Instead her lips twitched into a smile.

She eyed the small room again and the solid grate that covered the not-so-secret entrance. "You know, this is a horrible secret hiding place. Anyone could have moved the grate in the, what, nine hundred years it's been here?"

"L.G. has her connections. Now, if you would move so I could climb out."

"Sorry." Because the 'closet' wasn't tall enough to stand in, she clutched the skull to her chest and one-arm crawled out of the tiny space. She exited next to a podium at the front of a cozy, little chapel. She pulled herself up using the podium as leverage, then froze when the barrel of a gun came towards her face, stopping inches from her nose.

She followed the weapon to its black-suit-wearing owner. He had square shoulders, blonde hair and cold, emotionless eyes that said he wouldn't think twice about shooting her in the head.

"Oh, shit," Mackenzie managed to squeak out.

CHAPTER 17

The man raised his index finger to his thin lips. It was the international sign for 'shut the hell up' and one she didn't want to challenge him on.

Mackenzie wanted to warn Darius, but Lippy, as she named her would-be killer, motioned towards her chest with the gun. It took her a second to realize he was motioning at the skull in her hands and another second for her to make out that he was miming out an order that said, 'give it to me.'

It was not a good sign when her knight, who was supposed to protect her sorry self, swore with derision when he appeared at last and noticed the homicidal interloper. All her confidence in him saving her shriveled up and died.

Lippy motioned towards the skull, again. "Give it to me."

Mackenzie looked down in hopes the skull had turned into an AK-47 or a Kevlar vest. It hadn't, but if Lippy wanted the skull, she had no choice but to obey.

"Do you know who this is? It's L.G." Darius spoke.

Lippy looked her up and down, unimpressed.

"Darius, I don't think it's wise—"

"Let me handle this," Darius ordered.

Mackenzie ruffled at his dismissal. He wasn't the one with a gun aimed at him. "You can take your order and shove it up your ass. Don't antagonize the man."

"Quiet!" Lippy snapped. "The skull, now."

"You won't kill her, you need her," Darius said in a calm voice.

"You're right." Lippy aimed his gun at her right shoulder.

Mackenzie knew deep down even if she handed over the skull he would shoot her, and maybe it was that knowledge that shut down the common sense in her brain. Or, maybe she was the one without any self-preservation skills.

All she knew was that to obey the man pretty much sucked, but not to obey sucked, too.

So, she gave the man what he wanted.

She tossed the skull high in the air. Lippy's attention followed it and his gun's aim drifted away from her. She lunged forward, batted the gun away with one hand and punched him in the nose with the other.

A shot rang out in the small chapel and still she pushed forward. Her body collided with his and he grunted when his back slammed into the wall behind him. She kneed him in the groin, but that only seemed to knock some sense back into him.

As she stared into Lippy's ticked-off glare, she came to two realizations: One, Darius was right, she had a violent streak. And two, she should have given her plan more thought.

Lippy struck her across the temple with the butt of his gun and she stumbled into a low wooden bench. Her legs tangled with it and she went down hard, her head colliding with the stone floor.

Starbursts filled her vision as she struggled to extricate herself. Finally free of the bench, she tripped over another one, her elbows and knees taking the brunt of it this time.

"Whose side are you on, benches?"

A hand grabbed her arm and pulled her to her feet. She let out a war cry, but cut it short when the cool, smooth surface of the obsidian skull was pushed into her hands and she was pulled into Darius's growingly familiar body.

"And you say I'm an idiot," he growled as he pulled her along with him towards the door at the far end of the small chapel. "What in the bloody hell was that?"

"What about the guy?"

"Dead. But the Illuminati don't send just one guy."

He all but dragged her out of the chapel and she did her best to keep her feet under her. Louis Vuitton heels were not meant for life or death situations. They were barely meant for regular situations.

She heard gunfire and stone chipped off the wall next to her face.

"Son of a bitch." Darius pulled her to his chest and turned so his body shielded her from wherever the bullets were coming from. He pulled a gun from somewhere on his person and shot back.

Mackenzie's fingernails dug into his back as gunfire erupted around her. The very real idea she could die hit her like a fist in the gut. Someone in the distance cried out in pain. She closed her eyes and tried not to scream.

"Come on." Darius grabbed her hand and jogged around the outside of the chapel.

There were no gunshots as they rushed down the same stone stairs Mackenzie had blacked out on earlier.

"Guns." She managed to keep up in her heels and not look over her shoulder. "There were guns shooting at us."

"Yes, Mackenzie, there were guns."

Panicked tourists darted around the lower castle grounds.

She looked back to see if anyone had followed them down the stairway. "What happened to the guns?"

"The people shooting them died." He said each syllable slowly as if speaking to someone who's first language wasn't English.

"Should we send flowers?" Gun-battle etiquette was lost on her.

"No, we don't send flowers to the people who were trying to kill us." Darius shoved his gun into a holster tucked into his belt and covered it with his shirt.

"Oh, yeah, makes sense. I should send them a picture of me flipping them off."

"That's more like it."

Mackenzie saw a couple cowering in a stone doorway of a small building. The guy clutched his girlfriend by the hand and pushed her into the building as he looked around wide eyed. When they ran past, the guy yelled out something in a language she didn't recognize and ducked farther into the building with his girlfriend.

Had he mistook Darius and her for the threat? That was messed up.

Darius slowed down their pace to a fast walk as they headed for the exit at the base of the hill. His whole body was tense and his gaze reacted to every movement around them. He actually looked like he knew what he was doing.

Good, because she sure as hell didn't.

Mackenzie just focused on trying to not look suspicious as she kept glancing over her shoulder. It was quiet, too quiet, and the adrenaline pumping through her veins made her want to kick something.

As they stepped through the portcullis, rough hands grabbed her upper arm and ripped her out of Darius's protective grasp. A new bad guy, stocky with a buzz cut, pulled her around and slammed her into the unforgiving stone wall next to the archway. Her head cracked backwards against the rock and the all-too-familiar starbursts flooded her vision again. Her fingers slackened around the obsidian skull and it fell to the ground. Her legs gave out and she slid down the wall.

The skull rolled downhill away from her to the feet of a nefarious-looking, bald-headed man with a scar along his jaw.

"No," she breathed.

She turned to her right and saw Darius engaged in a struggle of his own with two Illuminati hit men. Damn, no help there.

Mr. Baldy picked up the skull and pulled a cell phone from his pocket.

Mr. Buzz Cut grabbed her by the arms and forced her to her feet.

"Let go of me." She fought to free herself, which only made him laugh. A hollow, cruel sound.

She struggled against him and her hand brushed a hard bulge under his arm. His jacket opened slightly and she saw a holstered gun. Without thinking, she tugged it out of the holster and pulled the trigger.

Mr. Buzz Cut looked down at his blood-soaked shirt and then up at her in disbelief.

She pulled the trigger again. His grip on her slackened and he crumbled to the ground.

She didn't have a chance to... what? She found herself in yet another situation in which she didn't know how to react. She pointed the gun at Mr. Baldy, who still held the skull.

"Put the skull down." She tried to sound menacing as she leaned back against the wall so she wouldn't collapse. Her head pounded in time to her thrumming heartbeat.

Mr. Baldy reached into his suit jacket, his intent clear on his face.

"I earned that skull, damnit. Now put it down." She raised the gun and aimed at his head.

She didn't want to shoot the man, she didn't want another death on her conscience, but when he pulled his hand out of his jacket, there was a flash of silver. She closed her eyes and squeezed the trigger. She squealed like a little girl and squeezed it again and again, the recoil jerking her arms each time.

She didn't stop until a hand gripped hers and she heard Darius's voice over the empty clicks of her weapon. "Enough."

Mackenzie opened her eyes as Darius pried her clenched fingers free of the gun.

"Who taught you to shoot with your eyes closed?" He wiped the weapon down with his shirt and tossed it onto the body of Mr. Buzz Cut.

"I never shot a gun before."

He picked up the skull and thrust the thing back into her hands. She fumbled with it as she followed him towards the now deserted exit.

She noticed movement in the window of the ticket booth and realized people were hiding from the mayhem. Wide, frightened eyes peered out at her as if she were the one responsible for what was happening.

They made it out of Edinburgh Castle without any more attacks.

The paved parking lot beyond the gates was more like an impromptu hideout for frightened tourists. As she and Darius weaved through the parked cars, she could see people popping their heads over the car hoods like meerkats.

Sirens of first responders blared from a distance, the very people who would have to deal with the dead bodies she left in her wake.

"I was conflicted."

"Conflicted?"

"I wanted the skull, but I didn't want to kill him. So, I thought if I closed my eyes and didn't see myself do it, then I didn't actually kill him... right?" She was hopeful, hell she was willing to convince herself it was true.

"Wrong."

It figured he would burst her bubble.

"However," Darius continued, "if you had kept your eyes open, you might've hit your target. He was only a couple of yards away, I might add. The only victim of your bloody-intelligent shooting spree was the five-hundred-year-old castle wall."

"I didn't kill him?"

"No, I did. Though the one who grabbed you, that was all you."

She paused, waiting for something like guilt to surface but felt nothing. "I'm surprisingly okay with that."

Just as they reached the end of the parking lot, Darius took a hard right and they made their way down yet another flight of steep stairs.

The sirens were louder now.

And maybe it was her pounding brain, or perhaps shock, but the sirens reminded her of ice cream trucks back home and she wondered if Scotland had their own ice cream trucks, and if so, did they play bagpipe music over their speakers?

Damn, now she craved a Rocket Ship ice cream cone.

They reached the bottom of the stairs and Darius stopped to look around. Mackenzie, however, continued walking right into the road.

"Watch it." He yanked her back just as three police cars sped past.

Their flashing blue lights only seemed to remind her more of the blue stripes in those rocket-shaped ice cream cones. "I want ice cream."

"What?" He turned her to face him and she grabbed his shoulders to keep her balance, because while she may have stopped moving, the scenery around her sure as hell didn't.

"Look at me."

She did, he was sort of hard to miss with both of his blurry faces mere inches away from hers.

"Your pupils are dilated, you have a concussion."

"I like those Rocket Ship cones, you know 'em? They're red, white and blue, although I can't remember what flavor they are. They're like colored pieces of shaved ice packed together with sugar."

"Right, and you also seem to be in shock."

CHAPTER 18

Darius peered around the semi-busy street to see if they were being watched. Empty, parked cars lined the narrow, two-way street that rounded the base of Edinburgh Castle and there was little in the way of foot traffic. From what he could tell, they were safe for the moment.

The fact the Illuminati found them at all was troubling. It meant L.G. had tipped them off somehow.

To what end, Darius couldn't fathom.

"Can we get some ice cream?" Mackenzie's subdued voice was at odds with, well, her.

"No." He stopped in front of a white compact car.

The vehicle was boring enough to go unnoticed in traffic and new enough to have electronic locks.

He pulled out his cell phone and typed the make and model into an app designed by one of the tech-savvy knights. He tapped the screen and waited for his phone to do its thing.

The doors unlocked and he scanned their surroundings once more for possible witnesses to their casual carjacking. Seeing no one, he ushered Mackenzie into the passenger seat of the car.

Mackenzie looked around with a frown. "Is this your car?"

"Yes." He slammed the door shut and jogged around to the driver's side.

He slid into the seat and started the engine with another tap of his cell phone app.

"Eight."

It was interesting how one single word could disrupt his calm. Now was not the time to be reminded that L.G. was calling the shots. Or, that the shell-shocked redhead sitting next to him didn't have much longer to live.

Mackenzie ran her fingers over the smooth surface of the skull in her lap. He stared at her, but must have stared at her longer than he thought because she turned her hazel gaze on him with a frown. "What? Why are you staring at me like that? You look like I dropped your favorite firearm in the ocean."

She was counting down to her death and she didn't even realize it.

He put the car into drive and drove them away from the carnage they had left behind at Edinburgh Castle. He checked the cars ahead and behind, and scanned the passing scenery for any obvious signs of a tail. There wasn't one as far as he could tell, but the Illuminati were almost as tricky as L.G.

Mackenzie strained to watch Edinburgh Castle until it vanished behind the blend of old and modern buildings of the city.

She hummed to herself and then looked at Darius. "You

looked troubled."

"You think?"

Darius glanced at his rearview mirror as he made an evasive turn down a side street.

"What's wrong? Well, aside from being shot at and killing a whole bunch of people." Mackenzie rubbed her forehead.

He looked over at her. Yes, she was definitely concussed. Even he wasn't this flippant the first time he killed someone, and he grew up in the dark ages.

"Oh my God," she blurted out. "I want ice cream soooo bad."

The girl almost died and now she wanted dessert. Part of him was intrigued, the other part wished she was a wilting flower, predictable and timid. Predictable, normal women did not attack evil, gun-wielding men.

"Don't ever attack someone pointing a gun at your head." The words erupted from him in a burst of anger he didn't realize he had as his mind replayed the horrific scene in the chapel. "What if he had pulled the trigger?"

Mackenzie hissed and cradled her head in her hands. "Stop yelling, my head is pounding." She pulled her hand away and stared at it. "I'm bleeding."

He glanced over at her and noticed a fine trickle of blood trailing down her right temple where the bastard had struck her with his gun.

"Holy crap, I'm dying."

"You should be more concerned by the fact he could've put a bullet in your skull."

She opened the glove compartment and pawed through the contents.

"Are you listening to me?" Darius was irked by her inability to appreciate the seriousness of the situation. Was she unaware how frail she was? How mortal?

"Um, this really isn't your car, is it?"

He let out a strangled groan of frustration and almost pulled over to shake some sense into her addled mind.

She removed a laminated identification card from the glove compartment and held it next to his face. She made a whole scene of looking back and forth between the card and him.

"Unless you're a gangly, redheaded teenage boy with acne, I think you stole this car."

Darius snatched the card from her fingers and tossed it into the back seat. "What you did back there was reckless."

"What did you expect me to do?" she snapped. "Simper and faint? Cry and beg for my life? Freeze like a deer caught in the headlights?"

"You could've–" 'Died' was what he was about to say but stopped short. There was a split second when the gun was pointed at her head in the chapel he forgot she was possessed by L.G. Man. In that moment, he realized he didn't want to see the light of life fade from her hazel eyes. And that was unacceptable, because that light was going to fade whether or not the Illuminati hit man pulled the trigger.

Even if they got the Mixtec Artifact to her in time, the odds were stacked against her. He caring whether she lived or died was a weakness they couldn't afford. "You could've lost the skull."

"Oh, and we can't have that." Mackenzie pulled a paper napkin from the glove compartment, held it to her temple and watched the buildings pass by her window. "Although, if I had died, the prophecy wouldn't happen."

He yanked the car to the side of the road, wrenched the gear box into park and faced her. "All you need to concern yourself with is staying alive. I'll prevent the apocalypse."

She looked down at the skull in her lap and he saw her hopeful conviction waver.

"You're telling me we actually stand a chance against this

demon possessing me." Her voice was cynical. "Your people can't even figure out what the skulls are really made of, let alone how to destroy them. What in the world makes you think we can stop her?"

He had no answer to that. "I'll figure something out."

"Seven."

Darius clenched his jaw and floored the accelerator. The tires squealed and the back end swerved as the car careened back onto the road.

"Darius?" Mackenzie's confused voice trickled over him.

He spared one last glance at her before he focused his attention on the road ahead. She looked at him like she believed he was the only person in the whole world who could somehow make this all better.

And, damned as he was, he wanted to be the person she believed him to be.

CHAPTER 19

"We need to get our things and relocate to a different location." Darius barked the orders and opened the car door for her, his chivalrous actions and he-man commands at odds with each other.

Mackenzie chose to keep her mouth shut on the subject, since he was all business at this point. It wasn't like she had any better ideas.

They entered the George Hotel and Darius checked out everyone they passed as if they all were would-be Illuminati assassins. He even scrutinized an old woman who stood by the concierge desk.

As they walked, Mackenzie tried to brush her hair forward with her fingers to hide the blood that had crusted on her temple. Her fingers fluttered over the wound and she discovered smooth, unbroken skin. "It's gone."

A middle-aged man who walked by stared at her. Darius

huffed, grabbed her hand and pulled her faster towards the elevators.

"L.G. has some limited healing capabilities," he said.

"Really?"

"Does your head still hurt?"

"Not anymore."

"In the eighteen hundreds, I shot a person she had possessed. It was a graze on the arm and when I saw her a few days later, she was fine, not a scratch." Darius let go of her hand and pressed the elevator button.

The old woman from the concierge desk joined them and they fell into silence.

Mackenzie gave her a polite smile and she smiled back. The seconds ticked along and Mackenzie couldn't help but fiddle with the hair at her temple again.

"You're fine," Darius grumbled next to her. "And stop looking guilty."

She glared at him. How could he look so calm and at ease? He just survived a shootout with a super-villain organization for goodness' sake.

When he gave her a smug I'm-so-much-better-at-this-than-you look, she contemplated kicking him in the shins. The elevator doors slid open before she could act on her thoughts.

Darius let the old woman enter first, then guided Mackenzie to the back of the elevator as he pushed the button for the fourth floor.

Silence reigned inside the old elevator as they slowly rose. Mackenzie had nothing else to do but stare at the back of the old woman, who faced the front. While Mackenzie wasn't as hyper-aware of everything around her as Darius was, something about the old woman's slightly hunched stance caught her attention.

The woman was the epitome of elderly frailty, dressed in

ugly old-people clothes and wearing a lot of the color beige. But Mackenzie could swear there was a faint protrusion at the old woman's neckline that seemed familiar.

Then it clicked.

Her uncle's shirt had the same crease when he wore his bullet-proof vest under his Santa Cruz County Sheriff's uniform.

The old woman opened her huge purse. "Now where is that key card?"

Mackenzie grabbed Darius's hand and squeezed.

"What?" Darius seemed distracted.

"Um..." How could she relate that something was off, however uncertain she was, without alerting the woman in front of her?

The old woman smiled at her through the reflection of the polished gold elevator door, which meant pointing at her was out of the question. "Something about a duck?"

If his frown was any indication, he recalled her earlier conversation with Lauren about their panic phrase. Unfortunately, he didn't have the years of friendship with her that she had with Lauren to interpret her subtle nudges and twitches like her friend could.

The old lady started to pull her hand out of her gargantuan purse and once again Mackenzie reacted without much concern for her own safety. Praying she wasn't wrong, she leaped forward and shoved the old woman face first into the closed elevator doors.

"Macken–" Darius's yell was cut off when the old woman dropped her purse and a small handgun skittered across the floor, followed by a syringe filled with an opaque liquid.

"Ah ha." Mackenzie pointed at the contents like a police dog that just sniffed out a bomb.

Darius pulled her back and incapacitated the would-be assassin with just a few moves. He caught the unconscious woman just as the elevator doors opened and carried her out.

Wide eyed, Mackenzie looked into the hall and let out a happy little sigh of relief when no one was there to bear witness to their elder abuse.

"Wait." She picked up the woman's purse, gun and syringe from the floor and raced after Darius as he strode down the hall carrying the woman. "You're not going to kill her?"

"Too messy."

"Um, hello." She waved the gun and syringe in his face. "She had no problem doing it to us."

He stopped in front of the door next to her room. "Front left pocket."

"Say what now?"

"Front. Left. Pocket. Is the key card to my room. Get it."

With pleasure. Mackenzie tried not to blush as she slid her hand into his pants pocket, pulled out his key card and opened the door.

Darius dumped the woman on the couch and motioned his head towards the connecting door to her room. "Get your things."

He pulled his phone out of his front right pocket, tapped the screen and held it to his ear.

Mackenzie dropped the syringe, gun and bag by the sofa.

"I need cleanup at the George Hotel and transport to a safe house." Darius's voice trailed off into quiet discourse as Mackenzie stepped into her room.

She grabbed her Birkin bag and Darius entered her room with his own small leather backpack. It was annoying at how good looking and put together he seemed after everything that had just happened. She didn't dare look at her own reflection in the mirror.

"Ready?" he asked.

"Are you asking? Or *really* asking?"

Darius grabbed her arm and took the Birkin bag from her. "What gets you out the door faster?"

"Oh, well then, I'm totally fine. Never been better."

The sarcasm wasn't lost on him.

CHAPTER 20

They took two cars and a train and not once did Mackenzie see Darius's 'people.' He would just get a text right when they needed their next transportation connection and, abracadabra, there would be a car ready and waiting next to the curb with keys hidden on the back tire, or train tickets reserved under pseudonyms.

It was all very James Bond.

After eight plus hours of travel, they finally stopped somewhere in the middle of the English countryside at a quaint, rustic cottage with a fire already burning in the fireplace.

Freshly showered, Mackenzie sat on a plush, queen-sized bed wearing cheap, drawstring cotton pants and a 'Keep Calm and Carry On' t-shirt she picked up at the train station. The shirt was a little cheesy for her liking, but it was clean.

The only thing that could have made the moment better

was not being possessed in the first place. If she hadn't been possessed, she would have never killed anyone. Not ever.

She could still see the man's shock and pain in her mind's eye. But instead of feeling bad, she just saw herself in his shoes. Her life was heading towards a similar end. Either the Illuminati would shoot her or she would beg Darius to kill her if the prophecy was too close to being fulfilled. She doubted she could kill herself. Even if it came down to her or the whole world, she wasn't that selfless.

A light knock on the door pulled her from her thoughts.

"Yeah." She got off the bed and ignored the chill when her bare feet hit the cold wood floor.

Darius walked in and held up a red, white and blue ice cream cone.

She stood corrected, ice cream could make the moment better.

She smiled. "I could kiss you."

"You won't hear any complaints from me."

She ignored him and took the ice cream, speaking to it as if it were the hottest man in the room. "My beautiful, sugary goodness. I don't care if you're bad for me, I'll devour you with love."

Darius cleared his throat. "I also had my people drop off some clothes." He grabbed a cloth bag from the hallway and held it out for her. "I thought jeans and sneakers would be a welcome change to L.G.'s choice in wardrobe."

"I could kiss you," she said again with a wide smile. She grabbed the bag with her free hand and hugged it against her body. In the bag were sneakers, a shirt, a jacket, some socks, a bra and a couple of pairs of simple lacey panties.

"Don't say things you don't plan acting on." His tone dropped a titillating octave that woke up parts of her that should have been too tired to function.

"Fine then, I'll just call you 'my hero.'"

He raised an eyebrow in question.

"My hero," Mackenzie licked her ice cream cone with innuendo, "who nearly got shot by a frail, old lady."

His steamy stare turned into a scowl and she couldn't help but laugh.

"And it was I, Mackenzie, Warrior Princess, who came to your rescue."

"Now, you're exaggerating. Come." He trudged into the hall. "There's hot food downstairs."

Mackenzie left the bag of clothing on the hope chest at the foot of the bed and followed him like a lost puppy, licking her ice cream as she went. The aroma of baked bread reached her nose as her foot hit the bottom step. The last semi-substantial thing she had eaten, aside from the ice cream, was a bag of chips she bought at the train station.

"Sit, I'll bring you a plate." He motioned towards a cozy, little loveseat in the living room and headed into the kitchen.

Mackenzie sank into the couch and tucked her feet under her with a happy sigh. For the moment she was safe. Well, as safe as she could be while being possessed, but she was too tired to care about that little discrepancy.

She finished off her Rocket Ship cone and her attention fell to a bottle of whiskey and a half-filled glass tumbler on the coffee table in front of her.

"Aw, Darius, you shouldn't have." She leaned forward, grabbed the glass and brought it to her lips.

"I didn't." He snatched it from her hand before she could take a sip and replaced it with a plate of pizza.

"Rude."

He tossed back the amber liquid in one gulp and went back to the kitchen. He returned with a plate of his own in one hand and a can of soda in the other.

"I don't think it wise to drink while under the influence of L.G." He handed her the soda and took a seat in a chair across from her, placing his plate of pizza on his lap.

"Buzz-kill."

He ignored her and took a bite of his pizza.

Mackenzie examined the two slices of cheese pizza on her plate. It wasn't the best looking pizza she ever saw, but it smelled delicious and made her miss her best friend. Pizza night usually meant watching wonderfully bad 'B' films together.

She smiled and shoved her home sickness aside. "Pizza. How very American."

"Indeed. I thought it would be nice for you to have something familiar. Considering."

"You make it sound like I have a terminal illness."

He choked on the food he'd been meticulously chewing.

"You okay?"

He quickly refilled his glass and washed his choking back with a swig of whiskey. "Fine."

"So…" She tried to sound as uninterested as possible as she opened the can of soda and took a sip. "Where's the skull now?"

She hadn't seen it since the first car ride out of Edinburgh, but didn't comment since he didn't appear concerned.

"On its way to a secure location."

A non-answer.

"Aren't you afraid that whoever has it is going to get possessed, too? I mean, one L.G. running around is bad enough."

Darius refilled his glass with whiskey and took another swig, then set the glass aside. "L.G.'s skull is the only one capable of possessing people because it's the only one that contains an entity. Think of her as the keeper of all thirteen skulls. She scatters them across the world when she doesn't need them, ensuring they all don't fall into the hands of any one individual, unless it's her hands."

"Seems like a lot of work."

Darius shrugged. "Scattering the skulls has prevented them from all being discovered by now. So, while it's a lot of effort, I can see why she'd do it. Yet somehow with all the effort to hide them, she's always had them on hand whenever she wanted to call her people in the past."

Mackenzie froze. "She's done this before?"

"Yes."

"When? How? Why are we all still here?"

"The last time they were gathered was millennia before me."

Yet another non-answer. She almost lunged across the coffee table to beat the truth out of him. Well, she would have attempted to beat him, but with his cat-like reflexes he'd have her pinned in seconds. Not a particularly bad predicament to find oneself in, but still. "Explain."

Darius studied her for an infuriating minute as if he contemplated whether or not she had a need to know.

"Hey, don't forget I'm the one possessed by the ender of the world. I should at least know what she's done before."

He capitulated. "Have you ever heard of the Hittite Empire?"

"Um, it's an ancient civilization?" That was a guess.

"Yes, an ancient civilization and a powerful one at that. It baffles the 'uninitiated' archeologists because it disappeared from history." He said the word 'uninitiated' as if it were an insult to be normal and unaware of the world as the Templars knew it. "For them, the Hittite Empire was a force in the east one minute and gone the next. As if the people just awoke one morning, decided to leave their homes, their land, their lives and vanish into thin air. The truth of the matter is L.G. saw the thriving cities and large population, gathered her skulls and called her people to come and collect. When they were finished, there was nothing left of the

Hittites. What remained of the civilization collapsed and was reclaimed by the sand."

"Where did they go?"

Darius shrugged. "Can't say, but L.G. has stated on more than one occasion that we made durable slaves."

Mackenzie tore her pizza slice into smaller pieces as she thought about that disturbing detail. When this was over she was definitely going to buy holy water and a few crosses.

"So they took the Hittites and just left L.G. here?"

He nodded.

"Why didn't they take everyone?"

Darius poured himself more whiskey and swirled the amber liquid around in the glass. "My guess is they didn't want to take so many they would risk future inbreeding or panic the entire population, which would have slowed the replenishing of our numbers. The Hittite empire wasn't the only civilization to disappear because of L.G., but they were the last we know of. That was three thousand years ago."

"Why wait so long? Our population has more than recovered."

Darius shrugged and sipped his drink.

"Well, if we're their supply of slaves, the world isn't going to end then," Mackenzie said. "That's good. Of course it's still bleak, but you made it sound earlier like we have an Armageddon situation on our hands."

"We do. L.G. has changed over the millennia. From what my mentor, Jonathan, told me about her, she's grown angry and resentful. He told me she more than wants to return home, but she's been waiting. For what, I don't know. Jonathan didn't know either. But for whatever reason she's gathering the skulls now, this time when she goes back to where she came from, she intends to leave nothing but wasteland behind her."

"But she wouldn't wipe out the entire population, that

would destroy any future slave profits." Mackenzie frowned. That was something she never thought she'd say or ever be somewhat happy about.

"L.G. always gets what she wants."

"And she will become a god herself and unlike man fall not from grace," Mackenzie said softly. At least that part of the prophecy made sense now. Sort of. "What about her body? I mean her people can't just consist of a bunch of obsidian skulls, and where do they live? Hell? The prophecy says they are coming from their home in the sky, but I doubt they're coming from heaven. What demon-like creature comes from the sky?"

"I honestly don't know." Darius ran his hand through his hair.

Mackenzie sipped her soda and then put the can on her empty plate, running over the prophecy in her mind.

"What about the Phoenicians?"

"They were a people who—"

"No, not who they were, I actually know that." Of everything she didn't know about ancient history, she knew about the Phoenicians thanks to the ride in the big Epcot ball at Disney World. "They're the ones that created our modern alphabet. And just like the Hittites, they're no longer around. So, how are they going to bear witness as the world ends?"

He shook his head with a contemplative look on his face that told her not knowing was frustrating for him. "I hope we shall never find out."

She watched the fire burning in the fireplace across the room and cleared her mind of her own frustrations. The past was done and she couldn't dwell on the 'what ifs' anymore.

While the future was filled with too many questions, the present, at least, had her safe, warm and protected by an immortal knight, who looked nothing like his seven-century age with his solid chest, strong hands and unending stamina.

Nope. She shook herself. She couldn't think about that either.

She shifted in her seat and forced her thoughts anywhere but on the fact they were in the middle of nowhere with a very empty and very comfy bed upstairs. A bed capable of fitting more than one person in it, even with his broad, muscular shoulders and over six-foot frame.

"So," Mackenzie cleared her throat, "how many times has the world been prophesied to end since you became a knight?"

"More than you'd think. Each knight is constantly working to prevent Armageddon."

Well, that was disturbing but wasn't her focus at the moment, she was more interested in her knight. No, she corrected herself, the knight. She had no claim on him, never would.

Her mind drifted to the face of the man whose life she took. What she should have felt, guilt and remorse, didn't surface. Not in the way she thought. Her actions, no matter how justified, had a price, she knew that much. But what that price was she didn't know yet. "Is it hard doing whatever it takes to keep the world from ending?"

Darius sat there for a second in silence. "Yes."

"And your mentor? Was he the one who introduced you to this life?"

"Yes." Darius pushed himself to his feet, gathered her plate with his and walked towards the kitchen.

"And where is he now?"

He stopped and looked back at her. His brown eyes were stormy, his expression hard. "You should focus on letting L.G. find the remaining skulls."

He disappeared into the kitchen, leaving her alone in more ways than one. It was a feeling that left her wanting to curl up in the comforting safety of her old, worn-in couch in her apartment back home. But even if the search for the obsidian skulls ended that second, there would be no returning to her home, no comfort from her favorite blanket.

She got up from the couch, unsure what to do with herself. She took two steps towards the kitchen and stopped.

She wasn't going to be that girl, the one who couldn't stand to be alone. Darius made it clear his only interest in her was because L.G. could help him find the skulls. At least Darius promised to de-posses her when this was over, but that was all she should expect from him. He had a job to do and she was just the means to an end.

He had far more important things to do than be her BFF.

Instead of the kitchen, Mackenzie walked towards the stairs, head held high with a confidence she didn't quite feel.

"I'm going to bed," she said loud enough for him to hear but didn't wait for a response.

CHAPTER 21

Darius strained to hear Mackenzie's every move upstairs. Even knowing L.G. could surface at any moment, he wanted to give her a few minutes alone. It helped that the entire house and surrounding land was locked up tighter than the Tower of London. If L.G. so much as looked at a window wrong, an alarm would go off.

He knew that to solely rely on technology was folly. Still, he remained at the sink, over-concentrating on the task of washing dishes.

If he was being honest, and this really wasn't the time or the place for such a thing, he needed distance from her. She was pretty, vibrant and smart, and he had lived far too long alone in his self-imposed exile. Man wasn't built to be solitary.

But she wasn't irresistible just because of that. No, he knew he would have been drawn to her even if he had met her under different circumstances.

He set the last dish on the drying rack and stared at the sudsy water in the sink. He should be happy or, at the very least, relieved that his hunt for the obsidian skulls was at last nearing an end. He had planned for this day for centuries, looked forward to it.

When he thought of the end now, though, he thought of Mackenzie's end.

He dried his hands on a dish towel and tossed it on the counter. He pulled his cell phone from his pocket and called Finley.

A guttural, Scottish-accented voice snarled over the line. "Och, someone better be dead."

"Finley."

"Darius." A bit of the harsh gruffness filtered out of Finley's voice.

Darius's free hand gripped the wood of the counter in a white-knuckled hold. "Did you get it?"

Finley huffed. "I'm not sure you completely remember the last time we dealt with the Vatican."

"I believe the Cardinal's words were, 'I hope God finds it in his forgiving heart to smite you and every Templar Knight from the face of the earth.' But I'm paraphrasing."

"And you think I've managed to get the very artifact that failed to save their Pope in just one day?" Finley laughed in a way that lacked any humor. "I'm good, but I'm not that good. I'm gonna need a bit more time, ya ken?"

"Do I have a choice?"

"Not really. I may be out of reach for a bit."

The piercing screech of an alarm cut through the air around Darius.

"Everything all right?" Finley's voice was almost drowned out by the siren.

Darius strode two long steps out of the kitchen and into

the hall. He stopped in front of a bare, wood-paneled wall, felt for the hidden button in the wood and pressed it. A panel slid to the side, revealing six small black-and-white screens. They displayed closed-circuit TV views of the cottage and the surrounding property.

In the upper left corner of the panel was a larger screen, displaying a digital map of the grounds and the floor plan of the small, two-story cottage. A red light flashed on the floor plan at the window of Mackenzie's room, designating the location of the security breach.

"Darius?" Finley said.

"False alarm." He turned off the phone, disabled the blasted siren and took the stairs two at a time.

He threw open the bedroom door to find Mackenzie straddling the windowsill. She looked over her shoulder at him, her metallic eyes glinting.

Not Mackenzie.

Darius stormed into the room as her pretty little mouth tugged into a coquettish grin. He snaked his arm around her waist and pulled her back inside. He tossed her on the bed and pinned her on the mattress with the entire length of his body.

"You said you'd work with me to find the remaining skulls." Darius shook with restraint from his need to force her into submission. "What the bloody hell is this?"

"I cannot in good conscience let an opportunity to escape pass by. Only a fool would assume I would become an amiable twit just because I agreed to work with you."

L.G. didn't struggle when he grabbed her left wrist with one hand. He pulled a pair of handcuffs from his back pocket, flipped one cuff around the wrought iron bedpost and clasped the other around her wrist.

L.G. let out a deep, throaty laugh.

He reached over to the nightstand and opened the

drawer. Nestled exactly where he told his people to place them was another pair of handcuffs, which he used to secure her other wrist to the bedpost. Her slender body was now spread out helplessly before him. Well her upper half anyway.

Her throaty laugh faded and L.G.'s auburn head drooped forward then jerked back up. She looked up at him, the metallic glint gone.

Mackenzie took in his face, hovering so close. Her gaze trailed downwards and studied his body pressed against hers.

Darius was surprised at the carnal heat that flared to life inside him. It pulled at his chains of control and brought to the fore a hunger that was best left to people who weren't trying to prevent an apocalyptic prophecy.

He shifted his hips away just enough so he didn't accost her splayed-out form with his own hard interest.

It was a herculean effort because he wanted to linger against her curves. And that was wrong on so many levels, the main one being she was a victim.

Mackenzie's hands twitched as if she wanted to touch him. The metallic clink of metal against metal rattled.

She frowned and turned her head to see what prevented her movement. "Oh, come on! What's up with you and shackling things to my wrists? Now, if we were talking kinky sex, that's a whole other story, but this..." She raised her wrists to prove a point. "This is neither fun, nor kinky. It's borderline psychotic and you know it."

He eased himself away from her, ignoring his tang of disappointment, and sat next to her on the edge of the bed.

"L.G. surfaced didn't she?" she said, sounding calmer.

"She tried to escape."

"I didn't—" She yanked at her restraints. "I couldn't stop her."

"I know."

"I'll try better to warn you." Mackenzie glared at him. "Please take these off."

"No."

In a huff, Mackenzie swung her foot up at his head. He caught the offending appendage before it connected with the side of his face.

He locked his fingers around her ankle, lowered it to the mattress and rubbed a comforting thumb over the exposed skin. It was smooth and soft and he wondered if the rest of her was as well.

Mackenzie didn't tell him to stop. If she uttered that single word, he would let go.

He watched her pull at her restraints one last time and let out a defeated sigh.

He understood her frustration, had experienced it firsthand to an extent. There was nothing worse than losing control over one's life, feeling it slip through your fingers and unable to do anything to stop it.

It was an exhausting way to live. Hell, he was one old bastard and if it wasn't for the constant threat of the skulls, he would have tired of his existence a long time ago.

"So, did she stab you again?" Mackenzie tried to give him a smile, but it didn't reach her eyes.

"No, nothing as... drastic as that this time. She just wanted to chat."

"To chat?" She didn't believe him.

"And remind me who's in charge."

"And that's not you."

"No." It was a hard admitted truth.

"How is that?" Mackenzie watched him. She had to know the extent of what he was up against by now, but true to a woman's nature, she wanted to talk about it. "You have L.G.'s skulls, shouldn't you be the one calling the shots?"

"She knows where the other skulls are and likes to

remind me from time to time that I do not."

"Right. Skull radar," she mumbled. "And the handcuffs?"

"I need sleep."

"And you can't afford that I might slip away or kill you while you slept." Mackenzie winced. "Huh, I can't even promise you I won't do that."

He wanted to pull her into his arms and say anything that would sound comforting, but he managed to keep his hands to himself.

"Finley's close," he blurted out without forethought. He cleared his throat when her hazel eyes focused in on him. "Close to getting the artifact for you."

Mackenzie shimmied back towards headboard and sat up a little bit. "And?"

"And..." Wasn't that enough?

Somehow he didn't think she'd appreciate his candor if he followed that up with the reality that her chances of survival got slimmer with every passing second or that L.G. could kill her before she ever saw the artifact.

"And..." He sat there like the village idiot grasping for anything to say but the honest truth. "And... Finley... is finalizing his plans to extricate the artifact as we speak. If he doesn't get killed in the process, there's a medium-to-high possibility of success."

There, good, comforting news. All the knights he worked with would have been more than emboldened by those odds.

"Wow, seriously?" Her head dropped back against the wrought iron headboard with a clang. "You could have just said the artifact is on its way and insert amount of time here."

"This is the Vatican. Anything we plan and prepare for will surely go to hell–"

She snorted.

"So, any timeframe I give you would be a lie. But Finley

knows what he's doing and doesn't take failure well."

"I guess it's better than nothing." She shimmied back down the mattress as far as her handcuffed wrists would allow. "When will we know that he has it?"

Darius reached over and adjusted the pillow under her head, bringing him close enough to feel the heat radiating from her body.

His attention lingered a little longer than was needed as he made sure the pillow was just right. When she licked her bottom lip, he almost lost it.

He tucked a stray hair behind her ear and her lips opened just a touch in silent invitation.

This was madness. She could become L.G. at any moment.

And just like that his desire fizzled and died. He pulled back and didn't miss the disappointment that flittered across her face.

"It's been a long day. Sleep." He turned off the light on the bedside table and stood.

"Where will you be?"

"Outside. If you need anything, all you need to do is yell." Darius shut the window, then stopped just inside the doorway. "Anything at all."

The only light in the cozy room drifted in from the hall. It was enough to make Mackenzie's pale skin look as if it glowed faintly of its own accord. She reminded him of a siren, or a ghost.

"Um..." She hesitated.

He knew if she asked him to stay, he would, and as stupid as that would be, he wanted her to ask.

"Okay." Her voice was breathy, but she said no more. Gave no invitation.

He nodded, stepped into the hall and shut the door behind him with a heavy breath.

He needed to get laid and by someone other than the fiery redhead handcuffed to the bed. Yet, he knew no other woman would hold his interest long enough to satiate his need.

An exaggerated yell came from her room. He yanked his knife from the sheath on his ankle and dashed back inside.

She looked up at him with wide eyes.

"What is it?"

"You said to yell." She tried to pull off an innocent expression, but her sly smile ruined it.

"What do you need?" He slid the knife back in its sheath.

She looked around the room before she raised her left wrist. "Can you at least take off the bracelet?"

"No."

That earned him a haughty raise of her eyebrow and a pout of her lips. He found he could get used to her being annoyed, especially if she wore a little less clothing.

"Won't or can't?"

He had no bloody clue how to get the enchanted piece of silver off her wrist and he loathed to admit that travesty out loud.

"Goodnight, Mackenzie." He shut the door again and went downstairs.

He reset the alarm, took a pillow from the couch and went back upstairs. He dropped the pillow on the hallway floor in front of Mackenzie's door and sprawled out on the threadbare runner. Then he closed his eyes and crossed his arms over his chest, just like he used to before the invention of memory-foam mattresses and central heat.

CHAPTER 22

It was difficult to sleep with one ear strained to any noise from inside Mackenzie's room. When the soft morning light crept in through the small hallway window, Darius couldn't take the hardwood floor anymore and pushed to his feet.

True to England, the entire cottage was enveloped in a layer of morning chill. He stretched his stiff muscles and made his way downstairs to the kitchen. He grabbed a pint of milk and a palm-sized block of cheese from the fridge, then went over to a loaf of sourdough bread sitting on a cutting block on the counter.

He didn't bother with formalities, he just ripped off a chunk of bread with his teeth, bit off some cheese and mixed the two together in his mouth as he chewed.

He enjoyed the morning quiet as he took another bite of bread, then cheese, and leaned against the counter. It wasn't until he was halfway finished with the loaf that he remembered he wasn't alone and Mackenzie might not be so receptive to his barbaric style of breakfast. She would be even less amused at having to eat something he had already gnawed on.

She was a woman who probably wanted things like eggs, bacon, pancakes and orange juice for breakfast.

He tossed his rudimentary meal aside and searched for a pan to make eggs, since he had no idea how to make pancakes. He pulled a pan out from the cupboard, went to the stove and hesitated. Concern over Mackenzie's breakfast preferences meant he cared, and that was a problem. He would have let anyone else figure out their own damn breakfast.

He set the pan aside, grabbed a knife from a drawer and cut off his bite marks from the bread and cheese. She would just have to be happy nibbling from each like he had. Or she could cook her own damned breakfast. But she'd have to do it without a knife, a pan or basically anything else that could be used as a weapon, in case L.G. surfaced.

He sighed and cut the bread and cheese into neat slices. Then he tossed them onto a plate and frowned.

Maybe frying some eggs and toasting bread for her wouldn't be such a horrific disadvantage to him. It could be seen as just caring for his ward. He could even lie and say he cooked breakfast for himself all the time. No one would be the wiser.

Then Mackenzie would look at him with those eyes that said he was truly her knight in shining armor. And if he was lucky, she'd be so grateful she'd allow him to show her how much fun being handcuffed to a bed could be.

During which time L.G. would surface and gut him before he realized the changeover had happened. What was he thinking? Cheese slices and cold bread it was. Mackenzie should be grateful he bothered to feed her at all.

Darius grabbed the plate, strode across the kitchen and then stopped at the stove when his attention fell on the discarded pan on the counter.

Bugger it all, he was going to make her eggs and toast.

The blare of an alarm cut through the silence.

"Oh, thank Christ." He tossed the plate on the counter and dashed over to the security panel.

He typed in the code to turn off the alarm and scanned the screens for the threat.

Mackenzie's room wasn't lit up this time. This time the red light blinked on the outside perimeter near the gravel driveway about a quarter of a mile away. The small CCTV screen displayed a dark sedan parked at the entrance with a very familiar-looking man leaning against the door.

The man Darius stole an obsidian skull from in Santa Cruz.

"Shite." The Illuminati had found them.

He ran upstairs and barged into Mackenzie's room.

Mackenzie was already awake, her disheveled hair reminding him of a lion's main.

"You kept me handcuffed to the bed?"

Nope, not Mackenzie.

"We're leaving." Darius grabbed the bag of her clothes and tossed them on her stomach. Then he released L.G.'s wrists from the bedposts and pocketed the handcuffs.

She swung at him with a furious growl and Darius batted her hand away. "We don't have time for this. Get dressed."

"Of all the indignities I have suffered over the millennia, this has to be the most humiliating."

He pressed his hand over L.G.'s mouth. "The Illuminati are here, so gripe at me when we're safe. Now. Get. Dressed."

L.G. made a muffled noise he could only assume was

more outrage. He ignored her and put a few feet of distance between them.

She reached in the bag and pulled out a pair of jeans, a t-shirt, socks, and a dark blue lacey bra and panties. She looked as if she had just pulled out a pile of steaming hot poo.

"Could you not afford something more appealing?"

He imagined how the lacey underwear would look against Mackenzie's pale skin and questioned L.G.'s tastes because they were quite appealing to him. "Hurry up."

L.G. pulled her night shirt over her head and grabbed the clothes from the bed. Darius tried not to stare, but he couldn't afford to turn his back on her either. Not that he could at this point even if he tried.

Mackenzie's body was a thing of beauty. She had a flat stomach, a nice perky round ass and breasts that looked just big enough to fill his hands. Her pale skin was smattered with freckles that called to him. She was beautiful and completely off limits.

He just had to keep reminding himself of that last detail.

When L.G. finished tying her shoelaces, Darius grabbed her arm and pulled her down the stairs into the living room. He checked the security monitors and discovered that half a dozen Illuminati soldiers had just breached the tree line surrounding the field wherein the cottage was situated.

"How did they find us?" L.G. went to the front window. The curtains were drawn, but she inched one aside just enough to peer out. "Do you have a traitor in your ranks?"

"Impossible."

"Is it though?"

Darius ignored her. He knew people were fallible, but they had more pressing matters at the moment than to discuss a possible leak among the Templar Knights.

He turned the coffee table on its side and pulled back the

rug. Nestled within the floorboards was a small keypad on a hidden door. He punched in the code and pulled it open, revealing a hidden compartment loaded with an arsenal of weapons.

He grabbed his backpack and filled it with two handguns, ten loaded magazines, a grenade, a box of cherry bombs, an assortment of knives, two ropes, two flashlights, a lighter, a pair of gloves and a roll of duct tape. He grabbed Mackenzie's purse from the floor next to the couch, removed a bundle of cash from it and dropped the offending bag into the hole. He shouldered his backpack, locked the hidden compartment and put the furniture and rug back to rights.

"Darius?" L.G.'s voice trickled over him like dirty water.

"What?" He went back to the monitors and saw that the Illuminati had surrounded the clearing, trapping them inside.

"I thought you said you liberated one of my skulls from the Illuminati."

"I did." He pulled out the duct tape and a grenade from his backpack and went to the front door.

"Then why do they have one now?"

Darius duct taped a grenade to the floor by the side of the door where it opened. With care, he trailed a length of duct tape from the grenade's pin to the door's edge.

L.G. glared at him when he stood, hands fisted at her sides. "I gave you one simple task. I damn near handed their skull to you myself and you failed?"

He yanked out a short length of duct tape, tore it off the roll and slapped it over her mouth. He turned her bodily towards the back of the house and urged her forward. He only stopped long enough to type a code into the security panel to wipe out all the hard drives and monitors. They crackled and fizzled, then went black.

He stopped her just shy of the back door and removed a small picture of a peaceful countryside from the wall. He

Insta-Prophecy Hotline

flicked a little switch he found there and a hidden door next to him opened a crack with a soft schnick sound.

L.G. pulled the duct tape off her mouth as he opened the door. He turned on the light, pushed her forward towards a narrow, wooden stairway leading down and shut the door behind them.

The wood creaked under their weight as they descended into the perpetual mustiness of the cellar. The room was littered with old tables, a grandfather clock and discarded boxes. A dozen broken chairs were shoved up against the left wall and a large wine rack took up most of the right wall.

L.G. went to the wine rack. Darius thought she was going to examine the dusty old bottles, but she knew far more about Templar Knight protocol than he gave her credit for. She ran her fingers down the side of the rack, feeling for the hidden switch that would unlock the secret passageway they both knew was there. He grabbed her wrist and stilled her expectant fingers.

"False exit. Nasty surprises that." He pulled her towards the stack of wooden chairs piled high above their heads. "This way."

He tugged on a sturdy chair leg that pointed out at an odd angle and the wall of chairs moved towards them as one, unveiling a narrow subterranean passageway. Darius pulled out a flashlight from his backpack and illuminated the tunnel for a few feet before the shadows engulfed the light.

"Clever," L.G. said as if in fact it wasn't.

"Go in."

"Oh, no." She slowly shook her head.

Darius reached forward, preparing to shove her into their only damned escape route when L.G. blinked. The metallic glint faded and her haughty expression cleared, only to be replaced by confusion as Mackenzie looked around at their surroundings.

"Mackenzie." He put an urgency in that single word and a subtext that demanded she trust him.

He gave her a flashlight and pushed her forward into the underground tunnel. He pulled the wall of chairs closed behind him and followed her.

The tunnel was tight and Darius had to hunch over to keep his head from skimming the ceiling.

Mackenzie walked at a steady pace, but her movements were hesitant. "I think I'm becoming claustrophobic."

"What doesn't kill you..."

"Hasn't killed me yet," she finished for him. "I don't want to press my luck, I didn't have much of it to start with."

"Aren't you part Irish? Aren't they innately lucky?"

"Half Irish, half Scottish. They cancel each other out."

A loud explosion surged around them. Dirt shook free from the low, rounded ceiling and dusted their heads and shoulders.

Mackenzie reversed until she pressed against him.

"What the hell was that?" she whispered.

"The Illuminati found my grenade at the front door. It'll only slow them down, so go." He nudged her forward again.

She didn't budge. "Any other surprises I should expect, like death by tunnel collapse?"

"When they find the false exit in the cellar, there'll be a bigger boom, if that's what you mean."

Mackenzie jogged down the tunnel and Darius chuckled. He caught up with her and put his hand on the small of her back in what he hoped was a comforting gesture. He almost snatched his hand away when he found he enjoyed the touch a lot more than he should. They were running for their lives, for God's sake.

He almost pulled away, but when her shoulders seemed to relax from their previous tightened rise to her ears, he lingered. He'd worry about the ramifications later.

Ten minutes of silent, fast-paced trudging and finally their flashlights shone on a solid stone wall that barred them from going further. Mackenzie threw herself at the wall, her free hand frantically searching for some hidden lever.

He pulled her back into his chest, grabbed her hand holding the flashlight and pointed it towards the low ceiling. It illuminated a dark, solid metal grate.

"Huh, you'd think I'd learn to look up by now," she said more to herself than to him.

Darius slipped past her, braced his hands against the grate set into the ceiling and pushed up until two fingers of sunlight spilled in. The light damn near blinded him.

He paused and waited for any signs of life outside. When he saw and heard nothing, other than the expected sounds of the forest, he heaved the heavy steel grate aside and pulled himself up and out. He took the flashlight from Mackenzie's outstretched hand and stuck it in his backpack. Then he offered Mackenzie his hand, which she took.

Darius lifted her up and set her on her feet in front of him. She had no reaction at being freed from the pitch black passageway, offered no sarcastic quip. She just stared off at a tree branch just above his shoulder. He pressed his finger to her furrowed brow, flattening out the frown line as best he could.

She finally looked at him.

"You all right?" He rested his hands on her shoulders.

"I'm fine." She peered at their surroundings curiously. "Where are we?"

"This, my lady, is our escape." He swept his arm out dramatically towards a small car covered with a camouflage-colored tarp, which was nestled between two trees at what seemed like the beginning of a vaguely marked forest road.

Her hands fisted at her sides.

Darius strode past her, grabbed the tarp and pulled it

free. He cursed at the tiny, two-door Fiat that mocked him. He needed to have a talk with his people about what they thought a proper getaway vehicle was, because the toy car he glared at, in his opinion, wasn't it.

"Well, I guess we'll have to make do." He turned back to Mackenzie and gave her a heartening smile.

Mackenzie slapped him with a force that wrenched his head to the side.

"You ingrate." The accented lilt in her voice was enough to raise Darius's hackles.

L.G. pulled back to deliver another blow, but he trapped her arms, spun her around and pressed her forward against the side of the car.

He brought his mouth to her ear. "That's quite enough."

"I gave you one simple task, get the skull." She glared up at him. "All you had to do was take it."

"And I did."

She scoffed.

"Get in the car." He pulled away to give her enough room to do as he ordered.

"I will not."

"You will."

She sneered at him. "Six."

He clasped his hand over her mouth and squeezed. Her fingers wrapped around his throat, but he refused to react. "You're going to get in that car and take me to the next skull. We'll worry about the skull the Illuminati have later, preferably when I have backup. But know this, I did take their skull back in America. It's not my fault if you forgot they had another."

She bit the fleshy part of his palm and he pulled his hand back with a curse.

"I forget nothing," she spat. "They only had one skull."

Darius moved her to the side and opened the passenger

door. He pushed her head down low enough to clear the car's roofline and then unceremoniously shoved her in.

"You have no idea what having my skull in their possession means, do you?"

"No and I don't care." He grabbed her wrist, pulled the handcuffs from his pocket and shackled her to the overhead safety grip inside the car.

"Have you never wondered why in the last eighty years the Illuminati have gotten closer to catching me than you ever have in over seven centuries?" She snarled the words as if he were the biggest failure on the surface of the planet.

Maybe he was.

"No, I haven't noticed." He lied and slammed the door on whatever else she was going to say.

He rounded the car, opened the driver's door and slid behind the wheel.

"I have met village idiots smarter than you," she said when he got in.

Darius pulled down the visor and the keys fell into his waiting hand.

"Jonathan would have figured it out long before now," she taunted.

The car whirred to life. Actually whirred. It was ridiculous. He felt like a giant as he pawed at the stick shift and tried to work the clutch and gas pedals while avoiding the brakes.

He guided the car down the narrow dirt road as fast as it would go, which wasn't close to being fast enough in his opinion. The car jolted and rocked over the uneven terrain as tree branches scraped the pristine, white exterior.

When his curiosity became too much to bear, he broke the silence. "Why are the Illuminati better at finding you than I am?"

CHAPTER 23

He jerked the car to the right to dodge a fallen tree branch. The tires spun on the loose dirt, sending debris flying into the air.

He yanked the car back onto the dirt road and the steering wheel groaned under his grip. If L.G. decided to be elusive now, he wasn't sure he would be responsible for his actions.

"Back in the thirties..." L.G. finally spoke, stopping him from doing something drastic. "I became impatient waiting for the prophecy to occur and thought I could expedite the inevitable." L.G. rested her forehead against her raised, handcuffed arm.

Her docile façade could change as quickly as a blink of an eye and he tensed waiting for that moment.

"You knew about the prophecy?" He couldn't say he was surprised.

"I knew about it since its inception." She let out a quiet chuckle. "I am surprised your own people felt the need to keep it secret from you."

An image of Allyanora's pitying face flashed in Darius's mind.

"The Illuminati reached out to inform me they had one of my skulls." She paused and damned if Darius didn't find himself leaning a fraction closer. "I wanted to see it in person and they wanted an act of goodwill before they would consider it. Of course, I could have stolen my skull from them, but that would have required time and I was tired of waiting."

"Because waiting eighty more years out of the three thousand was just too long."

"Exactly. In a moment of weakness, I taught them how to use the skulls to find me wherever in the world I may be. It was the only thing of value I could offer on such short notice."

"Wait, what?" He twisted his head to look at her and the car swerved. He righted it a second before wrapping them around a tree.

"Of course, they can only find me when I actively possess someone, like now."

"The skulls can be used to find you." He was skeptical.

"If I can always find them, do you not think they could always find me?" Her question was rhetorical, they both knew he couldn't answer that. "Afterwards, they agreed to meet me on one of their airships, the Hindenburg. I believe they wanted to impress me with how sophisticated and technologically advanced they thought they were in the nineteen thirties. In all reality, it was nothing more than a metal box attached to an oversized, flammable balloon."

Darius pulled out onto the deserted main road.

"Go left." L.G. said.

Darius turned left and headed away from the cottage and, he believed, towards London. He quickly turned on his phone and peeked at a road map. Yup, towards London.

He thrust the phone at her. "Put in the address for the next skull."

She placed the phone in her handcuffed hand and used the touch screen to type in the address with a familiarity that was unnerving. Darius didn't even know what half the icons on his smart phone did. He never needed to use them, nor wanted to.

"The Illuminati," she continued, "thought to convince me to work with them."

"Fools."

"Indeed. Unfortunately, they did not bring what they promised." She played with his phone some more. "All it took was one little spark and in sixty seconds the entire craft went up like kindling."

He remembered the Hindenburg, had watched transfixed as a news clip flickered on the black and white screen in a movie theater. The entire airship shuddered and collapsed within itself like a writhing, living creature taking its last breath.

"I did not burn, of course, although the Illuminati men with me met a gruesome end."

"And you ran."

"I do not run." She shot back. "I departed. I learned fate cannot be rushed."

Darius filled in the blanks in his head with what he knew had happened after the airship disaster. He had picked up L.G.'s trail almost ten years later and chased her off and on until that disastrous plane ride in the nineteen seventies.

L.G. resumed typing on the phone as she spoke. "It will take them about half an hour to realize we are gone, then they will give chase. Now we know how they found us in

Edinburgh. And it is why I wanted you to get the skull from them in America."

"I did."

She studied him as if trying to read his mind. Maybe she could.

"Then they lied to me back then." She went back to toying with the phone. "Interesting."

"You didn't already know?"

"My skulls give me inklings of the general area they are in, not detailed reports. When I want to find one, I focus on it and know the direction to go in."

Darius leaned across the tiny space between them and snatched the phone from her hand. "It takes you that long to type in an address?"

"No."

He glanced down at the screen and saw the GPS was pulled up directing him to another location. He clicked out of the app to see what else she accessed, but no other apps were running.

She gave him a small, knowing chuckle and turned to watch the scenery go by.

CHAPTER 24

Mackenzie fought for consciousness. It felt like trudging through waist-deep sludge while fighting against a rampaging current. With every small victory, she was rewarded with another layer of consciousness until finally she was able to blink open her eyes.

She squinted from the bright sun as grassy fields spanned out from her window. The car rumbled as they sped down the country road.

It should have been calming, a picturesque scene of rolling English hills, tall wispy grass swaying in the breeze and a blue sky with a smattering of puffy, white clouds. Yet, all she felt was dread.

Waking up was never this hard before. And now in the back of her mind she could feel L.G. bearing down on her, suffocating her from the inside out. She wasn't even sure how long she'd been out. Her handcuffed hand tingled and ached, indicating it had been a while.

The last thing she remembered was staring up at Darius after he pulled her out of the tunnel. Then nothing.

Just a day before, L.G. had to struggle to take her over. Now it was like L.G. just flipped a switch. L.G. could kick her out of her body forever without any trouble. Not even Darius could protect her from that.

Mackenzie shivered, but not from the cold.

"Pull over," she whispered. The car felt like it was closing in on her and she forced herself to steady her breathing.

"Mackenzie?"

"Pull over." She yanked on the handcuffs and slicing pain shot down her arm, a reminder she was still alive. "Now."

Darius stopped the car on the gravel shoulder of the two-lane road. He got out as Mackenzie opened her door and yanked harder on the handcuffs. She hissed in pain.

L.G. never had issues with taking control, Mackenzie knew that now. The struggle and feeling of drowning was only for her benefit, or her torture. She was only ever in control because of L.G.'s whim.

Without the idol Darius spoke of, she was going to die.

And soon from the feel of it.

No one should have that knowledge, ever. She always figured she would die in her sleep at the ripe old age of a hundred and three. That or she would die in a blaze of glory of action-movie proportions. Not withering away while a parasite stole her body and her life from her.

Darius crouched in front of her, his expression a sad mask of knowing concern, like he understood her struggle.

How many people did he watch fall to L.G.? How many had he saved? What were her odds?

She avoided his gaze, she couldn't tamp down the sudden wave of jealousy she had of him being all alone there in his head.

"Unlock it." Her voice was harsher than she intended, but she didn't care. She was going to die soon. She felt it, down to her bones. No, not her bones anymore, L.G.'s bones.

"Now." She yanked then hissed again.

His gentle hand stilled hers and he unlocked her shackle. She surged out of the car and ran.

Gravel turned to long grass that reached her waist. She vaguely heard Darius calling her name, but her only concern was escaping.

It was pointless. No matter how hard her legs pumped, L.G. was still there.

She wanted the world to just stop moving forward. She needed a moment to think about what was happening to her, let the weight of the situation not crush her for a second or two.

"Mackenzie, stop." Darius's large hand wrapped around her arm and pulled her to a stop in the middle of the field, her back still to him.

A searing-hot, bitter tear ran down her cheek and she furiously rubbed it away. "Call Finley. Tell him to bring that artifact thingy here now."

"He doesn't have it, not yet, but he will."

"We're out of time."

His grip tightened. "Why do you say that?"

"I've–" 'Lost.' She couldn't say it out loud, but she had to warn him, even if she feared what he would do. "I'm losing to her."

Darius turned her around. She stared at the ground so she wouldn't have to see his face and the look of pity, resignation or disgust that might be there.

"Mackenzie, look at me." His voice was low, soothing.

She didn't want to be soothed, she wanted something more abrasive, something painful. Anything that would remind her she was still alive.

"Look at me." His calloused, warm hand cupped her cheek with such gentleness it hurt her.

"Stop." She jerked her head back, but his hand followed.

"Look at me."

"Why?" She glared at him. "So you can tell me it's going to be all right? We're past those lies."

He was quiet for a minute. "I never said it would be all right. I have only ever said you had a chance. One chance."

She wanted to scream at him, hit him, make him show any other expression than quiet determination and confidence. "It's so easy for you to be calm and accepting. This isn't happening to you."

"There's still time." He was so adamant, so insistent, she wanted to believe him.

"And you know this because you know so much about L.G.?" She pulled away from him. "She's the one who's been yanking your chain for the last few centuries, so what do you know?"

"I know you can't give up." He closed the distance between them, a calm to the tumultuous storm that whirled inside her. "I know you're too stubborn to just allow any old entity to take you over without a fight."

"But it's not a fight, not for her. I can feel her now." She slapped her hand against her head. "I didn't feel her before."

Darius pulled her offending hand away and cupped her face in both his palms. He invaded her personal space with his body, filled her vision until she could see only him. He commanded her attention the same way he took down the Illuminati at Edinburgh Castle, with fierce determination and the belief he'd never be disobeyed.

"That's good," was all he said.

"How so?"

"It means you have a target, something tangible to fight

against, even if it's in your mind."

She had the Illuminati to fight, and she couldn't stop them from attacking her or blowing up her home. Before that she had a crap boss who fired her for no good reason, and she couldn't do a damn thing to stop that either. She couldn't even stop a stupid prophecy from playing out as someone else predicted.

She was an inept fighter with tons of tangible enemies. What chance did she stand against an enemy who had supernatural powers?

"I am fighting... I think." What she was, was exhausted from her world being upset every five minutes.

"You're giving up. You can't give up."

Something in his expression made her freeze. There was a note of desperation in his voice. "I don't think I'm strong enough for this."

"You are, more than you know," he said in a whisper as he pulled her into his chest. "We have a chance. You just have to keep fighting." He rested his chin on top of her head and wrapped his arms around her shoulders in a secure embrace.

She closed her eyes and let him stop time for her. She realized it wasn't a weakness to need someone, to use their lent strength to shoulder her burden for even the briefest of moments.

She just needed a second to come to terms with what had happened to her and what was yet to come.

Darius's warmth seeped into her.

"Please," he said in a beseeching way.

And just like that, time moved forward, but the foundation of her strength had been reinforced and she could build on that.

She pulled away from him, although it pained her to do so. His hands dropped to her waist as if to hold her in place should she run away again. His gaze was haunted, so different from the Darius of the previous night, the one who pushed her away and made her feel alone. He mirrored what she felt and she had the sudden urge to kiss the expression off him, lend him the strength he had given her to help him continue on.

"Fine. I'll keep fighting." She cleared her throat and resisted the urge to press her lips against his. "But if I find myself alone and underground again, all bets are off."

"That won't happen."

She touched his arm, needing his strength for just a moment longer.

His gaze dropped to her mouth and another sort of charge filled the field around them. She wanted to embrace this new feeling, the feeling of life emanating from him in its most basic, virile nature. That celebration of being alive.

She brushed a strand of hair out of her eyes and inched closer to him.

Darius blinked down at her and she saw the moment when he realized what she was about to do. She saw his need get locked down and his 'knight on duty' expression take its place.

She was once again reduced to being a means to an end, but it wasn't as big of a slap in the face this time, just more like an obstacle.

"We have to go." He shoved his hands in his pockets and they walked back to the car. "L.G. gave us another location."

CHAPTER 25

The GPS directed Darius to the posh side of old London. Of course L.G. never did anything in locales she considered seedy, gritty or downright dirty.

During the drive, he caught Mackenzie studying him with her hazel eyes, as if measuring him up to some invisible standard. Did she find him lacking? He almost demanded the answer, but at the last possible second he staved off the urge. He knew she lusted after him, but he refused to ask her whether she liked him or not, like some adolescent schoolboy.

He was not going to moon over a girl who was quite literally a ticking time bomb.

But he couldn't shake off his growing need to kiss her.

"The GPS said you're supposed to turn left here." She motioned across his vision to the intersection he was about to drive straight through.

"Shite." He spun the wheel and cut off the car next to him. In a blare of horns, Darius made the turn.

"Okay. A bit drastic," she said.

"In one mile, your destination will be on the left," the female GPS voice droned.

Posh little boutiques, cafes and pubs lined the busy streets. The words Soho Chic came to mind. How he knew those words, he didn't know. Every building was on the attractive side of old and they were meticulously kept, even though they were constructed in the middle ages.

He couldn't help but wonder how one of the obsidian skulls managed to be hidden here. From the looks of it, the buildings underwent routine refurbishment to keep from looking dingy. In all reality, he doubted there was much left of the original structures, having long since been remodeled with new exterior stone, new interiors and everything else brought up to code.

He pulled up to a stoplight and tried to get a bead on where the skull would be located on sight alone.

The passenger door opened and Mackenzie leapt out of her seat. She turned and smirked at him.

"Do try to keep up." L.G. flashed him a smile, her eyes glinting in the sunlight. Then she ran around the back of the car and down the street, disappearing into the crowd.

Why didn't he re-handcuff her to the overhead handle? Darius slammed his hands on the steering wheel and looked up at the light. It was still red.

"By the saints." He grabbed his backpack from the back seat and abandoned the car in the middle of the street. Horns blared as he pushed past two chatting women in business suits on the street corner.

He tapped the screen on his cell phone and cut off the person who answered. "Car pickup on..." He searched for the street signs, then read their names over the line and hung up.

L.G. had already vanished, but his phone still guided him a few yards more towards a quaint little pub.

"You have arrived at your destination," the GPS informed him.

"The hell I have." He ran through the front door and peered around at the clientele for L.G., but she was nowhere in sight.

He shoved past a heavyset man standing in his way and confronted the bartender.

"Oi." The man he shoved tried to push Darius back. It was almost laughable.

Darius ignored him and stared the bartender down."Did a redheaded woman rush past here?"

The bartender motioned towards the back.

Darius brushed past the fat man again, who was now trying to intimidate him. Darius wanted to explain that girth of waist didn't quite measure up to the amount of muscle and defensive skills Darius had, but there wasn't time.

He went through the swinging doors that led to the back kitchen, past an angry chef who cursed at him in Italian, and was out the back door in less than five seconds.

The street he came out on had less foot traffic, store fronts that weren't as showy, though still well kept, and a fraction of the cars.

He looked left and right, trying to figure out where the bane of his existence had run off to. His fingers itched to wring her neck.

In his peripheral vision, he saw a shock of red hair enter the double glass doors of a store across the street and to the left. The store took up most of the block and had a sign overhead that read 'Diedrich's Antiques.'

Darius hurried across the street to the store. He opened the door and a little bell chimed, killing any element of surprise. He heard L.G.'s voice within the bowels of the room, but he couldn't see further than a few feet in front of him because of all the ornate, antique furniture that turned the inside of the store into some historical labyrinth.

"It would seem my associate has honored us with his presence," L.G. said as Darius rounded a large Rococo-style bookcase.

He entered a cozy, little sitting area that felt like a peaceful island in the middle of the chaos. His full field of vision was limited, though, by display cases, book cases and other odds and ends that once graced castles, mansions and homes of extreme wealth. The musty smell of old wood and fabric filled the air.

Now this was where he expected to find a skull.

The weak sound of a clearing throat caught Darius's attention and he turned to face a middle-aged man whose hair was a tad too long for the sophisticated slicked-back look he was trying to achieve. It didn't help that his hair was over greased to the point that Darius could easily see the thick comb lines in it. He also sported an unattractive, too-thin mustache and pasty skin. The only thing on the man that seemed to fit the high-end richness of the decor that surrounded him was his fitted, expensive, dark gray suit.

"My name is Anton Diedrich," he said in a high-pitched, German accent. He stepped out from behind his large, ornate desk and offered Darius a limp-wristed handshake.

Diedrich's palm was moist and when Darius let go he couldn't help but wipe his hand on his jeans.

Anton waited, staring at him in expectant silence. Darius stared back, unrepentant in his lack of courtesy by not offering the man his name in return.

"Ignore him, he is a brute." L.G. cut in.

"Yes, well." Anton rounded his desk and waved a hand towards the empty chair next to L.G. "Please, sit."

Darius preferred to stand. He opened his backpack and palmed the smaller of his two handguns. He didn't like being out of his element and with L.G. he needed to be prepared for anything, even the possibility this greasy little man might be capable of doing something unpleasant.

"It would seem Diedrich's is doing very well for itself," L.G. waved a nonchalant hand at the opulence that surrounded them.

Anton nodded and sat back in his leather wingback chair. "Yes, my family has been in the antiquities business since before the first World War. We offer one of the most extensive collections in London."

"I bet you do."

"What can I help you with?"

"I am looking for something very particular." L.G. spoke in a slow, measured tone, as if she was toying with the man.

Anton, unaware of the psychotic murderer sitting before him, pulled open a drawer and plucked a tablet computer from it. He turned it on and tapped the screen. "What are you inquiring about exactly?"

"A map."

"I have several antique maps in my inventory." He held up the tablet and scrolled through images with a flick of his finger across the screen. "But if they're not what you're looking for, I can put feelers out and see if we can acquire what you want. But you must be aware that will cost more, for it takes extra time and effort on my part."

"I'm looking for an ancient map that will guide me to a treasure."

A treasure? Darius didn't have patience for games. He put his gun in the back of his waistband and moved towards L.G. to drag her out of the shop.

Anton stopped scrolling and Darius could swear the air around them dropped about ten degrees.

When the man moved, he was stiff and forced as he placed the tablet on the smooth surface of his desk. "Unfortunately, I do not deal in novelties like treasure maps. I deal in high-end, reputable antiquities. Now, if you'd excuse me."

He stood and L.G. just grinned.

That smile made Darius grab his gun again. Shit was about to get real. Damn, he was starting to think like Mackenzie spoke.

L.G. stood and leaned her hip against Anton's desk. She picked up a dagger that rested on a display holder. The placard underneath it read 'Damascus Steel Dagger 100 B.C.' It was a blade of myth and legend, smelted in a particular way that made it indestructible.

And L.G. was using it to clean the dirt out from underneath her fingernails.

"Now, if you would show yourself out." Anton ignored her and walked towards the back door behind his desk.

When his hand touched the doorknob, L.G. spoke. "I believe your great-grandfather told you about the map he was commissioned to find."

Anton went rigid and his shoulders rose up, doing a fine imitation of a greasy turtle.

"If he did not," L.G. continued, "I pity you."

Anton turned around, the façade of the calm, sophisticated antiquities dealer gone. In its place was a slimy, little man, who knew how to deal with black markets, shady dealers and, most of all, threats to his life.

"That was a long time ago," he said.

"Let me see if I remember the name I was using when I commissioned the late Diedrich." She toyed with the blade in her hands with the ease of someone comfortable wielding edged weapons.

"I'm going to have to ask you to lea—"

"Oh, yes," L.G. cut him off. "Fraulein Tod."

Fraulein Tod, Darius knew, meant Lady Death in German.

"You couldn't have possibly made that inquiry." Anton strode back to his desk, pressed his hands flat against the top of it and leaned forward. "And I won't stand here and be threatened."

L.G. grabbed the back of Anton's head, slammed it against the desk top and pressed down on his skull until the man let out a pained gasp in protest.

"It is best you learn to whom you are speaking. I am the very same Fraulein Tod who walked into your great-grandfather's shop eighty years ago. Like you, he did not think I was serious." She sunk the dagger into the desk within slicing distance of the man's sweating face and gouged out a little hole in the dark wood.

Anton squealed. One false move and she could slice off his nose.

"I noticed you do not keep clerks like he did."

"B-because they can be used against us. My great-grandfather learned that w-when Fraulein Tod murdered the th-three clerks he had working for him."

"It is good to see that some humans do not have as short of a memory as I have associated them with. Now, the map."

"My great-grandfather looked for it every day for the rest of his life."

"And I paid him well for his time. It is how your ancestor went from selling trinkets and forged antiquities in a run-down shop in Munich to the high-end wares you deal in now." She pulled the dagger free of the desk and yanked the man's head up by his hair. "My map."

"I don't have it."

"What?" Her voice was so calm, it was almost a whisper.

Darius wasn't sure if he should be relieved or alarmed Anton didn't have this map. He wasn't sure how he should feel about the situation in general, but he saw where it was going and he inched backwards to give himself more space to maneuver.

Anton licked his lips and a light sheen of sweat slicked his forehead. "My great-grandfather never found it. He told the family Fraulein Tod would return, but we didn't believe him. Even so, after he died, my grandfather searched, my father too, even me. It's become the Holy Grail to my family. We have used all our contacts, been around the world. If this map existed at all, it doesn't now."

"It existed. Exists." L.G. hissed and corrected herself. With a growl she slammed Anton's head against the table again.

Darius wondered where this rage was coming from. She didn't care for anything on this 'puny little planet.' Her words, not his. Why would a map mean so much to her?

"Then it's beyond my family to find it."

"That is unfortunate." Her voice steady again. She leaned back against the desk and toyed with the dagger. "You were warned what would happen should he or, in this case, you fail?"

"However..." Anton held his head. "My search has brought me in touch with some very interesting people of late."

Anton glanced towards a tall display case. Before Darius could move, a silencer attached to the barrel of a gun poked out from behind it and pointed straight at L.G.'s head.

"Fraulein Tod, meet the Illuminati."

Damn the antiques store, damn Anton and especially damn L.G. Man.

Darius sidestepped around the display case and a bald-headed man with dark eyes came into view. The fellow didn't even blink at Darius, his sole focus was on L.G. as he stepped closer to her.

L.G. sighed. She shifted from her perch on the desk and peered down the barrel of the gun. "What are you going to do, shoot me?"

"L.G." Darius inched closer towards her, but he couldn't chance taking the shot.

"You humans." L.G. shook her head. "Once in a very long while you have a moment of sheer genius, then you piss it all away with actions as ridiculous as this."

She batted the gun from her face, spun on her heel, and using her momentum, sunk the Damascus steel blade into the bald man's forehead. Anton let out a little cry. And as if the finality of her action wasn't enough, L.G. wrenched the knife's handle and broke it off, leaving the blade wedged in the man's skull.

The man collapsed, eyes still wide in shock.

L.G. snatched the gun from the dead man's slackened grasp. "Now, had the blade been real Damascus steel, it would not have snapped. With this little demonstration, I was able to correct an atrocious error on your behalf, Anton. Had anyone else discovered the forgery, your reputation might have been ruined."

Anton stood frozen halfway between his desk and the back door. His mouth opened and closed like a fish, his confidence in the Illuminati's protection vanquished.

"P-p-please. I will continue to look for your map, I'll do whatever it takes."

"Time has run out." She raised the gun and shot him between the eyes.

Anton's head jerked back and his body followed the motion all the way to the floor.

L.G. faced Darius then, her eyes wild. The gun shook in her hand and a snarl marred her features.

He had never seen her like this. She was the one with infallible control, always fifty steps ahead of anyone she faced, including him.

Now, she looked like she was on the verge of snapping.

"What the hell is going on?" he blurted out.

L.G. opened her mouth to speak and stopped. Instead of answering, she raised her gun and aimed it right at him.

CHAPTER 26

Darius aimed the sights of his own gun between Mackenzie's eyes. He wasn't surprised it had come down to a standoff.

L.G. sneered and pulled the trigger. In that exact moment, Darius's reflexes should have kicked in, causing him to fire back, but he hesitated instead.

L.G.'s bullet grazed his shirt sleeve as it flew past. Behind him he heard a surprised grunt, followed by a thud as a body fell. He turned around and found another Illuminati foot soldier with a bullet in his heart.

"Son of a bitch." Darius knew if there was one Illuminati foot soldier, there was always another close behind, yet he had dropped his guard.

He turned back and saw L.G. slip through the door behind the desk.

"L.G., wait."

Out of nowhere, a wall of muscle rushed forward and tackled him. They both clattered to the floor in a flurry of fists and kicks.

Darius's backpack slipped from his shoulder and his gun jarred out of his grasp. The dark-haired man landed on top of him and laid blows like a professional boxer. He matched Darius pound for pound, muscle for muscle. Darius took the hits on the back of his arms, protecting his head with defensive moves as he gathered his bearings.

He saw a flash of silver slant towards his gut and he grabbed the man's wrist just before the knife sliced him open. With his other fist, Darius delivered a tooth-breaking blow to the man's face. Darius punched him again and blood spurted out of his nose like a broken faucet.

The man wrenched his hand free and brought the knife back down towards Darius's head. At the last second, Darius rolled out of the way and the knife ripped into the carpet.

Darius kicked the man away from him with both legs and then half-lunged, half-crawled to his fallen gun that lay a few yards away. He wrapped his fingers around the grip, swung around and fired three times as fast as he could pull the trigger as the man dove towards him. The bullets tore through the man's chest and he landed heavily on top of Darius. The man's knife clattered across the floor.

Darius hurriedly shoved the lifeless body off him, sat half-way up and swept the room with his gun, anticipating more attackers. When none came, he relaxed a little and took one second to catch his breath.

He scrambled to his feet, grabbed his backpack and ran through the back door, which led him into a narrow hallway. The first room he came to was a small bathroom. He moved on. The second room was an office with an overturned desk, papers strewn about in careless abandon and a few antique lamps littering the floor in pieces. A large upright vault that took up the entire far wall stood shut, untouched by the frantic violence.

He moved on to the end of the hall. There were two doors on either side. He peered into the room on his right, which looked like some kind of maintenance supply closet. Metal shelves had been pulled away from one wall. Cleaning supplies and open lacquer cans covered the floor, their glossy, thick liquid oozing out. Paint brushes and towels were piled on top, absorbing the mess.

Built into the wall the shelves had been up against was an old, smaller safe with an electric keypad, left untouched by whoever had ransacked the room.

Darius crossed the hall to the final door, which stood ajar.

He pushed it open and walked into a huge, well-lit warehouse. L.G. stood with her back to him, studying the bracelet locked around her wrist. In front of her was a panel of electrical wires. She turned her attention to the panel and then without warning grabbed the live wires with her bare hands.

"L.G." Darius sprinted towards her.

The wires sizzled with electricity as she pulled out one handful, then another. The lights overhead died and a fire alarm beeped at the loss of power. Darius stopped inches shy of L.G., his hand outstretched too late to prevent the death by electrocution that should have happened.

Instead, L.G. dropped the wires, pleased with herself. "It would seem the bracelet you forced upon me is designed to deflect all foreign energy away from this body, not just invading spiritual energy. Quite interesting."

He snapped out of his shock and spun her around. "You could have killed her."

L.G. raised a delicate brow. "Oh? One would think you would be more concerned over my safety. You need me."

"And the map? What is that for?"

L.G. slipped past him towards the doorway. "I will tell you when I get it."

"Anton claimed he didn't have it."

"Anton was lying." She stepped into the hall and he followed after her. "His family has a unique gift of finding whatever they are looking for. Their abilities border on the paranormal and they are relentless. I watched his great-great-grandfather ferret out extraordinary relics years before I sought out Anton's great-grandfather."

She walked into the room with the smaller, older wall safe. Darius pulled out a flashlight from his backpack and pointed the light at it. The safe's door was now ajar.

"Why not check the bigger safe first?"

"Because," L.G. ran a hand over the front of the safe. "A trick of the Diedrich family is that they use the bigger, flashier safe for all the valuable antiques they are expected to have, the safe they show to their public clientele. Their antiques acquired through less than pristine sources, they hide in here. Yes, this safe might be easier to crack open or have a major flaw like a power surge releasing the electronic lock, but it does not matter if no one knows to look for it."

She pulled the door open. The safe was filled with papers, a few rolls of papyri and a couple cardboard tubes. She pulled out the papyri first and unfurled roll after roll. She tossed aside the antiquated papers and moved on to the tubes. Three held rare paintings. One Darius could have sworn once adorned the walls of the Louvre. The last three tubes held handwritten pages on yellowed, cracking paper that crumbled as she forced them flat.

"It has to be here," she said more to herself than to him.

She dove on the stacks of papers and tore through them in a damn-near frenzy.

"No!" She screeched the word and tossed the last of the papers aside. "No."

She slapped her open hand on the safe door and slammed it shut. The clanging metal reverberated throughout the room. She screeched again and turned on Darius.

"The prophecies, are they ever wrong?"

It took Darius a second to register her shouted question. "No."

"Lies. Five." She spat the word in cruel glee.

He clamped his hand over her mouth. "What's so damned important about this map?"

She shoved him away and walked out of the room. "Everything."

"What do you mean everything?" Darius followed her back into the warehouse.

She stopped, her back stiff, her hands clenched. The windows high up on the walls let in enough muted light to see by, although there wasn't much too see. Wooden crates with shipping labels on them were stacked on industrial-sized steel shelves along one wall, packing supplies filled shelves on the opposite wall and wooden pallets were neatly piled in the middle of the room.

"Do you know the last civilization I took?" Her voice was deceptive in its calm.

"The Hittite Empire, twelfth century B.C."

"Did you ever wonder why it has taken me three thousand years to gather my skulls again?"

"Of course."

"Did you think I grew soft? Began to care about humans?"

"Not once. Jonathan said you seemed to be waiting for something."

She snorted at that and leveled him with a look of such rage it would have seared Pompeii faster than Vesuvius. "I ask you again, have your Seers ever been wrong?"

"Not once."

"Then the map is here."

"Clearly, it's not."

"Then there is another safe somewhere. We will have to check his residence and the two vacation homes his family owns."

"How about telling me what's on the map?"

"It shows the location of the one skull I cannot find." She said the words as if slinging the worst curse in the books.

"L.G."

That brought her attention back to him and she clicked her tongue. "After I destroyed the Hittite Empire, I traveled to the coast and chartered a ship to take me north. I had grown tired of heat and sand." She stared at a point on the wall to her left as if she were standing three thousand years in the past. "I chartered the vessel from a Phoenician named Pelagios. He was smarter than I gave him credit for."

"The Phoenicians." The prophecy played in Darius's head.

"Yes, the Phoenicians. It would seem word about the fall of the Hittites had traveled faster than I had anticipated. I was moving my skulls with me, all thirteen. Pelagios must have heard the stories, somehow saw through the face I was using at the time and figured out what I was." Her thoughts were no longer focused on the present. In her distraction Darius moved closer.

She grabbed her gun that had been lying on a shelf next to the power box and pointed it at him.

"I have waited so long to leave this planet and I am beginning to think I may never see my home again." She turned the gun towards her own head and rested her finger against the trigger. "I should just destroy her now and end this, rot in whatever hole you put me in."

"Don't."

Her lips twitched. "Or what? You plan to do the exact

same thing when you are done using me. And I grow bored of this body."

"Stop." His heart pounded in his ears as he dared a step closer.

He wasn't ready to let Mackenzie go, wasn't about to give up on her. Not when Finley was out there getting the one thing that could change everything.

As if reading his mind, L.G. rolled her eyes. "You believe the artifact will work? Mackenzie may be naïve enough to believe such farce, but I am not."

"You still have two skulls to help me find." He inched closer.

"And if we cannot find them? I wonder if Mackenzie will like you as much if she knew your vow to stay with her 'till the end' means you putting a bullet in her brain."

"It's a hell of a lot better than what you plan to do to her. At least her soul will survive."

L.G. shook her head. "Sentimentality does not suit you, Darius."

He didn't answer. He could save Mackenzie, do what he had failed to do for Jonathan and the other victims. Save one out of the many.

"She cannot be saved. Accept that and it may not destroy you."

Darius saw victory in her eyes.

He grabbed the gun from her hand and pressed her up against the shelves. L.G. let him, but her expression didn't change, as if she had caught onto something he had yet to figure out. Then it hit him, it wasn't anger and frustration he had suffered all these years. It was the pain of defeat, the anguish over every life he had failed to save.

All those shortcomings faded when Mackenzie was around. She gave him peace, something to strive for other than failure.

The look of triumph in L.G.'s eyes said she already knew this.

"What did Pelagios do?" Darius finally asked.

L.G. gave him a strange look. "I do not know how he did it. After we made land in Scotland, I discovered three of my skulls had been stolen. I searched for his ship, but he had already sold it and he and his men had disappeared."

Darius fisted his hand in her hair and forced her to look at him. "Get to the point."

"I tracked down the first two skulls easily enough, but when I tried to find the third one, I felt it." Her hand rubbed idly over her heart.

"What?"

"Each skull has a tendril of awareness in my consciousness. It connects them to me and me to them. Nothing on this planet can sever that connection. But somehow..." she trailed off.

"Pelagios did," he finished for her.

"I discovered later he had chartered a dozen seafaring ships with a crew of a thousand and was never seen again."

"And you think he made a map of where he was going before he left?"

"I think he made several maps. The Phoenicians were a seafaring people and he was comparable to an emperor in their culture. They made maps of the entire world, accurate maps of places that were yet to be officially discovered by humans."

"He could've destroyed the maps."

She shook her head and even in the shadows of the warehouse she looked frustrated. "The Phoenicians were the Knights Templar before the Knights Templar. They made it their mission to protect people from objects powerful enough to influence the world. There would be a map of where Pelagios went, so his people would know where the treasures were hidden and could keep watch over them."

"But you couldn't find it back then."

"Not for the lack of trying. I am the reason Phoenicia fell apart. I hunted every man, woman and child connected to the Pelagios family and tortured them, the only pleasurable moments in this entire fiasco. They either did not know where their revered leader went or they were loyal enough to hold their tongue."

"And you think you stand a chance now? That somehow three thousand years later this map has managed to survive?"

L.G. looked lost for a split second, even hopeless.

If Darius cared, he would have felt sorry for L.G., stranded on an alien planet, all alone. But he didn't. In fact, he silently thanked Pelagios for putting that expression on her face because he never could. "It doesn't matter. We still have two other skulls I need to recover. Plus the one the Illuminati have."

"No."

"The longer you help me, the better chance you have at finding your map."

"Give me your phone."

He pulled his phone from the front pocket of his backpack and handed it to her.

She played with the screen for a second.

"Calculating route." The electronic GPS voice echoed in the warehouse.

"Take it. There are notes." She held the phone out to him. "It will lead you to the location of the next skull. We part here."

He ignored the offered phone. "You're coming with me."

L.G. stepped into him, pressed her body against his and ran her hands up his chest. "The skulls cannot be the only reason you wish me to stay.

"It is."

"Do not make me count down some more. She is running out of numbers." L.G. wrapped her arms around his neck.

His brain knew it was a trick, but his body didn't care. L.G. looked like Mackenzie, smelled like Mackenzie and, if he ignored the metallic glint in her eyes and she didn't open her mouth to speak, he could be fooled into believing it was Mackenzie.

"I guess I shall keep counting down." L.G. rested her hands on his chest and smiled.

She was goading him into crossing a line and he knew once he did, it would shatter the illusion of him keeping distance between them.

Damn the saints. He was tired of being a mere pawn in L.G.'s plans. He let out a frustrated sound from deep in his chest.

She wanted confirmation of his attraction to Mackenzie? Fine, she would have it.

He crushed his lips down on hers and all coherent thought fled his mind. Her body stiffened and then she relaxed into him, and his thoughts became consumed by her. Her fiery temper, her violent streak and the playful passion she kept just beneath the surface.

He cupped her soft cheek as his tongue ran across the seam of her lips, begging for entrance. He groaned in victory when they parted and he slipped inside, tasting her for the first time. She tasted of woman and peaches.

He tightened his fist in her hair and angled her head for better access. She moaned against his mouth and his need ratcheted up tenfold. The kiss was no longer enough, but his overwhelming need to rip off her clothes and take her up against the wall snapped him back to reality.

He broke the kiss and rested his forehead against hers, his breathing labored. He wanted to curse L.G. and himself.

In a moment of weakness, he stole something from Mackenzie that wasn't his to take, making him an utter bastard.

"You win, L.G. Man." Darius closed his eyes and concentrated on controlling himself.

"L.G.?" Her accent-less voice sliced through his thoughts. "Man?"

He opened his eyes to find Mackenzie staring back at him, wide-eyed. An array of emotions flew across her face, lust, surprise, need, hurt, anger and then nothing. The emotionless mask that settled barred him from knowing what was going through her mind.

"Welcome back." He tried to give her a half grin that had many a woman swoon in the past.

"Make a u-turn in approximately 500 feet," the GPS interrupted.

"Darius," Mackenzie said in a low, calm voice.

Good, he needed her calm. Pushing aside his need to kiss her again, he rested his hands on her shoulders, prepared to explain.

Her knee connected with his groin and pain exploded through his body like an A-bomb had just gone off.

"So this is what goes on when you're with L.G.?" She pushed past him and stomped towards the back of the warehouse. "Perverted asshat."

Darius bent over, put his hands on his knees and fought for consciousness. He sucked in air through his mouth and wondered if she had finally succeeded in making him a eunuch.

Mackenzie brandished the cell phone at him like it was a weapon.

"I should have known something was up when I woke up yesterday handcuffed to the bed. You lying son of a—" She cut herself off with a frustrated yell.

The moment he got feeling back in his lower extremities and he was positive he wasn't going to projectile vomit the entire contents of his stomach all over the warehouse floor, he'd chase after her and fix this mess. Until then he had to keep taking deep breaths.

The voice of the GPS trailed back to him as Mackenzie disappeared around a stack of crates. "Recalculating."

Yeah, no shit.

CHAPTER 27

Before Darius could put the SUV in park, Mackenzie burst out of the car and slammed the door for all she was worth.

She had just endured eight hours of Darius dodging her questions as if she didn't have the right to know why he was making out with the enemy.

She was tempted to slam the car door again just in case he missed how pissed off she really was. By the nonchalant way he was acting, he apparently needed someone to spell it out for him.

She thought about chucking the cell phone at his head.

"You have arrived," the GPS on the phone chimed. "Your destination is on the left."

"Bloody hell." She groaned. Great, she was starting to talk just like the ass.

Mackenzie shoved the phone in her back pocket and

looked at the field that stretched out before them. In the soft light of the moon, everything was cloaked in long shadows. A wind rustled the bushes that sprinkled the grass. Beyond the field was a hill, which had a small copse of trees at the top that reminded her of a bad toupee.

In the light of day, the scene could have been something picturesque, peaceful even. But right then, in the dead of night, it looked and felt like it was straight out of a horror movie. And like in a horror movie, their destination, the Dashwood Mausoleum, wasn't nearby. Nope, it was on top of the hill, enshrouded by the toupee of trees, next to a small church and a graveyard. And given her track record, there was definitely a chainsaw-wielding maniac lurking in the shadows just waiting for her.

Gravel crunched as Darius walked towards the closed, metal gate that blocked the road. Even his footfalls sounded calm. What she wouldn't give to get him off balance, just once.

"It's locked. We're going to have to go on foot," he said.

"Of course we do."

"What was that?" He strode around the car, then opened and closed the trunk before joining her on the side of the road.

"I said you're an ass." She knew she sounded like a petulant child. Whatever.

When he was close enough, Darius held out a flashlight to her and she grabbed it with a huff. The man should have been groveling, not offering her something to help her see in the dark.

She stepped over the little trench that lined the road and tried not to cringe when her foot sunk into thick, spongy grass.

"Mackenzie, watch—" Before he could finish, she took another step and her shoe caught on something hard. She fell forward and flung her arms out in a fruitless attempt to catch herself.

"I was going to say, watch out for the fallen fence." Darius offered her a hand, but the smugness in his voice made her ignore it.

"Oh, no." Ignoring the offending hand, she pushed herself to her feet, picked up the flashlight from the ground and stomped past him. "I don't need, or want, your help."

"Yes, you do."

The truth of that statement pained her, so she threw the flashlight at his head. The dolt just caught the thing with those superhuman reflexes of his.

"Violence..." Darius said, chastising her. Her!

"Ground rules." She clutched her hands into fists, her silent brooding gone. "I can't believe this needs to be said, but no more tonguing the enemy. Especially, when said enemy has control of my mouth."

"Anything else?"

"Oh, don't you dare sound annoyed with me. Right now, I have no idea whose side you're on."

"Yours."

"I don't believe you."

"You have no choice. And all you need to concentrate on—"

"—is finding your blasted skulls," she mocked in his accent. "You're a cold bastard, you know that? Have you had so many skull radars you've forgotten we're people, too?"

Before she knew it, his hands gripped her arms hard and he pulled her against his chest until she wasn't sure where he ended and she began. "Are you quite done?"

"Why did you kiss L.G.?" She had to know. Had to put it to bed. Call her a hopeless romantic, but she still held out hope he had feelings for her. Her. That he saw her as something more than just a means to get what he hunted. How many other girls before her craved the same with him? "Why?"

"To keep you alive long enough in order to save you. You said you could feel L.G. gaining ground inside you. Did you ever think L.G. is letting you stay? That at any given moment, without warning, you could be gone?"

His dark gaze seemed to glow with an internal fire, his expression a combination of pity and longing.

"I'm as much at her mercy as you because she knows I'll do anything not to lose you to her." He shook her gently, letting it be known she wasn't the only one frustrated with their situation and helpless to change it.

She opened her mouth once, twice, but nothing came out. She still didn't understand why he felt the need to kiss L.G., but the intent behind it was clear. It was for her and it was more than a little weird she felt comforted by that.

However, what little hope she had to live through all this took a staggering blow, and fear threatened to beat out the rest.

Darius released her arm and cupped her cheek.

"This is why I didn't tell you. I'd much rather have you furious with me than lose hope."

His thumb brushed over her lips, and he gave her a small mischievous grin. "Truth be told, if you hadn't stopped me, I would have had you right then and there in the warehouse. And I'd only be thinking of you."

"Cheeky monkey." She had to laugh, as weak as it sounded. It didn't do much for her fear, but nothing would have. "You're like if Darth Vader and Casanova had a love child, and not in a good way."

"In what scenario would there ever be a good outcome to that?"

"Exactly."

Darius shifted his backpack around and pulled out a

small stack of printouts. "You forgot these in the car."

She took them and the flashlight, although it wasn't as if she needed the papers anymore, she had already memorized the information printed on them. Eight hours of seething with nothing else to do but read and re-read the research materials could do that.

After the warehouse, Darius had ordered up a new vehicle for their driving pleasure and the papers were on the passenger seat when she got in. If they hadn't been, she would have killed him at some point during the extra-long route he took, backtracking over and over to make sure the Illuminati wasn't following them.

So now she had basic knowledge about the mausoleum they were headed to, the St. Lawrence Church next to it and the nearby Hellfire Caves, which were all built in the 18th century by the same eccentric nobleman, Sir Francis Dashwood.

"Thanks." She rolled the papers in her hands and headed up the hill. Darius pulled another flashlight out of his backpack and matched her pace through the empty field of short grass.

Mackenzie pulled her jacket closer against the rising chill in the night air and the foreboding sense of danger. All that was missing from the long-reaching shadows and eerie full moon was the howling of wolves and the gates of hell opening beneath her feet.

By the time Mackenzie reached the gravel parking lot near the top of the hill, she was panting and sweating, but at least she was no longer cold.

Darius didn't break his long-legged pace and walked straight into the toupee of trees ahead of her. She lingered behind just long enough to catch her breath and for the axe murderer to start in with the slicing and dicing of her knight. When she heard no screams from Darius, she trudged in after him.

Their walk through the towering trees was brief and opened up to a smattering of headstones and a good-sized, simply built brick church with a large golden ball mounted on top of its bell tower. An odd fixture for a church, but the man who built it was anything but normal.

"Sir Francis Dashwood added the golden ball to the church when he built the mausoleum. He never bothered to explain why," she recited the research from memory as she tried to keep her mind off the old graveyard that stood between them and the mausoleum beyond.

Again, Darius didn't stop to take in the information or their surroundings, he walked straight into the graveyard.

"Guess if you've seen one graveyard, you've seen them all," Mackenzie mumbled to herself as she followed him, mindful of the tombstones in her path.

He might have been used to walking over graves in the middle of the night like a grave robber, but she wasn't. Every rustle of leaves, chirp of crickets and odd shadow cast by the moonlight made her look wildly about half-expecting to see a ghost.

"Sir Francis Dashwood and the secret society he created met here. Well, in the Hellfire Caves." She rambled to break the chilling silence. "Some say he threw orgies and practiced the dark arts. I hope they didn't summon anything from the other side. I don't think I could stomach running into a demon or a ghost."

"Come now, Mackenzie. Everyone knows ghosts can't hurt you."

"Oh yeah?" She stepped over a flat gravestone. "What about poltergeists? My aunt told me one threw pennies at her when she stayed at an old hotel in Wales and almost hit her in the eye."

Darius didn't answer.

She stepped over another gravestone and cringed. "What, no witty comeback?"

"If I say anything, you'll just react in the same violent manner as every other time I say something you think is unpleasant."

A shadow moved in the corner of her vision and she shined her light on it. It turned out to be a bush. "Well, what were you going to say?"

"That perhaps your aunt over exaggerated."

Mackenzie stopped beside a half-toppled-over headstone. Her verbal comeback of condemnation fizzled and she shrugged. "You could be right."

"What?" He raised his voice and turned, his flashlight blinding her in the dark. "You're joking."

"A girl presented with a plausible alternate explanation can't consider another possibility?"

"In the short time we've known each other parts of me would have to disagree."

"Well, my friends would say otherwise."

"Do they have a choice?"

"My friends also know not to ask stupid questions." She walked past the last gravestone with a sense of relief since no zombie had reached out of the ground to drag her to hell and no ghosts had appeared and yelled 'BOO!'

Things were looking up.

They rounded the small, stone church and the mausoleum came into view. It was a large, one-story, roofless, hexagonal structure with arched openings that served as windows and doors. Moonlight spilled through the rounded arches and reached out as if beckoning them closer.

Even though Mackenzie knew what to expect, the image she had in her mind of what a stereotypical mausoleum should look like contradicted the structure that stood before her. From the mere definition of the word mausoleum, she pictured a closed fortress, designed to keep the living outside and the dead, undisturbed, inside. The only things here that blocked anyone's entrance were iron bars bolted to the arched windows and a gated entryway.

She walked up to the gate and saw it was chained and padlocked. She rattled the bars and pulled on the lock for good measure, to no avail. "What's the plan here?"

Darius's response was to nudge her out of the way. She was glaring at him when she noticed a small crowbar poking out of his backpack.

She eased the crowbar free without drawing his attention from his examination of the lock. She tossed the rolled papers and flashlight aside and raised the improvised weapon over her head. "Move, I got this."

"You do?" Darius sounded far too amused as he turned around.

He took one look at her stance, weapon in hand, and sidestepped out of the way just as she brought the crowbar down. Metal clashed against metal and the violent motion jarred the crowbar right out of her hands.

"Son of a—" She could feel her teeth rattle together. The padlock remained unscathed. "What's that lock made of, titanium?"

"What was your plan there?" He picked up the crowbar from the ground.

"Well," Mackenzie rubbed the ache from her arms. "In the movies, they always make it look so easy to beat the lock open, or shoot it. But I figured you wouldn't let me use one of your guns."

"You are correct."

"So what did you expect me to do, make out with it until it opened?" She snatched the roll of papers and flashlight from the ground. "You seem to be pretty good at that."

"I've had hundreds of years to work on my technique."

"And I bet you took every opportunity to practice."

He didn't respond as he took his place in front of the lock again.

He was a pig, an ancient pig, and yet she still took a moment to admire his ass. He had a fine one and if he was just going to stare at the lock until it opened, they could be there a while. Perhaps she could throw the crowbar on the grass again and this time enjoy the view of him bending over to retrieve it.

Darius pushed the wrought iron gate open.

"Did you really just make out with it?" She stared at the open lock dangling on its chain. "What are you?"

"Relax." He motioned her inside with his head as he shoved small metal sticks into a leather case. "Lock picks."

"Then why not open the gate on the road, so we could have driven here?"

"If I'm being honest—"

"I didn't know you had stopped." She threw the roll of papers at his head and he batted them aside.

"I wasn't entirely sure the Illuminati weren't already here and I didn't feel it necessary to alarm you over the possibility. I thought we would draw less attention to ourselves on foot."

He was as calm and collected as if he were telling her the weather was lovely outside, not that gun-wielding men with homicidal tendencies might be laying in wait.

"Next time we're heading into a possible trap..." Mackenzie walked up to him, happy to see him tense up. "You warn me and then act as my personal, bulletproof shield."

"I didn't say trap."

She balled her fist and aimed a swift punch to his chest. Darius wrapped his hand around hers and held it there.

"I just thought there may be a few scouts watching possible locations L.G. may visit."

"A location you didn't even know about?"

"There's a lot I don't know about L.G.," he said quietly.

He looked every bit his ancient age then. Weary, like he was tired of living with the constant struggle of it.

Mackenzie didn't like that, not one bit. She was foolish, of course, to have any sort of feelings for the ancient knight, but she couldn't help but want to wrap her arms around the big oaf to comfort him somehow.

His grip on her hand tightened as if he sensed the direction of her thoughts. But he didn't let go.

"I'm learning a lot about you, you know." She gave him a playful smile she didn't quite feel and he raised an eyebrow in question. "Like here I thought my knight in shining armor would never lower himself to petty criminal activities. Come to find out he's quite skilled at breaking and entering."

He drew close to tower over her, but she was more titillated than intimidated.

"Sometimes it's far more appealing to be naughty," he said.

Oh, lordy. She almost leaned in for the soul-searing kiss that should have followed a comment like that. Instead, he turned and entered the mausoleum, and she was left out in the cold, literally.

Right, skulls. Why else would someone be standing in the middle of a horror movie set in the dead of night?

"With a full moon no less," she mumbled under her breath.

"What?"

"I said–" She turned on her flashlight and peered around. "Where do you think the skull is?"

"Don't know."

"Not even a guess? Did you even look at the papers your people left us?"

"I figured we'd just search until..." He trailed off and at

least had the decency to look sheepish.

"Until L.G. decides to surface? Well, she's not coming. So, what now?"

"Start over there and work your way around. Unless you have a better idea."

She didn't. Not once while reading the documents was there any mention of an obsidian skull.

She slowly turned around in a tight circle to fully take in the eerie, high, marble walls marred with sporadic gouges of archways and several smaller, rectangular alcoves.

Having given the exterior walls the once over, she focused on a large monument in the center of the mausoleum. It consisted of a roof, four Grecian-style marble pillars and a three-foot-tall wrought iron fence with pointy posts surrounding a large stone urn perched on top of a marble pedestal. But it was too open to hide anything, much like the rest of the mausoleum.

"Sir Dashwood had that made for his late wife, Sarah." She motioned to the monument. "And he also filled all the alcoves in the mausoleum walls with busts of his dead relatives." She waved her arm in a sweeping motion at the walls around her. "No bodies, just busts in their memory. What I don't understand is why call this place is called a mausoleum?"

"Why not?" Darius moved to a section of wall and ran his fingers over the stone. "Mausoleums are large, stately, above-ground tombs that house dead people."

"Okay, then tell me, genius, where are the bodies? The obsidian skull? All I see are bare walls and one urn." She paused. "I wonder."

She stepped up to the wrought iron fence surrounding the urn and jiggled it. It rattled against its bolts but didn't break free.

She contemplated the sharp points of the posts, then

stepped up on the large base of one of the pillars and carefully threw one leg over the iron fence. Straddling the top railing between the posts on the tips of her toes, she made a small hop and landed on the other side, all without violating herself. With care she stepped up on the dais supporting the stone pedestal and large urn. A small placard at the base of the urn read 'Sarah Ellis.'

The skin on her arm tingled as she reached towards the urn. She felt a sense of guilt over the fact she was about to deface a dead woman's cenotaph. It looked big enough for a skull and she hoped it was going to be that easy.

"Please, please, please, Sarah, don't haunt me for this." She shoved the urn off the pedestal before she could convince herself her actions were ludicrous.

The urn shattered against the wide stone dais loud enough to wake the dead, if there had been any there.

"By the saints, what are you doing?" Darius looked furious on the other side of the fence.

Her flashlight illuminated the rubble. And rubble it was. There wasn't a skull in sight, not even a handwritten note from L.G. with the words 'made you look' on it.

"I could've sworn..." She nudged a piece of broken urn with her toe. "The outside walls don't look thick enough for a hidden room to hide the skull in and of all the places that belonged to Sir Francis Dashwood, this mausoleum would be the last on my list to hide anything. The church back there, or better yet the Hellfire Caves, would make more sense. For all we know, the skull is hidden in one of the lost caverns."

"Then L.G. would've sent us there instead of here."

A headache stirred beneath Mackenzie's eyebrow. She rubbed her forehead and tried to think. "Then there's something we're missing. L.G. had to have said something more than just handing you the phone with this address already typed in the GPS."

"Notes." Darius said the word with as much frustration as she felt as he walked back to the walls to continue his search.

"Say wha–" Mackenzie struggled back over the wrought iron fence to get him to repeat what he said but the bolts connecting the fence to the stone pillars loosened and the entire fence toppled over, taking her with it. Mackenzie hit the grass with a grunt and then groaned when the fence landed on top of her.

When this quest was all over and Darius went on to save his next damsel in distress, and if she ever got her life back to normal, she was so becoming a hermit and never leaving the safety of her 'new' home ever again.

"Are you trying to kill yourself?" Darius lifted the fence off her and tossed it out of the way.

"I think the universe is conspiring against me." She took his hand this time and he pulled her to her feet. "And what did you mean by notes? Musical notes? Handwritten notes? Did she conveniently etch on a wall 'Skull is here'?"

"I don't know. She handed me the phone and said 'there's notes.'"

"Aw, come on, you gotta give me some–" Her mind clicked and she pulled Darius's phone from out of her back pocket. Luckily, it had remained unscathed during her multiple encounters with the cold, hard ground. "You do realize there's an App on your phone called Notes, right?"

"What?" The question rumbled in her ear as Darius huddled at her back and stared over her shoulder at the phone's screen.

She tapped on the Notes App and found a single note titled 'I was Sarah Ellis.'

CHAPTER 28

Mackenzie tapped on the title of the note displayed on the phone, a new screen popped up and she read the words aloud. "Take twenty steps and rest awhile. Then take a pick and find a stile. Where once I did my love beguile. 'Twas twenty-two in Dashwood's time. Perhaps to hide his cell divine. Where lay my love in peace sublime. Paul Whitehead."

The note ended with no further explanation.

"A detailed map would've been nice, preferably one with a fat 'X' marks the spot." Mackenzie mumbled, but the poem rambled around in her head sparking a tendril of recognition.

"Bloody riddles." Darius stepped back, scratching his head. "The alcoves along the walls could be considered stiles, if you take creative license."

He strolled over to the wall, and Mackenzie walked back to the entrance of the mausoleum where her rolled papers lay on the grass.

"Twenty two." She ruffled through the papers and found the image she was looking for. It was of the Hellfire Caves. About halfway down the cave system was a roman numeral twenty-two etched into the chalk wall.

"Again with the caves."

She skimmed the pages in her hands. It was believed a secret passage branched out somewhere near the wall where the Roman numerals 'XXII' was carved, which led to a few lost rooms where Dashwood hosted his secret society meetings.

A few people who used to attend the gatherings mentioned at a later date that the caves had once been much larger. The remaining rooms in the Hellfire Caves that used to fit twenty or so people with ease, could now barely squeeze in half a dozen. A moat that was once so wide it had to be traversed by a small boat, was now just a glorified stream.

But that meant nothing to Mackenzie. She skimmed the theories on the pages about the forgotten rooms and found the poem that was assumed to be about the famous Roman numeral 'XXII,' the same one L.G. typed into the phone, but there was one major difference between the two.

"The poem was written by Anonymous," she yelled over to Darius, who walked back towards her.

"I thought you said it was written by Paul Whitehead."

"L.G. wrote it was written by Whitehead, but the research says it was written by Anonymous. Again it doesn't make sense."

"L.G.'s playing games with us."

"And the poem is believed to be tied to the Hellfire Caves below us." Mackenzie tried to break the puzzle apart piece by piece and hoped that in smaller chunks something would click. "But Paul Whitehead is tied to the mausoleum."

"How?"

"His heart. When he died he requested in his will that his friend, Sir Francis Dashwood, put his heart in an urn and let it rest here in the mausoleum."

"Where's the urn?"

"It was moved to the Hellfire Caves but someone had already stolen his heart by then." She stared at the empty pedestal that once held Sarah Ellis's urn.

"Then where should we look?" He sounded as frustrated as she felt.

She didn't know and wished she could be of more use than stating pointless facts about people who died long ago. But L.G. wasn't surfacing, which frustrated her most of all. The fact she was dependent on the demon that possessed her made her feel like she was somehow lacking.

"I refuse to be outdone by a body-snatching squatter with a clichéd motivation to destroy the world."

"Would it be clichéd if she was actually the first one to devise a plot to destroy the world?"

She shot him a look she hoped seemed threatening. He just smiled.

She went back to sifting through the facts. "Paul Whitehead was the secretary of Dashwood's secret society, he knew all the secrets, and days before his death he was seen burning stacks and stacks of paper."

"And the point you're trying to make?"

"He wanted his heart to be buried here, in a not-mausoleum, which is rumored to be located over the great gathering room of the Hellfire Caves. No, wait, I just confused myself. Again, why are we here and not in the caves?"

"Because L.G. told us to come here."

"Great, we're back at square one asking the same question, where is the skull?"

They stood in silence. The air temperature was now

firmly on the wrong side of cool and goose bumps pockmarked Mackenzie's skin.

Mackenzie was wasting time and was unsure what to do next. "The stupid roman numerals on the wall in the cave don't even make sense. They're farther than twenty-two steps from anywhere relevant and there are no signs of any hidden passages. And what could possibly change from being twenty-two steps one day and twenty another and why a heart? Symbolically hearts are romantic. Cartoon hearts, not real ones that is. But where's the romance here? There's an empty urn dedicated to a dead wife who may have been possessed by L.G., and there are walls that used to be filled with busts of Dashwood's relatives who Whitehead would have never met."

"When was the Hellfire Club active?" Darius asked.

"From about seventeen forty-nine to seventeen sixty-six."

"And when was the Mausoleum built?"

"Seventeen sixty-five."

"So this wasn't even here during most of the time the club was active. So the twenty-two reference in the poem could mean anything."

Catching on to his thoughts, Mackenzie flipped through the papers. "Except this monument to Sarah Ellis was erected when she died in seventeen *sixty-nine*." She couldn't help but snicker.

"That's mature." Darius shook his head.

Details of the poem and what she knew collided together in her mind, nagging at her. "There are rumors and myths of hidden or lost rooms in the caves. The first rumor is that the caves actually reach all the way underneath where we stand. The second is that there were various rooms and sections that once existed but don't anymore. There are discrepancies in those stories that make the supposed lost rooms a myth. There's even a story about a secret entrance so the more prominent members of the Hellfire Club could come and go unseen." Mackenzie read the poem again, it was no clearer than before. She walked back to the entryway of the mausoleum. "The mausoleum was built by Dashwood during the height of his secret-societies reign. But the monument to Sarah wasn't built until after the decline of the club."

She walked from the entry arch and counted her steps towards the center of the mausoleum. When she reached twenty, she was standing at the Greek columns surrounding Sarah's monument. At twenty-two steps, she would have stood at the pedestal that once held Sarah's fake urn. "Could the pedestal cover the secret entrance to the Hellfire Caves?"

They stared at the empty marble pedestal in silence. She hoped the stone would produce a skull by the sheer force of her will alone.

Nothing happened.

"Very well." Darius handed her his flashlight and stepped up to the marble dais.

She pointed the light in his direction, but he just stood there with a frown.

"You gonna look for a secret lever?" She broke the silence. "Or are you going to call your people for a bulldozer?"

"No." He stepped up to the marble pedestal and shoved. The pedestal grated against the stone base beneath it, then tipped over and broke into pieces on top of the rubble of Sarah Ellis's urn.

"The he-man act works, too."

Darius wiped his hands together. "It was hollow."

And empty. Damn.

The remaining stone base was four by four feet by Mackenzie's guess, and it was in their way.

"A jackhammer would be nice right about now, you

should call your people."

Darius took the flashlight from her and crouched. He ran his fingers over the stone as if willing it to speak.

"It's hollow, too. There's a crack here." His fingers ran down a darkened line.

He stood and pulled the crowbar from his backpack.

"Careful, the backlash is a bitch." She took his flashlight again.

He swung and the crowbar connected with the stone. Once, twice, three times and he kept swinging until the crack gave way to a larger crack. She raised her light and saw an enticing sliver of black darkness through the slight opening.

If this was how archeologists felt when they made a discovery, she was in the wrong profession.

Darius wedged his crowbar into the opening and pushed down. When the far side of the base lifted, he rotated it on its edge and dumped it on the grass, revealing a manhole-sized void in the ground where the stone base had been.

Mackenzie should have been focused on that hole, instead she watched Darius wipe sweat off his brow. No, not sweat. Sweat was a much too common word for it. His skin glistened in the light, like he stepped right out of one of those Firefighter calendars.

It made her wonder if he glistened after another type of strenuous activity.

"Mackenzie."

"Hmmm?" She blinked, knowing full well she'd been caught gawking.

He wiggled the fingers of his already outstretched hand. "Torch."

She gave him the flashlight and his hand grazed hers before he pulled it free. It was an unnecessary embrace and her toes curled for it.

She rounded the wrought iron fence that blocked her

path as Darius knelt and examined the opening. It was just wide enough to squeeze his shoulders through, which meant she would have no problem.

Five feet below the opening was a staircase cut into the white chalk stone.

"I hate to be that girl, but it looks dark and scary and I don't want to go in there."

"And I hate to break it to you, but you have no choice in the matter. I could always throw you over my shoulder if that helps."

"You look way too happy saying that."

"Anything to assist a damsel in distress. Besides, the last time I did that, I rather enjoyed the view." He offered her his hand. "Come on. You're stalling."

She let him lower her down through the opening, but she kept her focus on him. When she reached the top of the stairs, she pulled the flashlight from her pocket and chased the shadows away, along with anything else that might be scurrying about.

"On the plus side..." Mackenzie made room for him to drop down beside her. "If I decide to give into my violent urges, at least I won't have to dig your grave."

"I have discovered I enjoy it when you threaten to perpetrate violence upon me."

"You have problems." If she wasn't so terrified, she may have just laughed. Instead she was fighting off a wave of debilitating claustrophobia.

CHAPTER 29

Darius led the way down the stairs with Mackenzie close behind. She ran her fingers over the cold, moist chalk walls and felt the gouges where pickaxes once marred the stone. The steps that spiraled downward had been hacked into the stone unevenly with rudimentary skill.

Even though she should have been comforted by the fact the caves had been there for centuries and hadn't fallen in, they were still made of chalk. She played with chalk enough as a kid to know that it was brittle. "L.G. is really tempting the universe here with all her subterranean hiding places."

"Someone is being a tad pessimistic."

"I don't see how I am." She crumbled a small piece of the wall with her fingertips. "I'm just stating facts. Statistically, if you tempt fate enough times, she's gonna take you up on it."

"She?"

"Yes, she. You think fate would be a man?"

"Yes."

"Anyway, this situation is no different than saying 'things can't get any worse.'" Mackenzie's tirade was cut short when Darius made an abrupt stop and she collided nose first into his shoulder blade.

"It got worse, didn't it?" She rubbed her nose.

"The passageway is flooded."

"Fate is definitely a woman." Mackenzie shoved Darius to the side and peered into the shadowy depths of her future subterranean-turned-watery grave. "Only a woman would see the obvious likelihood of being buried alive and still manage to come up with something as ironic as drowning."

Both their flashlights illuminated a narrow, tunnel-like passageway. The right side gave way to a large, cave like room. To the left, the view was blocked by a bend in the wall.

Mackenzie ignored the looming, low ceiling and focused on the glassy surface of the water that covered the floor. It didn't even reach the first step of the staircase.

"You call this flooded?" She turned her flashlight on him. "I was expecting the hallway scene from the movie *The Shining* and you give me a big puddle."

"I'm saying you're going to get your feet wet, Ms. Doom and Gloom."

"Call me DAG for short." She took his offered hand and stepped into the dark, cool water. An errant thought occurred to her about the dangers of stagnant water, like flesh-eating bacteria, but she shoved it away. She had far bigger issues to deal with.

She took a step and cringed as bacteria-laden water sloshed up her pant leg. But she couldn't dwell, Darius had headed to the right, so she sloshed after him. The passageway flared outward to form a large cavern big enough to fit at least thirty people, three times bigger than her research indicated.

"So this is how Lara Croft must feel." She spun around to take it all in.

"Who?"

"Lara Croft, the fictional, kick-ass archeologist." Mackenzie patted Darius on the chest. "Sorry, I forgot, you're old. Of course you wouldn't be up to speed with all the high falootin' things us youngins' are doing now-a-days."

"I'm not amused."

"Well..." She smiled at her hand that lingered on his chest and discovered she had gone from playful patting to a far more intimate caress. She pulled away. "Congratulations then, we just discovered one of the lost rooms of the Hellfire Caves."

"There's no skull. Let's move on."

"Seriously? Not even an 'oh, that's nice'?" She didn't let his unimpressed attitude dampen their discovery. Instead, she made a sweeping gesture and lowered her voice an octave as if she were about to divulge the meaning of life. "We just discovered one of the lost rooms of the Hellfire Caves."

"Restating it won't change the facts."

"The facts being that we're awesome? Or that you're a douche?"

"I hardly see a need for personal attacks."

"Everyone thinks the missing rooms are a myth. A myth! The caverns known today are a fraction of this size. Yet, everyone believes all the rooms to be found are already on display, and we just proved them wrong. The very least you can do is go 'ooooh and aaaahh.'"

"Oooh. Ahhh." Darius walked down the hall back the way they came.

"Fun sucker," Mackenzie said to his back.

They trudged past the stairway and stopped when they

came upon an arched opening just before the bend in the hall. Mackenzie shoved Darius aside and entered, refusing to let him be the first to discover another lost room. It was rectangular in shape and could probably hold about ten people with ease. Carved into the upper portion of the far wall were two arched alcoves on either side of a wide shelf.

Mackenzie let out a steadying breath of air when her flashlight lit up a dusty obsidian skull that was perched on the middle of the shelf. "If L.G. was Sarah Ellis, then this is definitely the lost room named 'Sarah's Cave.'"

"No secret society is complete without an ancient artifact to worship." Darius sloshed past her, grabbed the skull and shoved it in his backpack.

"How many skulls does this make?"

"Eleven of thirteen."

"Oh." She eyed the alcove on the right. Centered in it was a small urn with a fleur-de-lis topper and a plaque covered in a layer of thick chalk dust. She stepped closer, wet her fingers in the murky water and wiped the surface of the plaque as best she could.

"Here lies the true heart of Paul Whitehead," Mackenzie read. "Okay, ew."

"It makes more sense to have part of you buried next to an artifact you worshipped."

"Still weird." She moved to the other alcove, where there was another similar urn. She brushed clean the larger placard. "To my love, your yearning heart now rests within." She couldn't help but make a face and wipe her hand on her jeans. "Please don't tell me Dashwood cut out Sarah's heart and put it here."

"Either way, we need to leave." Darius turned to go.

"In a second." She re-read the plaque. "Why not just say Sarah's heart is here? Whitehead's plaque is straightforward." She knew she was overthinking it. With the whole trying to figure out the riddle in the poem business, she was starting to see double meanings everywhere. Why the people of the past didn't deem it necessary to be straightforward was beyond her. It would have made her life a lot easier.

She set her flashlight aside.

"What are you doing?" Darius almost sounded bored.

"Something incredibly stupid that will possibly scar me for life, so give me one fraking second." Her fingers wrapped around the stone fleur-de-lis topper and she took a silent moment to pray to the universe not to give in to the temptation to traumatize her further.

"Quick question." she said as she pulled the urn's lid off, but hesitated to peer inside, "what does a two-hundred-year-old decomposing heart look like? Dust, goo, or jerky?"

"Jerky, if no moisture got in. Dust, if it did."

She set the lid on the mantle and tipped the jar close to Darius's flashlight. There was no decomposed heart withering away inside. Instead, she found two rolled up, leather bound tubes.

"What in the–" An explosion cut her off.

Chalky chunks fell from the ceiling into the water.

Darius wrapped his body around her and tucked her head against his shoulder in a protective embrace. Though that didn't protect her from the reverberating noise of the huge cave-in happening just outside.

When the rumbling stopped, Mackenzie held her breath and just waited for the rest of the cave to crumble down around them.

Darius's hands ran down her arms in a soothing caress before he stepped back and turned his flashlight towards their only exit. From what Mackenzie could tell, the doorway hadn't caved in.

"Please tell me that's a natural occurrence in underground tunnels." Her words echoed in her harsh whisper. "Because if someone is trying to kill us, we're so screwed."

"Shush."

Faint voices echoed towards them from at least two people, possibly more.

"Shite." Darius didn't need to explain, she knew who they were.

He pulled out a hand gun from the backpack and handed the bag to her.

Mackenzie slid the leather-bound tubes in the bag, shouldered it and followed after Darius who was already in the hall. She came to a stuttering halt in front of large boulders that now blocked the entrance to the stairs.

"Oh, no, it's happened." She wanted to scream, cry, panic and faint all at once. She settled on screaming. Darius's warm hand clamped over her mouth before she could emit a sound.

He turned her towards the bend in the passageway and guided her forward. Unfortunately, it was in the same direction as the voices and their only way out.

"Stay quiet," he whispered in her ear, "and do everything I tell you to do. Understand?"

She nodded and his hand fell away.

They sloshed forward until her footing faltered as her vision doubled and the world tilted.

"Oh, no, no, no, no, no." She grabbed the wall for support as she felt her very soul being pulled from the surface, almost drowning in the sensation. "Not now."

She struggled to take a breath and her vision blurred.

"What's wrong?" Darius was there in front of her, all two of him.

"It's L.G., she wants to come out."

CHAPTER 30

Darius and Mackenzie were trapped in a bloody cave with the Illuminati blocking their only exit and now L.G. wanted to make an appearance?

"Don't let her, Mackenzie, I can't face what's coming for us head on if I have to watch my back as well." Darius kept his voice low, steady and calm, but inside he was frenzied.

He also wouldn't admit it aloud, but every time L.G. surfaced there was a chance Mackenzie wouldn't come back. He didn't want his last moments with her to be in some dank, dark, chalk-covered cave.

"Stay with me." He knew he demanded the impossible but prayed L.G. could hear him and for once listen to his demands.

Mackenzie's breaths shortened and fearful tears filled her eyes. She was shutting down. He'd seen this more times than he could count with lesser-trained soldiers.

Insta-Prophecy Hotline

"Look at me." She shook her head. He stepped closer, forcing her to react to him. "Look. At. Me."

She looked up at him with wide, hazel eyes.

"Don't let L.G. win, she can't take over if you refuse to leave." A lie, but he didn't care at this point.

"Four."

"Stop counting down," he shook her, frustrated he could do nothing else.

"I'm counting down?" Her voice raised in alarm. "What am I counting down to?"

"Just fight." He was not going to lose her, especially not here in this watery, suffocating tomb. He was going to pull her through this whether she wanted to fight or not. "I order you to fight and you will obey."

She was too far gone to even get annoyed. She just looked sorry. The feisty flair that burned in her eyes dimmed for a split second and he feared Mackenzie was about to be snuffed out for good.

Her eyes flickered between beautiful hazel and that dangerous metallic. "Three."

Damn it all.

He slammed his lips down on hers with a bruising force. There was no kindness, no gentle urging like before. This was a kiss demanding total submission and he would allow no other reaction.

It felt like a jolt of electricity shot through his body and into hers. Still, he didn't relent and he nipped her bottom lip demanding entrance. His fingers trailed up from her cheek and snaked in her hair.

Mackenzie quietly moaned, her stiff body softened and her mouth opened. When her tongue touched his, he shifted his stance and shoved her against the wall.

She squeaked and pushed at his chest. With much reluctance, he stepped back, though he couldn't look away from her lips. He didn't dare look at her eyes, afraid it wouldn't be Mackenzie staring back. "You still with me?"

"Damn backpack," she mumbled and shifted the backpack straps.

He dared a glance and found her eyes were still hazel and even in the faint light the fire that was all Mackenzie burned bright. And there was no doubt in his mind that if the backpack hadn't gotten in her way, she would have soon demanded some submission of her own.

Whether L.G. had been beaten back or not he didn't know, but he still had time. Not much, but it would do.

"We need to move." He adjusted the gun in his grasp and focused on what lay further down the damnable cave.

Since he couldn't take his frustration out on L.G., the bastards who damn near buried them were soon going to feel his wrath.

CHAPTER 31

Her lips tingled from his kiss and her ears still burned with his order to not give up as they trudged down the hallway. Mackenzie might have resisted L.G.'s takeover, but she knew full well the only reason L.G. retreated was because L.G. wanted to.

There was no fighting her like Darius thought, but Mackenzie couldn't tell him that. Not after the look of utter desperation he gave her.

Darius stopped and she ran into him, again.

"What?" She looked around but saw nothing of importance.

"Torch."

"Hmm?" She looked at the flashlight he held and found he had turned it off. She clicked hers off, too. "Oh."

The passageway was cast into darkness, except for the faint light coming from their enemies beyond where the hall took a blind turn. Their echoed voices were louder now.

Half of her self-preservation instincts screamed at her to flee, the other half demanded she close her eyes and crouch down until the scary stuff was over. By no means did any part of her scream out 'fight the enemy.'

Darius pressed his back against the wall and inched closer to the corner. He closed his eyes for a brief moment and then took a quick glance around it.

"Well?"

"Three, maybe four men. There's a reservoir of water in a large cavern between them and us. They're traversing it in a small raft. We have some time before they get here."

"What's the plan?"

"You go hide until I get you." Darius checked the magazine in his gun.

She liked this plan, yet she hesitated. "What if you don't come back?"

"I'm very hard to kill." He gave her a boyish grin that she wanted to smack right off his face.

"That's not comforting."

He cupped her cheek and crouched until he matched her height. "Then you do what you must to survive. They won't kill you. Last long enough to get out and call the Hotline. They'll send another knight."

She didn't want another knight. She wanted Darius.

"You need more ammo." She shoved the backpack into his chest, giving him no choice but to take it.

With as much care as she was able, and while he was distracted pulling magazines out of the pack, she peered around the corner to get a glance of the cavern herself.

Where she found the courage to do so, she had no idea.

The cavern was big, at least the size of a football field in length. Boulders had fallen from the rounded ceiling overhead, marring the still water. Well, at least now she knew why the caves they stood in were flooded.

She saw four people on an inflatable raft with two lanterns mounted to it. Beyond them was a gaping hole in a once pristine off-white cavern wall. It was a miracle they managed to blast a hole in the soft chalk without collapsing the whole place.

Darius pulled her back into the shadow. "What the hell do you think you're doing?"

"You need to calm the frak down."

"You need to hide. You'll be fine, I'll make sure of it."

For that she had no doubt. Yet her feet wouldn't move.

He gave her the backpack and gently pushed her away from the cavern, back the way they had come. She turned to say something pithy, like he could take his order and shove it up his backside, but he had already turned towards the bend, as if he couldn't fathom being disobeyed.

Pompous ass.

She tore into the backpack looking for something, anything, she could use. She found a hand gun, which she shoved aside. She wasn't confident she could shoot the thing with her eyes open.

Hadn't Darius mentioned earlier using a grenade? She shoved aside the leather bound tubes, a large knife, a length of rope and the skull.

Her hands shook as she reached the bottom of the backpack. All that was left was a lighter and a packet of cherry bombs. Why cherry bombs she didn't know, but they were better than nothing.

Darius peered around the corner again and when he pulled back he was swearing under his breath.

"Go," he said when he noticed her still standing there.

She pulled the backpack on and shoved the cherry bombs into her pockets, except for one and the lighter. "Do you trust me?"

"You have L.G. in you."

"Not what I asked."

She could see the struggle in his shadowy features, the doubt and uncertainty, and ignored the fact that the light from the four men coming towards them had gotten a whole lot brighter.

Then Darius's features relaxed. "Yes."

It was comparable to saying 'I love you' to her at that moment. But if she were smart, she would have taken his confession and hid. Let the trained knight deal with this alone.

Instead, she lit the cherry bomb and lunged out into the open cavern.

CHAPTER 32

Her feet landed in the water with a kerplunk and four pairs of eyes focused on her. One man secured the raft and the three others reached for their weapons.

Mackenzie lobbed the cherry bomb at the gun wielding goons. "Grenade!"

The cherry bomb exploded, catching the closest man in the chest.

Darius shoved her behind him.

She lit two more cherry bombs and dashed back around him. Shots rang out, hitting the wall behind her. She threw one cherry bomb at two of the darkly dressed men to her right, and another at the goon to her left, who was checking on her first victim.

"Grenades!"

The two men on her right dove into the dark water. The man on her left didn't dive fast enough and the cherry bomb took a chunk out of his leg.

"Are you insane?" Darius yanked her back and opened fire on the two injured men who had enough sense to start shooting back.

Darius took out the one with the chest wound, ejected the magazine from his gun, and replaced it with another in one swift movement. "When I say hide, you hide."

One of the two men who had dove into the water surfaced and Darius moved towards him, shooting off two rounds. They hit him in the stomach and he fell back under the water with a splash.

The man with a chunk missing from his leg tackled Darius from the side and they both went down.

Mackenzie pulled out another cherry bomb and waited for the right moment to light it.

The fourth goon shot out of the water like a breaching whale on her right. She yelled and dropped the cherry bomb as he lunged for her with a knife clutched in his hand.

He slashed at her, grim intent set in his features and her only defense was the useless lighter clutched in her hand.

A thick arm came up from behind the man and wrapped around his arm holding the knife. Another arm wrapped around the man's throat and her attacker was thrown back into the shallow water.

Darius dove on top of him and the two grappled for dominance in a brutal display of force. Even in the dim lighting, she could see both men were equally matched. The only unfair element was the knife Darius had yet to wrestle away from his enemy.

The Illuminati soldier lunged, his blade aimed to sink into Darius's chest. Darius grabbed the offending arm at the last moment and twisted until the bone snapped. The man screamed in pain and dropped the blade into the water. Darius grabbed the man's head and wrenched it until his neck cracked and the screaming stopped.

The body fell lifeless into the water and Mackenzie clutched the lighter in her hand even tighter as an odd silence fell over the room. The lights from the lanterns on the raft illuminated the three other lumps in the water, still and unmoving.

It was an odd dichotomy. One second there was screaming, adrenaline and action, and now there wasn't.

Darius took the backpack off her and pulled out the other gun. "Get in the boat."

She turned away as he took aim at the still forms in the water. She flinched as four shots rang out. Kill shots, if they weren't dead already. She was aware it was a necessary evil, but it wasn't great to hear regardless.

She climbed into the raft and did her best to ignore the unpleasant squish of her pants as she sat on the inflatable seat. Darius shoved the raft off the ledge and jumped in. He grabbed the two oars and started to row.

"Of all the irresponsible. Stupid. Foolish. Dangerous. Things to do." Every word was punctuated with a row of the oars, propelling them towards the other side of the cavern.

"You know I have strange reactions to high-stress situations." She flipped the lighter on and off. "And what would you have me do while the Illuminati shot at you? Wait a minute." She frowned and glared back towards the bodies. "Those guys shot at *me*."

"Which is why I specifically ordered you to hide."

"They actually intended to kill me."

"I want to spank you for the danger you put yourself in."

"Oh, please, that's not a threat, that's foreplay." She snapped her mouth shut.

Naughty, Mackenzie.

Darius paused, mid-row, his anger vanished.

He leaned forward and she found herself unable to resist

doing the same, closing the distance. He let go of an oar, reached out and toyed with a lock of her hair. All her attention focused on that one hand as it warmed her cheek.

"The bullet nearly hit its mark," he said through a tight jaw and tugged a lock of her hair. The fire of his anger back, full force.

"Huh?" She reached up.

"I saw your hair move as a bullet grazed past. You nearly died because of your foolish action." He went back to rowing.

It was one thing to know L.G. was slowly killing her. It was another to know she almost died at the hands of someone other than L.G. No warning, no preamble, just death.

A part of her couldn't help but wonder if that would have been a kinder fate. At least death from a bullet to the brain would stop the prophecy and there was the added bonus that she wouldn't have seen it coming.

Then again.

"Good job, Mackenzie, way to kick some arse," she mumbled to herself, mocking Darius's British accent, trying to shove aside that tightened, panicked feeling in her chest. "You really saved the day with the element of surprise. Jolly good."

The raft nudged the flooded landing on the other side of the cavern. Darius abandoned the oars and jumped out.

Mackenzie pocketed the lighter and grabbed the lantern from the front of the boat. She climbed out and trudged towards the ragged, blown out hole in the wall. Wet jeans clung to her legs and she tried not to cringe at the soggy feeling as she stepped over the rubble into a small, round room with a dry floor. Out of the corner of her eye she caught a glimpse of a person hiding in the shadows and cried out.

Darius was there in an instant, blocking her body as he

Insta-Prophecy Hotline

faced the danger head-on like the knight he was.

She expected fighting and violence with someone getting shot. But instead Darius relaxed.

"What are you doing?" she hissed. "Shoot it."

"It's a mannequin." He turned enough to give her a clear view of the supposed attacker. Four more mannequins dressed in colorful, period costumes were strewn in a haphazard pile against the wall.

"Shoot it anyway."

"Look who's becoming bloodthirsty." Darius took the lantern from her.

She toed one of the fallen mannequins aside and found another underneath it. "I bet you a hundred dollars there's a prophecy about mannequins coming to life and taking over the world. And I wouldn't be surprised if it started here."

"I don't bet with money." He tugged her out of the small room, away from the flooded caves and towards their only exit.

"Then what do you bet with? Horses? Camels? Goats?"

He stopped and she almost ran into him. "Think less livestock and more..."

"Pervy? Your guy friends must hate making bets with you." She didn't miss the tick in his jaw when he glared at her from over his shoulder.

"I bet jobs with them. With you, however..." He helped her step over a small stream that intersected the hall.

He let the silence linger. If that didn't get Mackenzie's mind to take a nose dive into the gutter, then she was already dead. She studied his broad shoulders. Even in the shadows, she could appreciate the vast expanse that teased her gaze. Her attention shifted downwards and settled on his ass and thighs. She never realized thighs could be sexy, but his set her mind a whirring with all the tantalizing positions a pair of strong thighs could achieve.

"So, are you going to make that bet?" His voice trailed back to her.

"Okay, I bet you an entire week of me naked with you in Bora Bora that the mannequin apocalypse starts here." The words blurted past her lips before she could reign in her libido.

Darius studied her as a new tension filled the air, one that promised such naughty things. Or perhaps he didn't appreciate her forwardness. It was hard to tell in the dim light.

When he shifted and adjusted his jeans, she realized he wasn't as unaffected by their conversation as she thought.

"I'll take your bet," his voice husky. "Should I lose, I'll treat you to an entire week in Bora Bora teaching you all the fun things you can do with a pair of handcuffs."

Oh, drool.

Then his words sunk in. "Wait, you're supposed to bet something that would be a sacrifice for you."

"Oh? And being naked at my mercy for an entire week would be a sacrifice for you?"

"Um…" She walked right into that one. "A girl likes her clothes?"

His deep chuckle sent a trickle of electricity down her spine. "You're the one who went down this path. You could've bet cooking for me for an entire week or doing my laundry."

"You can do your own damn laundry and I don't cook."

"I could just eat you."

Breathe, Mackenzie, breathe. It was hard to do when one naughty scenario after another played out in her mind.

Darius squeezed her hand and continued to guide her down the hallway. They walked in silence, her hand nestled in his, until the passageway split.

She knew exactly where they were. "Choose either side, they both wrap around and meet again down-a-ways."

Darius nodded and chose left.

A gunshot rang out and Darius fell backwards. She stared for a second at her hand which had been holding onto his and then down at his still form as her brain scrambled to make sense of the situation. Blood oozed from a hole in his chest and spread across his shirt.

"Darius?" She crouched over him, oblivious to the possibility of more shots coming her way. He was far too still and there was far too much blood.

Someone yanked her to her feet as a lantern switched on down the hall.

"Got you." The man who grabbed her turned on a flashlight of his own. He motioned with a jerk of his chin at another man who strode towards them and then dragged Mackenzie down the other hallway.

"No." She struggled as the other man neared Darius, who wasn't getting up. "Darius."

She felt numb, he couldn't be dead. He was a Templar Knight, super-healer and knower-of-all in the weird world she found herself in.

He couldn't be dead.

The man yanked her around the corner, and Darius and the other man disappeared from her sight.

"You no longer have a knight to keep us from you, Fraulein Tod."

She gaped at him then. His firm jaw, while sexy on Darius, was overly pronounced on him, making him look like a cruel brute.

"I'm not Fraulein Tod, I'm Mackenzie."

"You must think I'm stupid." He squeezed her arm.

"No, I don't." She looked back hoping to see Darius. He promised he wouldn't leave her. He promised he would stay with her to the end. He promised a week of naked fun, damnit.

"I'm well aware, Fraulein Tod, that once you possess your victims, there's nothing left of the host. No one survives you."

"Wait, what?" She snapped her head around.

They passed through another large chamber, this one with a vaulted ceiling patched together with metal mesh to keep the fragile stone from crashing down on their heads.

"Now, you're going to tell me where you've hidden your skulls."

Her brain was still stuck on 'no one survives being possessed by L.G.' Did Darius know this? Surely he would have said something.

The man squeezed tighter until she cried out in pain. "The skulls, where are they?"

The passageway fractured ahead of them, split by a small, gated cave-like room, behind which two more wildly dressed-up mannequins were lit up by a lone, eerie spotlight.

A gunshot echoed throughout the passageway and Mackenzie jerked her head around and looked back.

The kill shot.

Her frightened mind stuttered to a halt. She needed to get free, but all she had was a sore arm and a lighter, not exactly foreboding weapons.

What would L.G. do?

"Unhand me." Unsure how L.G. acted, she made it up and pulled out her best impersonation of Queen B from her old job.

The man turned on her with eyes so dead she doubted he had any semblance of a soul. She almost broke down right then to plead for mercy she knew he'd never give.

"You're no longer in a position to dictate how things are done." He gnashed his teeth in a vicious display of a smile.

"What are you going to do, kill me, like your buddy almost did back there?" She tried to keep the wobble of fear out of her voice, not sure if she succeeded. "Death threats won't get you anywhere. Without me, need I remind you, there's no hope for you in finding the other skulls."

He leaned forward. He reeked of three-day morning breath and she turned her head away in disgust. "Then, I guess I'll have to keep you alive. Torture is a personal favorite of mine."

Nope, she didn't do torture.

She slammed her forehead into his face. Pain blossomed between her eyes and the man's fingers slackened. She yanked free and stumbled into the wall, shaking her head as she tried to free her vision of starbursts.

Why did movies always make that move look so easy?

She shoved away from the wall and lashed out at the cold-eyed man, knowing she couldn't outrun him. He grabbed her arm and swung her back into the wall.

She slid to the floor and fell to her side. She was kicked in the stomach and the air slammed out of her lungs.

So this is how she was going to die.

A pair of booted feet stopped in front of her face. The man grabbed her by the hair and forced her to look up at him. His face was a blur. Tears filled her eyes and she struggled to take a deep breath.

"Now, Fraulein Tod," he said with a smile that made Mackenzie wish she had passed out. "You will lead me to your skulls."

When she just wanted to break down, wallow in fear and have a good cry, the words 'What would L.G. do' reared their ugly head yet again.

She struggled to brace herself up on her elbow. With her other arm she motioned for him to come closer and the bastard, cocky as he was, did.

She licked her lips, took a breath and yelled, "Not bloody likely."

The crack of gunfire sounded, the hand in her hair slackened and the man jerked around. Another gunshot rang out and the man dropped to the ground. She couldn't even feel relieved as she lay there watching his still form because her lungs felt like she was breathing around a wad of razor blades.

"You okay?" Darius, who was apparently back from the dead, crouched in front of her, bloody as hell. The bullet hole still gaped in his chest and he was still bleeding, although less than before, yet he seemed more concerned about her.

"Never better," she choked out as she sat up. "I thought you died."

"Only for a second."

"I didn't realize you were immortal."

"Immortal, no. Harder to kill, yes."

He put the gun in his back waistband and helped her to her feet. Mackenzie hoped L.G's healing abilities kicked in soon because she almost crumbled back to the ground when her ribs protested. She leaned against the unforgiving wall behind her in an attempt to not appear weaker than the bullet-ridden Darius.

Her attention fell on the lantern that had been dropped and forgotten. Bending over to get it required too much effort, so she willed it to her hand.

It didn't move. Shocker.

Darius picked up the lantern with his free hand. That would do.

He wrapped his arm around her waist, adding support without putting pressure on her ribs, and they made their way down the hallway.

Mackenzie jumped at every reaching shadow, half-expecting them to be filled with more Illuminati jerks.

Not Darius, though.

He didn't show hesitation or wariness and he didn't jump at the sight of yet another horrid mannequin.

She couldn't help but wonder that if she lived as long as he had, would she still walk with such self-assuredness or would she break?

The Illuminati henchman's words haunted her. *No one survives you.*

The cruel man seemed so sure.

But she was still here. She survived what he said she couldn't.

They must have been the obvious ramblings of a nut case because Darius... looked like he was going to bleed out at any moment.

"Are you sure you're okay?" Even in the faint light, his shirt glistened with blood.

"'Tis but a flesh wound."

So, he was a nerd for Monty Python as well as immortal. "And look how well that turned out for the Black Knight."

"The Black Knight wasn't me."

She wanted to laugh, even chuckle. But she could only muster a faint smile.

At long last the exit came into view and the night's brisk air filled her aching lungs.

Darius didn't hesitate or slow his pace as he walked towards the doorway and the unknown beyond, but Mackenzie had a few remaining brain cells left.

"Wait." She pulled him back into the shadows of the tunnel, turned off his lantern and set it on the ground. She gasped when the effort tweaked her bruised ribs.

"You okay?"

She ignored his question and dug out another cherry bomb from his backpack.

She neared the exit but stayed in the shadows as she peered into the relatively peaceful night. All she could see was a smattering of picnic tables, an open gate in the distance and a darkened storefront she hoped was empty, but knowing her luck it was a way station for lurking evil doers.

"Mackenzie?"

She winced at how unsure he said her name. She lit the firecracker and lobbed it through the doorway into the quiet, open area outside.

"Grenade!" She gasped the word as pain stole her breath, but it was worth it.

The cherry bomb hit the ground and exploded. Silence followed. No cries of alarm. No footfalls of an enemy preparing for an attack. Just the sounds of crickets and the ringing in Mackenzie's ears.

"Is this going to be a recurring event with you?" Darius snaked his arm around her waist again and urged her out the exit.

She noticed that while Darius acted all calm and unaware, he now gripped his gun in his other hand while scanning their surroundings with hawk-like precision.

"Well, who's gonna stop and check to see if I'm wrong?" She wrapped his arm over her shoulder and attempted to help him instead of the other way around. "Besides, one day I plan to have real grenades to throw at my enemies."

"Lord, help us all."

CHAPTER 33

With her feet propped up on the empty chair across from her, Mackenzie chowed down on a crumbling scone.

All it took was one phone call to Darius's mysterious 'people' and they had a clean, but modest, motel room waiting for them an hour away from the Hellfire Caves, along with a care package containing among other things new clothes, a bakery box with half a dozen scones and a large bottle of aspirin.

Now that she was clean, warm and content, she found it a little creepy she had never been asked for her measurements and yet they somehow knew what bra size she wore.

If only she could get Darius's contacts, she would never have to shop for clothes again. With all the time she'd save, she could take up a hobby like martial arts or learn the proper way to shoot a firearm.

She finished off her scone and looked at the alarm clock nestled on a nightstand between two full-sized beds. It was beyond late, but she wasn't tired. Funny how being shot at, almost buried alive, twice, and assaulted to within an inch of her life brought out her insomnia.

She grabbed her coffee mug off the round, cheap motel-grade wooden table in front of her and sipped her lukewarm, caffeine-free tea.

Her ribs still ached but L.G.'s super healing powers were taking care of it.

The words the goon spoke at the Hellfire caves still played over and over in her mind. Surely, he had been trying to scare her, but that look in his maddened gaze said otherwise.

If he was right, how had she managed to survive? Not that it mattered at this point, she was so close to death she could almost see the Grim Reaper beckoning her to the afterlife. The constant pressure in the back of her mind now felt like L.G. sat atop her soul, smothering her beneath the weight.

"You seem troubled," Darius said from behind Mackenzie.

She jumped and banged her elbow on the wooden armrest of the chair, nailing her funny bone. Lukewarm tea sloshed onto her hand and she abandoned her cup on the table. She wiped her hands on the chair's cheap upholstery so she could rub her elbow.

"In your advanced age, you should know better than to startle..." She turned in her seat to yell at the oaf face-to-face. Instead she trailed off when Darius's naked body came into view.

Well, there was a towel wrapped low around his waist, but he might as well have been naked for all the bare skin he revealed. His muscled chest called to her, taunted her to run over every indentation with her fingers.

He grabbed a canvas bag from the bed closest to the bathroom and pulled out clean clothes.

She knew she was staring but couldn't help it. The towel was held up by one mere corner tucked into the fold around his waist. She knew from years of trying to make her towels stay in place while combing her hair that all he needed to do was make the slightest bend or twist and the towel would drop.

He bent forward and the towel stayed in place. He twisted and the towel still didn't budge. He dropped his shirt and bent over to pick it up, still the towel protected his modesty.

Thus proving Darius a sorcerer.

"What are you thinking about?" He sauntered back into the bathroom and closed the door just enough so he had privacy without shutting it all the way. Right when he was out of sight, she thought she heard the towel flop on the floor. Damn.

"Mackenzie?"

Right, he asked a question. "Um, nothing?"

"You sure?"

"Yeah." It was a good thing he couldn't see her face, because she knew her cheeks burned fifty shades of red. She rubbed her temples and tried to get an imaginary, naked Darius out of her head by thinking about her imminent demise and the burning question of how many people Darius was unable to save because of L.G.

Why did she want to know? Because, it would seem, she was a masochist.

Darius walked out of the bathroom fully clothed and grabbed the backpack from the floor next to the bed. "What's wrong? Is it L.G.?"

"Isn't it always?" She tried not to glare at his black jeans and t-shirt, but wasn't sure she succeeded. She liked the visual of him in a towel better.

Darius sat in the chair across from her and looked like he wanted to say something.

She cut him off and motioned to the backpack. "Are those two leather-bound rolls still in there?"

He pulled them out. "Was there a reason you took them from the caves?"

"Seemed like a good idea at the time." And now they served as a great distraction.

The rolls were darkened with water stains and a bit crunched in places but otherwise undamaged. If she was lucky, what they contained would still be dry. She set one roll aside and pulled the damp leather tie on the other.

Darius took out his handgun from the backpack and did what men always did with their guns. He fondled it.

She pushed her cup of tea farther back on the table and set the roll in front of her. With slow and deliberate movements, she unrolled the leather. Light crunching sounds filled the air as the disintegrated remains of whatever had been left in the tube for three hundred years was revealed.

"Aw, man." She poked at the pile of yellowed, gritty bits and they crumbled further into dust. "Well, on a positive note, at least the leather kept the contents dry."

Darius pulled ammo out of the backpack. "What's on them?"

"A recipe for chicken noodle soup. How would I know?"

"You grabbed them."

"Because it was in an urn dedicated to Sarah Ellis." She rolled the leather back up, trying to keep the mess contained, and set it aside.

She swiped the remnants off the wood table and moved on to the second roll.

With a tug, the tie came free and she unrolled the leather. This time, two dry, yellowed sheets of paper remained intact.

The bottom sheet was large, the size of two place mats side by side, and was covered with the delicate lines of an old map. The smaller piece of paper, however, coiled in on itself and rolled across the table.

To keep the map from doing the same, she flattened it and put her cup of tea on one corner and Darius's gun on the other, ignoring his raised eyebrow. Then she spread out the smaller paper, which was filled with such elaborate calligraphy the words were nearly indecipherable in their elegance.

"My dearest Sarah," Mackenzie read aloud. "It has only been a few years since I buried the body of your human vessel, yet I find myself hoping you may grace me with your presence one last time. While I understood your reasons for leaving, I was never content with them. I continued your search after you departed and came across this ancient Phoenician map in the archive of the Ottoman Empire. I had it transcribed for I do not think the original map may fare the test of time much longer. I cannot know for sure this will lead to anything fruitful. I am old, too old to make the trip dictated on the map to see for myself. I know you will come for the skull you left in my care, so I leave this as my last testament of my devotion to you. It is my sincerest hope you find what you have been searching for. To my heart, my Sarah. Francis."

Mackenzie set the letter aside. "I wonder if Francis knew she was a homicidal megalomaniac."

Darius rounded the table and stood behind her. "In his defense, he most likely had no idea what she intended to do with the skulls once she gathered them."

He rested his hands on the arms of her chair. His breath teased her ear and his chest pressed against the back of her shoulders as he cocooned her within his arms.

She did her best to concentrate on the task at hand. So, she studied the hand-drawn lines on the right side of the yellowed map that looked like the coastline of what she assumed was Italy and the rest of Europe, including the islands of Great Britain and Ireland. Below Europe, was Africa. On the other side of the map was the familiar east coast of America and to the west beyond.

Of course there were no border lines outlining countries, nor convenient state lines or other useful hints that adorn modern maps. There was writing scribbled across the Atlantic Ocean, but it was written in a language she didn't recognize. She assumed it was Phoenician.

Her gaze was drawn to a detailed drawing of what she could only describe as a large gash across the lower, southwest portion of America.

"Is that the Grand Canyon?" It was a rhetorical question, she knew it as soon as she saw it.

The canyon was drawn out in great detail, even showing where a smaller river joined a larger river. What was especially interesting was that a hooked 'X' was drawn on the smaller river.

"Isn't that the Knights Templar symbol?" She pointed out the 'X' to Darius.

"So is that." He tapped a drawing of a double-headed eagle above the darkened lines of the canyon. There were more words scrawled next to it in the same odd language as the rest of the map.

"The Templars hid an obsidian skull?"

"This predates us by about two thousand years."

"Holy shit. You know what this means?"

"That if Dashwood refrained from taking any creative liberties while transcribing the map, then we may have discovered the location of L.G.'s lost skull, and that there's more to the Templar Knights than I gave them credit for."

His fingers traced the double-headed eagle symbol and he seemed surprised, perhaps even a little dazed. At least he displayed an emotion other than disinterest.

Once again she felt just like Lara Croft and the excitement thrummed in her veins.

"So long, Christopher Columbus. Sayonara, Leif Ericson. America was discovered by the Phoenicians." She let out a breathy laugh. "We just rewrote history."

She looked up at him when he didn't answer and caught him looking at her instead of the map. A small curve played at his lips. His face was inches from hers and although he didn't move a muscle, she could feel when his emotions changed from amusement to hunger and it stirred her own.

Mackenzie reached up, sunk her fingers into his thick, brown hair and pulled him closer, and then she pressed her lips against his.

She turned in her seat, pulled herself up on her knees and wrapped her arms around his neck, seeking more contact. Three pounding heart beats was all it took before Darius returned the kiss. His strong arms wrapped around her waist and he pulled her flush against him. He growled when the back of the chair blocked him from pulling her closer. The sound of his frustration made her tingle with anticipation.

Without breaking their kiss, he hooked his arm under the back of her legs, and with impressive strength, lifted her over the back of the chair and carried her across the room.

Mackenzie urged him closer.

If L.G. thought to surface now, Mackenzie would find a way to make her pay.

"You're thinking about something and it's not me." His voice was low and coarse against her nerve endings as he set her on her feet next to the bed.

"I'm thinking you're wearing too many clothes." She pulled at his t-shirt, fully aware her hands shook with expectation, "Off."

She pulled his shirt up, revealing inch after delectable

inch of his flat stomach and defined chest, and ran her fingers through the slight dusting of dark hair that graced it.

She tossed the shirt aside and reached for his pants, but his hands stilled hers. "Your turn."

His gaze could have seared her clothes off with the fire burning within them. Instead, she shivered as his fingertips skimmed up her arms, leaving a trail of goose bumps in their wake. He angled her head for another toe-curling, soul-shaking kiss. His tongue slipped passed her lips as his fingers trailed down her spine.

She moaned into him as they battled for dominance in her mouth. Oh, she was losing, but that was how she wanted it.

His fingers trailed under her shirt and up the skin of her back, taking her shirt with it. When he reached her shoulders, she raised her arms over her head and let him pull her shirt free and toss it aside. With one hand he undid her bra and pushed the straps off her shoulders until the lacy material pooled at her feet.

Darius cupped her cheek and his thumb played with her swollen lips as his gaze drank her in from her head to her toes. He paused at her breasts and her nipples pebbled, eager for his attention.

Mackenzie nibbled the fleshy pad of his thumb. She didn't have the peace of mind to feel bashful over her top-half nakedness, she wanted him too damn much. She ran her fingernails down his chest, wresting a groan from him.

She stopped at the waistband of his black jeans.

Again, he stilled her. "Patience."

"Fuck patience." She tried to tug them open and he pushed her hands aside. He scooped her up and laid her on her back in the center of the bed. He followed her and pressed his body against hers.

She moaned at the feel of his weight and the way he fit

against her curves. He trailed kisses from her mouth to a newfound erogenous zone where her shoulder met her neck. She tried to pull him back to her lips, but he grabbed hold of her wandering hands and pinned them above her head.

"Stay." He gave her a no-nonsense look that promised retribution, naughty retribution, should she disobey. "Stay."

She was tempted to see what he would do if she reached for him, but grabbed the wooden slats of the headboard instead. He continued to kiss his way to her right breast. His tongue circled her nipple, then he took it into his mouth and sucked.

Mackenzie let out a strangled moan, her head dropped back onto the pillow and she let the sensations assault her. Nibble, suck, nibble, pull.

A quick tweak of her nipple brought her back to awareness. She looked down to find him smirking at her with such male cockiness it should have sent her into a fit, not make her beg for more.

He started to move away again and she was tempted to kick him for stopping, until his mouth reached her other nipple.

"Oh, God." She clutched the headboard in hopes it would help keep her grounded, it didn't.

His naughty hands toyed with the skin just above the waistband of her jeans. One tug and the button slipped free. Another and the zipper slid downwards. His fingers found the juncture of her thighs without much effort. He kissed down her body as his fingers rubbed the little bundle of nerves at her entrance through her panties.

She gasped. She dug her fingers into Darius's dark brown hair, tugged him upwards and devoured his lips with a desperate kiss. He then trailed kisses to another sensitive spot on her ear.

"Darius." She tugged on his hair again, trying to put to

words what she needed.

He grabbed the waistband of both her pants and underwear and slid them down her legs. "Patience, Mackenzie."

"Fu–" She was about to remind him of her stance on patience when he slid his fingers inside her.

Her orgasm hit her hard and her senses exploded. Darius swallowed her cries with his lips and kept sliding his fingers in and out, knowing all the right places to prolong the rapture until her legs were shaking and she was begging for mercy.

When her orgasm could be prolonged no more, he slid his fingers out of her and climbed off the bed.

He shucked off his pants and she let out a victorious cheer in her mind. He crawled back on top of her and she met him with her lips. Her hands explored his chest, arms and back. He pressed her into the mattress with his weight and he spread her legs apart with his knees until she wrapped them around his waist. His length, hard and long, nudged against her entrance and she almost came again right then.

He stopped, frozen above her like a damn conquistador taunting a bull, and pulled his mouth from hers. "I've wanted you like this since the second I saw you walking down the street in Santa Cruz."

It was her turn to growl. "Then what the hell are you waiting for?"

He chuckled and claimed her mouth. The moment their lips connected he thrust into her and didn't stop until his hips pressed against hers.

The sensations made them both moan and he pulled out until just the tip of him remained and then pushed back in with tantalizing slowness. Her nails dug into his back as every inch of him hit every erotic spot of her.

"Faster." She met each of his thrusts with a roll of

her hips.

He reached down with one hand and held her hips still as he continued his controlled and skilled assault on her senses.

But she didn't want him controlled and skilled. She wanted him as wild and frantic as she was.

"Darius, please." She moaned his name in his ear and followed it up by nipping his earlobe.

It was enough to shatter her knight's hard-won control and his hips quickened their pace.

"Come. For. Me. Again." He punctuated each word with a thrust of his hips.

The pressure that grew inside her halted at the precipice between frustration and ecstasy. She arched her back and whimpered, hovering on that line. She needed... something.

He licked her neck, then bit. Hard. The shock sent her rocketing over the edge. Mackenzie cried out, as her world tilted on its axis, only this time it had nothing to do with L.G.

Darius followed after her, barked out a yell and with two more powerful thrusts, he stilled.

The room went silent, except for their heavy breathing. Darius's weight on top of her kept her grounded, for she was sure if he hadn't been there, she would have floated away in a happy cloud of post-orgasmic bliss. She trailed her fingertips along his sweat-glistened back, enjoying the moment of peace.

On the heels of that peace, she felt the tendrils of sleep reach out and take hold.

Mackenzie wasn't sure how long they stayed like that. It was Darius who broke their connection first. He slid out of her, rolled to his side and pulled her into the warmth of his body.

She was only half-conscious when he covered them with blankets.

"Mackenzie." Darius's chest rumbled under her ear.

She mumbled something she hoped was a good response, but she was too tired to know for sure.

"When this is over..." He trailed off.

Her mind finished the sentence for him. When this was over, L.G. would be gone and she would have to return to her old life without Darius and the adventure that came with him.

The nightmare of a normal life plagued her as she drifted off to sleep.

CHAPTER 34

Mackenzie snuggled up to her body pillow. Her muscles felt like goo and she had found that rare perfect spot for her head that didn't throw her neck out of whack in the morning.

"Good morning," her pillow rumbled.

"Morning, pillow." She drifted back to sleep. Then it dawned on her. "Pillow?"

She shot her head up and stared into the dark, penetrating gaze of Darius, man extraordinaire. Judging by his lazy grin, he knew it too.

"Not a pillow." She lifted the blanket and took in their nakedness. Damn, that man's body was fine. She dropped the blanket and burrowed her head back into his warm, welcoming chest. "Give me a second, my brain needs to reboot."

Darius chuckled.

"Wait." She looked at him again. "Did we rewrite American history last night?"

"We did something."

She swatted him and he pulled her on top of him and kissed her with the heat of a man yet to be satiated. Her mind went to mush. So much for rebooting her brain, Darius just fried her system.

"History can wait." She straddled his hips and slid down his fully-cocked member.

They moaned as she tortured them both with her slow descent.

Two hours passed, maybe three, before the rumble of Mackenzie's stomach pulled them out of their sexual haze. She took a shower, towel dried her hair, and put on the same clothes Darius had taken off her. Muscles she had no idea existed ached, not that she minded. It served as proof she hadn't imagined the entire thing.

Was it lame to say it had been the best sex of her life? Maybe. Did it make it any less true? Nope.

She was already planning more. More Darius. More sex. More time.

"Way to go, you secret romantic," she chided at her reflection in the bathroom mirror. "You're getting attached."

She needn't bother listing every reason why she should keep her distance from the immortal knight. There were too many and they were all complicated.

Just once could something be simple? Boy meets girl, they share a moment and boom, they ride off into the sunset madly in love. Not, boy meets girl, girl knees boy in junk and, bam, they end up in a high-end hotel in Scotland where girl nails boy in junk. Again.

Mackenzie tossed the towel on the floor and brushed out the snarls in her hair with a comb. When she finished, she put the comb back in her canvas bag. "Remember, he's temporary."

Her reflection didn't look convinced.

She left the bathroom to find Darius hovered over a tray of food on the table.

"Ooh, breakfast." At least she had something else to do besides brood over what she couldn't have.

Darius put a plate in her hands. "Have some waffles. When you're done, we'll leave for the airport."

He didn't look at her as she sat at the table. It was then she noticed the map. Or lack thereof.

"Where'd the map go?"

"While you slept, I passed it on to my people to analyze and translate."

"Oh." Apparently she'd been the only one knocked out after their sexy time.

Challenge accepted.

Darius ran his fingers through his hair. He stilled as if he noticed the action and dropped his hand to his side in a clenched fist. His back was rigid, his shoulders stiff and his features drawn taught.

He looked stressed and it dawned on her why. He wanted to give her 'the talk.' The one where he told her that what they shared last night and this morning had been equivalent to a one-night stand. That he was an immortal knight and she was just a normal girl. That they had one objective and them being together wasn't it.

All right, she had already given herself 'the talk.' It didn't make her feel great, but she was realistic enough to understand. It didn't mean she'd make it easy for the guy. "So, what's wrong?"

While she knew what was coming, if he started with the 'it's not you, it's me,' speech, she'd have to punch him on principle.

Darius started to pace. "It's Finley."

It took a moment for Mackenzie to remember who Finley was. "The guy in charge of retrieving the artifact?"

Darius nodded.

"Oh, God, he's dead. And he didn't get the artifact, did he?" She plopped her face into her hands as her one hope at survival vanished.

She'd worry about her lack of concern over Finley's life later.

"He's alive and headed back to the states to lead the search at the Grand Canyon."

She lifted her head. "Does he have the artifact?"

Darius nodded yes.

Okay, not as bad.

"He should have contacted me first," he said as if reading her mind.

Mackenzie picked up a waffle, passed on smothering it in butter and syrup and munched on it dry. "We're going there too, right?"

"Yes."

"Then, no worries." A lie of course, but there was no use stressing over what they couldn't change.

He crossed the space between them and pulled her out of her chair. He took her seat and tugged her onto his lap with a contented sigh.

And she let him because he surprised her with his display of affection. Or was it dominance? Either way, it wasn't the action of a man trying to put distance between them.

It still didn't mean she was sure how to act. So, she sat there and tried to take interest in her waffle.

He wrapped his arm around her waist and kissed her shirt-covered shoulder. He then upset her fragile mind further when he turned her head and claimed her lips.

Then, while her mind was dizzy with lust, he stole a bite of her waffle.

"Hey." She flicked his forehead. "Mine."

"I'm hungry, too."

She motioned to the second plate on the table. "Yours is over there."

"Perhaps I'd rather eat what's right in front of me." He looked at her with such hunger that parts of her tingled in anticipation. She could see forever in his eyes and it was a cruel joke. This could only be temporary.

Holy crap on a cracker, she was seriously falling for the man.

She was already halfway there by the feel of it. As it was, she knew there would be a long road to recovery when this ordeal was over. And if she fell further, there would be no going back.

She refused to acknowledge the sudden pain in her chest as if her heart were already breaking, and convinced herself it was heartburn.

"Here." She shoved the waffle in his mouth and stood.

If he noticed her change of attitude, he didn't say as he chewed with such methodical slowness one would think he was divining the meaning of life.

It unnerved her, almost broke her into admitting her feelings right then and there. She retreated back to the bathroom instead and packed her toiletries into her canvas bag.

"As much as I want to get to Finley," she called out, "shouldn't we wait for some sort of confirmation? I mean this is the Grand Canyon, it's huge and popular. Actually, you'd think someone would have found the skull there by now."

"I think someone may have."

She grabbed her bag and strode back into the room. "What?"

"I remember back in the early twentieth century, an article was printed in a small local paper. It reported the discovery of a cave in the Grand Canyon. Inside were mummies, statues, tools and other ancient Egyptian artifacts."

She dropped the bag on the still-made bed closest to the bathroom. "But no skull?"

"There wasn't a skull mentioned, no." He gave her a look that said 'I'm telling the story.' "We sent one of our men to investigate the validity of the find, but we couldn't locate the man who made the claim, G.E. Kinkaid. We looked into every lead from his name to the organization he claimed to have worked for, the Smithsonian Institute."

"Sounds legit." Even being as uninterested in history as she was, she knew of the famous museum.

"No man by that name ever worked for them. In fact, G.E. Kinkaid never existed in any database from that time."

"Maybe he wasn't an American."

"Perhaps, but we were thorough." He stood and grabbed his backpack from the floor. "We sent a team to the cave's location described in the article but found nothing. We just assumed the story was faked, meant to drum up readership."

"How about now? Still think it's a hoax?"

"I think if we have any chance of finding that cave, it'll be with this map. I hope Sir Francis Dashwood made no transcribing errors."

"What if we get there and still don't find it?" She sat on the unused bed and tied her shoes. "Wouldn't it be better if the skull remained lost?"

"In my decidedly long life there is one thing I have come to understand, secrets and mysteries don't remain as such forever. The skull's location will be found and when it is, I endeavor to be the one who finds it."

She jumped when he touched her arm.

"Can't you stomp your feet or something?" She stood up, shouldered her bag and glared.

"I don't stomp." Darius stepped closer and she retreated until she was cornered with a wall behind her, a wall on her left, the bed on her right and Darius in front of her, all tall, dark and brooding.

His gaze promised such naughty things.

She couldn't do this. She wasn't the casual-dating type.

She was screwed. Figuratively. And if he continued to look at her like that, she would be screwed. Literally.

She bolted over the bed, jumped onto the other one and landed on the carpet on the other side by the door. "Coming?"

She didn't wait for him to follow and walked out with a plan forming in her head, which was get to Arizona, use the artifact to eject L.G. and then help find the root of the skulls with Darius. All the while not touching or getting any more involved with the man in question.

That sounded easy enough.

CHAPTER 35

Darius tried to keep his focus on the road as he drove down the A1 motorway. Whenever he thought he had his focus wrangled, he discovered he was watching Mackenzie out of the corner of his eye. She wasn't doing anything to draw his attention, just sitting there in the passenger seat, staring out the window, and looking sexy as sin.

His red-hot, violent minx was more subdued since breakfast. He didn't like it one bit, but he wasn't sure what to do or say to fix it. Somehow ordering her to return to her normal self didn't seem like the smartest course of action.

Dealing with men was much easier. He'd bark out an order and they would obey without question. If a man had a problem with that, fists would be thrown until they were both nice and bloody and the issue resolved. But Mackenzie wasn't a man, she was one hundred percent redheaded woman.

He wanted to twine his fingers with hers to take comfort in her warmth but refrained. He wanted to say something to break the silence but nothing came to mind. All he could think about was that any second now he could look over and find Mackenzie no longer there. Fear wasn't a feeling he was familiar with, yet he felt that panic-stricken emotion now stronger than he ever imagined. He feared losing what he just found, something that made his life... better.

Bloody hell.

He sounded like his love-struck brother.

But now that he had been with Mackenzie, had come with her, had laughed with her, he understood what Bastian felt for the eccentric Allyanora. More so, he now understood his mentor, Jonathan, who in the end was broken and beaten with no will to live. If he lost Mackenzie now, it would be a staggering blow.

She was precious because she made him forget. Forget he was an immortal knight, forget every name on the list of people he had failed to save and forget the burden placed on his shoulders when Jonathan died. All Mackenzie had to do was look at him and the bleakness of his life disappeared.

He was going to punch Finley for running off to America with that artifact.

Mackenzie leaned forward, dug into his backpack at her feet and pulled out the skull. Her fingers trailed over the smooth surface.

"I cannot tell you how happy I find myself at this moment." She smiled at him with a metallic glint in her eyes.

It was strange, when Mackenzie flashed him that smile, all seemed right with the world. When L.G. did it, a tremor of disgust went through him.

"L.G." Darius had to clench his jaw to keep the string of expletives at bay. "Bring her back."

"Two."

"Don't."

"You keep saying that word. Have you noticed it does not work?"

"If you destroy her, I'll kill you, slowly and painfully."

L.G. chuckled, unbothered as she continued to gaze at the skull in her lap. "We both know you do not have the stomach to do that at this point."

He focused on keeping his face blank and his breathing slow. It would do no good to start yelling. Yelling would imply desperation. And desperation would reveal weakness.

"I would have never expected the Phoenicians to have crossed the ocean with their archaic ships and antiquated navigation. I thought Dashwood a failure after years of searching, even with all his connections, but he has managed to surprise me. That is rare."

Darius took the exit ramp off the A1 towards the private airport. When he stopped at a red light, he reached into his pocket, pulled out a set of hand cuffs and locked one cuff around L.G.'s left wrist. He locked the other one around the overhead hand grip above her door.

"That was unnecessary," she said, although she didn't resist.

"I won't risk you running off."

"Why would I do that?"

He didn't answer the question.

L.G. went back to admiring the skull. "The redhead was a good choice after all."

"Let her surface." The light turned green and he pressed on the gas. "We're about to get on a plane for a very long flight and I know how much you hate being bored."

"Should I remind you there is still a skull here owned by the Illuminati? We can acquire it before we leave for America."

"No."

L.G. put the skull back in the backpack and stared at him. "Like teacher, like student. He thought he could save one, too. Do you know why his defeat came on so suddenly? Why one day he was haunted by his failures and the next he was consumed by them?"

"You." It was the only word he could push past his tightening throat.

"Yes. I picked someone I knew he would enjoy. Even though he was a strict Spartan warrior, he was a man after all." She leaned forward. "He actually thought a witch could cast me out of her body. He thought wrong."

In some ways the revelation was a relief. Darius always wondered why he couldn't see that Jonathan needed help in the end. The last time he saw his mentor and friend, he seemed fine. Two months later, he had committed suicide-by-battle and the Illuminati sent his head to Darius in a box.

Why hadn't his old friend come to him for help before it came to that? He answered his own question, because falling for a civilian involved in a prophecy was strictly against the rules, and if nothing else, the old Spartan was a stickler for the rules. He wouldn't have brought attention to his fallibility.

"He did everything to save the girl. What makes you think you have even the slightest chance?"

He tightened his grip around the steering wheel until his palms dug into the leather. He knew he had a chance with the Mixtec artifact. If Jonathan had known about it, he would have tried it himself, but it wasn't until after his death that the Templar Knights re-discovered it in one of the many old Templar artifact caches.

The artifact would work. It had to because there was no plan B and he wouldn't allow L.G. to destroy Mackenzie's soul. He would kill her himself before then.

They arrived at the private airport and he pulled through

the gates. The engines on Insta-Prophecy's newest jet were already running. The cabin door was open and a flight attendant was waiting at the top of the boarding stairs.

Darius stopped the car next to the plane, grabbed his backpack at L.G.'s feet and got out. He tried to shove aside what he had just learned, tried to let the cool, outside air calm his nerves. But his path was too similar to his old friend's and he began to doubt his outcome would be any different.

He rounded the car, opened L.G.'s door and removed the handcuffs.

"I must admit..." L.G. stood with the elegance of royalty. "I am rather impatient to finally have my lost skull returned to me."

He pushed her back into the car and tightened his fingers around her throat. It was just enough to get her attention, not enough to hurt. "The only thing you'll have is a passing glimpse of your skull before it's lost to you forever."

His words put a smirk on her face.

CHAPTER 36

Mackenzie was in so much trouble.

She was weak, but it wasn't her fault. She had ten hours to burn on a plane with its own private bedroom and a sexy knight hell bent on seducing her. Any red-blooded woman in her right mind would have caved. And oh, did she cave, faster than a blade of grass on a soccer field.

Now she was wrapped around Darius like a blanket, her head resting against his chest as she listened to his heartbeat.

She needed to get out of bed, right now, to rebuild her proverbial walls and put some literal distance between them

But...

She traced the hard lines of his chest with her hand.

The fact that she could die, lose to the entity inside her without so much as a fight, spurred her on to play with the fire that was Darius Cooper.

"Why are you frowning?" Darius ran his finger between

her eyebrows where they furrowed... in dread.

She swatted his hand out of her face. "I'm fine."

The cabin bell dinged and the flight attendant's soft voice eased out of the intercom. "We're twenty minutes from our destination, please prepare for landing."

Mackenzie sat up with a groan and the sheet that had kept her somewhat modest pooled at her waist.

Her instinct was to grab it and cover herself, but she had tried that before and ended up with no sheet and Darius on top of her.

Mackenzie shook herself.

Darius followed the line of her spine with his finger and she leaned into the trailing warmth. One would think after the marathon love fest they just had, his interest would have waned. Or hers for that matter.

News flash, it didn't. But she needed to focus.

She shoved herself to her feet and searched for her clothes. Darius watched her, sprawled on his back, arms pillowed under his head.

She tamped down the urge to slip back under the sheets and snagged her socks from the floor instead.

"This is a pretty shnazzy plane. I thought you said the Templar Knights were the good guys?"

"What would give you the impression we're not?"

"Um, how about this private jet, for instance? And those people you have on speed dial at your beck and call for any situation, and the unending string of cars? Oh yeah, and a safe house in the middle of nowhere rigged to explode? All of these imply something shady."

"It's one of the perks of working with an organization that can peer into the future."

"See? Shady." She snatched her underwear off the handle of the door that led to the main cabin. She slid her panties and bra on and Darius moaned.

Horny bastard.

Yet, she couldn't help the smile that toyed at her lips as she grabbed her jeans. "I think it's a bit unfair to use those powers of seeing into the future for one's own gain." She paused mid-shimmy. "I can't believe I said that with all seriousness."

"Perhaps it's not the best use of those abilities, but without money we'd be in no position to prevent these prophecies from occurring. Money is power, Mackenzie."

"Sounds like something a politician would say." She snorted and pulled her shirt over her head.

She found Darius's shirt draped across his backpack next to her on the floor and threw it at him. He caught it with one hand and gave her a heated look.

He pulled off the sheet, revealing inch after inch of tasty, toe-curling skin. She turned her back to him, then reconsidered. Ten more minutes of naked fun wouldn't hurt. It wasn't like the prophecy would start without her.

Holy crap, how weak was she?

She noticed the skull nestled in the open backpack and picked it up. It didn't seem like anything special. She could order one that looked identical to it on the internet.

It was weird how something so normal looking, well normal-ish, could destroy the world.

"What about ejecting one into space? If you can't destroy the skulls, surely you can separate them." She turned around and was a little disappointed to find him dressed.

"We tried that a few times. Like I said before, they always came back."

"So magic keeps them here?"

"Something like that."

She caught the subtle clench of his jaw and the small hardening of his gaze. It wasn't much and on any other person she probably would have thought he was thinking about something mundane like laundry. On Darius, he might as well have been shouting. He was worried about something and she would bet her entire life savings he was thinking about L.G.

Darius reached for her, but she shoved the skull in his hands. "There has to be a way."

"I'm willing to try anything new you can come up with."

"Isn't there a lab in Switzerland doing work on wormholes?" She saw her shoes under the bed and sat down to put them on. "I remember the controversy when they started that project."

He was already shaking his head before she finished. "The wormholes they create aren't big enough to shove anything through."

"Dump one in the deepest part of the ocean."

"Came back."

"How?"

Darius shrugged. "Not sure, but it kept popping back up on deck. Don't worry yourself, it's my duty to watch over the skulls. Your job is to survive and when all this is over, to go back to your normal life."

She stilled. It was one thing to tell herself she needed to keep her distance, it was another to hear it from his lips.

"When this is over and L.G. is out, what if I want to make it my job to watch over the obsidian skulls? With you?"

"No."

She blinked. He said it so fast she had to repeat the word several times in her head to make sure she heard it right.

Another ding from the intercom filled the air. "Please take your seats, we're about to land."

"Why not?" She turned to Darius.

"This isn't a life I'd wish on you. You're a civilian."

Being a civilian sounded like an insult, yet not too long ago she would have given anything to have her civilian life back.

"I see." She left the private cabin.

Darius's sigh followed after her. "How can you be mad over going back to your normal life?"

"I'm not. It's just that Lauren works at the Hotline's warehouse now, so it's not like my life returns to normal when this is over." She sat in a seat next to the window and buckled her seatbelt. "Maybe I don't want the adventure to stop. Maybe I could apply to work at the warehouse, too."

"Absolutely not." Darius barked out the words so loud she jumped.

"Excuse me?"

"I don't think you understand. This life isn't for everyone, it's rough on the strongest of people."

"And you don't think I'm strong?"

"I think you're strong." Darius sat down hard on the leather seat next to her. "Let's just focus on stopping the prophecy, we'll worry about the rest later."

In man-speak that meant he was finished talking about it. Forever.

Did rejection have to hurt so much, even if she was expecting it? The answer was yes.

Darius put his head back and closed his eyes. She stared through the window at the vast desert that sprawled out below.

So many places to hide Darius's body, so little time.

Right in the midst of contemplating the very cathartic demise of the man pretending to nap next to her, she spotted a small private airport, and just beyond that was the beginning of the Grand Canyon.

This was it.

All she had to do now was survive until they reached Finley. With the apocalypse averted, she would make Darius regret thinking she wasn't strong enough to stay. Somehow.

Her fingers traced the cuneiform bracelet and she glanced at Darius, his eyes still closed.

She had a gut feeling she would never get over him. "Damnit."

Darius's hand gripped her fingers that played with the bracelet and squeezed. "You all right?"

"No, I love–" She stopped before admitting aloud what she could barely admit in silence. "-flying. You've ruined me, you bastard."

No truer words ever said.

CHAPTER 37

The landing was quick and a hell of a lot less stressful than her landing in Scotland. Granted, it helped that this time she knew where she was headed and how she got on the plane in the first place.

Backpack in hand, Darius ushered her down the stairs of the private jet and onto the tarmac. She looked around expecting to see a car, instead they walked around the plane and headed towards a black helicopter that seemed to have the unfortunate condition of missing its doors.

The helicopter's blades were already rotating and a man wearing a helmet with a mouthpiece ushered them inside the cabin. She had just managed to buckle herself in before they surged off the ground and sped towards the canyon in the distance.

Without doors, she had an unobstructed view of the desert stretching out around her. Or, her mind chipped in, she was one seat belt malfunction away from plummeting to her death. She was optimistic like that.

Someone nudged her shoulder. The man who had ushered them onto the helicopter held out two helmets with mouth pieces. She put one on and Darius did the same.

"It's good to see you back on missions, Darius."

Back?

"Markus." Darius nodded in the man's direction.

Markus had olive skin, light brown eyes and brown hair that curled at the edges. His face was slender, his jaw square and he draped his arm over the back of his seat like a man who knew he was sexy as sin.

"Seriously?" She sounded tinny over the microphone. "Is it a rule that all Templar Knights have to be hot?"

Markus flashed her a quick smile. "You must be Mackenzie. It's an honor to meet the girl who will be responsible for the end of the world."

His gaze was warm and he looked more amused than accusatory, but he might as well have hauled off and slapped her. If L.G. got her way, Mackenzie would quite literally be the ender of the world, bringer of destruction, slayer of civilization. Not any titles Mackenzie wanted.

"What information do you have?" Darius bit out the question like it was an interrogation and it wiped the pleasant smile off Markus's face.

"We're taking you to the location on the map. Finley already made camp."

"Good."

Markus looked at Mackenzie and opened his mouth to say something else when Darius reached over and turned off her headset.

She elbowed Darius in the ribs and he just wrapped her arm around his, tilted his head back and closed his eyes, again. Markus shrugged.

As they crested the edge of the canyon, the desert floor dropped away. It was like a giant had tried to rip the earth in half with his bare hands and failed, leaving a massive tear in the ground. It made her wonder if giants ever existed to begin with, which she would have asked Darius if she knew how to turn her headset back on.

In a sort of violent, beautiful display, the beige, rocky desert floor at the top of the canyon turned into a reddish, orange color on the canyon walls, as if the world itself had bled. At the bottom of the canyon far below, a narrow river intersected the ragged stone.

They followed the river until it split and they took the narrower of the two paths. They continued upstream until a red tent emerged on a narrow strip of land that formed alongside the river.

They flew just past the tent to where the narrow outcropping of land widened. It looked uneven even from their height, but the others on the helicopter didn't seem daunted by that fact.

Or they were blind.

Darius still had his eyes closed, so Mackenzie wrote him off as clueless. Markus gave her a thumbs up, a gesture that looked out of place on the man.

As they descended, gusts of wind cycloned through the cabin's missing doors, which made her think of all the helicopter crashes she had seen in movies. The helicopter rocked and jerked, and Mackenzie's grip on the arm of her seat tightened until her muscles ached.

Finally, they landed with a jostle and the engines were cut. Mackenzie mirrored Darius and pulled off her helmet. Markus jumped out of the helicopter and offered her his hand. With his help, she landed safely on the rocky canyon floor, with Darius landing next to her.

"Welcome to the Grand Canyon." Markus smiled down

at her with a boyish charm that made her smile back.

"It's about time you got here," said a man in a thick Scottish brogue, whom she could only assume was Finley. He strode up to them, looking more bored than annoyed. "I was wondering if this was Allyanora's way of playing a practical joke on me, or what she likes to call 'such fun times.'"

He was at least six foot two and built. He wasn't bodybuilder built, but there was no mistaking the strength and power hidden underneath his jeans and black t-shirt. He had dark red hair and a trimmed beard that he managed to pull off without looking like an over-coifed hipster. The only flaw, if you could call it that, was the crook in his nose that said he broke it one time too many before he became a knight and acquired those fast healing powers.

"Finley." Darius chuckled and embraced the man with a loud, pounding slap on his back. Then they exchanged a few words too low for her to hear. They must have been good friends because the rough edge Darius had with Markus softened and he seemed to relax. The familiarity made Mackenzie miss Lauren, who would have been in heaven at being surrounded by such male hotness.

She kicked a tiny pebble across the rocky ground, skittering it into the river. Then she peered up at the sliver of the late afternoon sun not blocked out by the towering red walls of the canyon.

"So, where's the idol?" Darius asked.

Finley gave him an odd look. "I'd think you'd be more interested in finding the skull first."

"Idol first."

"It's in the tent. I'll get it."

They followed Finley to the tent, then waited as he disappeared inside. Mackenzie noticed wooden crates piled on the ground nearby. Some were opened as if they had just been rifled through. They were filled with supplies like food, water, ropes, climbing harnesses, guns and ammunition. There was a small box off to the side, away from the others. It held foil-covered bricks. She ambled over to it and crouched to get a closer look. A sticker across each brick read C-4. She had never seen explosives up close before.

"Is this real C-4?" She held a brick up for Darius to see.

"Yes." He plucked it from her hands and set it back into the box.

Finley exited the tent in a flourish. "I wasn't sure what we'd be needing for this little outing of ours, so I packed the essentials."

"Did you bring any grenades?" She looked around, hoping to spot a box of them.

"Dear Lord." Darius ran his fingers through his hair.

Finley handed a green stone to him. "No, I didn't. What's wrong with grenades?"

Mackenzie couldn't help the wicked, little chuckle that escaped. "I've discovered people take grenades very seriously in your line of work."

"Lassie, people take grenades seriously in any line of work." Finley handed her a flask from his back pocket.

"What's that for?"

"Something to calm the nerves and add a bit of much needed luck."

"Is it like holy water or something?" She took a swig and choked as the liquid burned its way down her throat.

"It's whiskey, though I tend to call it holy water."

She coughed and handed the flask back to him. "Thank you?"

"The lassie is a light weight, isn't she?"

"Enough, Finley."

Finley's ginger eyebrows shot up. He motioned towards the stone in Darius's hands. "I have to tell you, I almost didn't get it. The Vatican upped their security since the last time."

"You guys break in to the Vatican often?" She almost laughed when Finley shrugged.

Darius raised up the stone sphere in his open hand. It was about the size of his palm and the richest green Mackenzie had ever seen. Engraved on the stone's surface was a bird with its wings spread wide as if about to take flight, and coiled beneath the bird was a snake ready to strike. A flickering light burned within the heart of the stone as if lit by an impossible candle.

"I've never seen anything like it." Mackenzie couldn't take her eyes from the glimmering stone. "This should be in a museum, not hidden away in the Vatican."

"The Mixtecs carved it from an emerald," Darius said. "We swapped it out for a fake one just before the Conquistadors wiped out their village. They used this stone to cast out invading souls from the human body."

"A necessity because that particular village had a blood feud with the Shadow Walkers." Finley took a swig from the flask and tucked it into his pocket.

"Shadow Walkers?" Mackenzie's eye twitched. "They sound downright terrifying."

"Aye, think of them as demons," Finley said.

"Don't worry about them." Darius held out the stone to her. "All you have to do is touch the emerald."

This was it, the moment she would finally be free of L.G. So many things went through her mind, the thrill of this nightmare at last being over, the fear it might not be. But more profoundly, she would find out where she stood with Darius once her part in the prophecy was over. With her eyes on him, she reached for the stone.

At the last second, Darius snatched the emerald away, pulled her towards him and kissed her with such passion it distracted her from the uncertainty of the moment. His actions said far more than his words ever had. He was worried for her. He wanted her to survive this as much as she did. He wanted to be with her after this and somehow make it work.

Well, maybe that last part was wishful thinking, but it didn't matter.

"Darius," Finley grumbled and Mackenzie almost kneed the Scotsman in the groin for the interruption.

He grabbed Darius's shoulder and judging by the whites of the man's knuckles, it was a none-too-gentle grip.

Darius kept his focus on her, the heat in his gaze searing her to the core. "You mind taking your hand off me?"

"Och, man. You know better."

Darius looked ready to slug his friend and Mackenzie was right there with him.

He may have been talking to Darius, but Mackenzie felt the words were also meant for her. She was acting like a love-sick moron. This was her moment to eject L.G. Man, she could worry about Darius later.

With the tingle of Darius lingering on her lips, Mackenzie snatched the emerald from his hand.

CHAPTER 38

The faint light that flickered within the emerald brightened and heated until it blinded her and seared her palms.

"Son of a bitch." She dropped the emerald and turned away. The instant it left her hands, the light within it dimmed.

She gaped down at the stone, her hands held out as if she still held the thing, her palms burning like she had stuck them on a hot griddle.

It didn't work.

The overpowering presence of L.G. still pressed down on her consciousness, the feeling of doom and dread growing.

Darius grabbed her hands and with tender care inspected her reddened palms and fingers. "What happened?"

"The damn thing burned me."

"Shite." Finley picked up the idol.

"Shite? What shite?" Her voice raised an octave and panic threatened to strangle her. "Why is L.G. still in me?"

With every passing second the two knights didn't answer, her hope shredded further.

It didn't help that Darius looked almost as lost as she felt.

"It was designed to cast out a demonic possession." Finley polished the emerald's surface with the corner of his black t-shirt. "Not an alien one."

"Finley," Darius snapped.

"Alien?" Mackenzie winced when Darius's grip tightened around her hands. "Like from outer space?"

Darius looked pained, sad even, but it warred with something she now deciphered as guilt. "We'll try again. It'll work."

"Aliens from outer space?"

"You said that already."

She kneed him in the groin, spun around and stormed off away from the camp, away from the helicopter and away from him.

"Aliens," she said to herself.

At best, she thought she'd been possessed by an evil spirit. At worst, a demon. Much to her surprise, she could handle those two scenarios. Magic, she could believe. Hell, even accept it as fact instead of fiction. She loved fantasy books, even wished they were true.

But aliens?

What she wouldn't give for a padded room, a straight jacket and a lot more whiskey.

"Mackenzie." Darius's voice sounded strangled and pained and a good distance behind her.

Good.

She saw it then, a cave entrance about two hundred feet up a sheer rock wall to her left. That had to be it, the entrance to the Phoenician cave. A creepy feeling of exaltation swept through her that wasn't her own and L.G.'s presence grew in her mind. There was no doubt about who has happy here. Mackenzie tried not to throw up.

"Mackenzie." Darius's voice sounded firmer, less pained and right behind her now.

She spun around and slapped him across the face. Her vision was blurry with tears and she swiped them away as if they had betrayed her, too. "Aliens?"

"Is it really surprising we're not the only ones in the universe?"

"Of course I don't think we're the only ones, but you lied to me."

"No, I just didn't tell you the whole truth."

She slapped him again. "Censuring the truth by omission is still a lie, Darius."

"It wouldn't have changed the outcome."

"It changes everything. With a demon, you at least have something to fight them with, like magic, incantations and holy water."

"Holy water is just water."

"With aliens we have nothing." Her words echoed off the canyon walls. "No magic, no technology, because they're far more advanced than we are. What can we do to stop them from winning?"

"Nothing."

Everything went still. Even the soft garbling of the water quieted as if Mother Nature herself held her breath waiting for someone to give an answer that didn't end with death and destruction.

She wrapped her arms around herself. "I was dead the second I touched L.G.'s skull. Stupid, defiant me. All I wanted to do was prove the crazy seer on the phone was wrong."

"Stop." Darius grabbed her and ignored her struggle to yank free. "You're not dead."

"I might as well be."

"What we have against L.G. is that stone, that emerald, which will work for you. It's just that your possession isn't like a normal possession."

"Is there such a thing as a normal possession?"

He looked away and didn't answer.

"How is my possession different?" She wouldn't relent.

"In a normal possession, the possessor needs the host's soul in order to survive in the host's body. It uses the soul's power to fuel its own. When you touched L.G.'s skull, an entire consciousness was put into your brain." He tenderly tapped her temple. "And she has the ability to not only run autonomous of you but she doesn't need your soul to maintain hers."

Mackenzie frowned. "It sounds like computer speak."

"Technically, we're like organic computers."

"Okay." She placed her hands on Darius's chest. She intended to push him away, instead she pulled him closer. "So a normal possession is like a virus that infects a computer's operating system, that operating system being my consciousness. But you're saying L.G.'s possession is like another operating system fighting mine for dominance?"

"Sure."

Nope, it was too ridiculous to think about. She pushed him away, but Darius held fast.

"Mackenzie, stop."

"I don't want to die, I don't want L.G. to win, I don't want to lose..." 'You.' That last word stilled her tongue.

He wrapped his arms around her and she buried her head in his neck. While she didn't want to die, feeling his warmth against her skin would make right now the best time to go.

"The emerald will work. It worked on Pope John Paul the First and he had a not-so-normal possession," His voice rumbled beneath her cheek.

"He died."

"Not because we failed to get the demon out. It did work, his body just couldn't take the strain. All you have to do is keep fighting."

That didn't sound too promising, to kick L.G. out only to die from the shock of it afterwards. But she wanted to fight, the need damn near choked her.

"Please don't let L.G. take you." His words were so quiet she almost missed them.

They weren't an order or a demand from an invincible knight who expected to be obeyed. They were a plea, quietly begging her to not give up. And she doubted this man ever begged for anything.

She drew away and that's when she saw it, how much a toll the hunt for the skulls had taken on him. She was close to death, but he was so much closer. Now that she was aware, she saw the dark tinge of sadness that permeated the air around him.

He cupped her cheek with such tenderness the walls she was trying to keep in place with anger and fear crumbled. She kissed him, seeking a connection that would give her the strength she needed to struggle on. The second her lips touched his, those doubts that threatened to tear her down quieted until there was only one voice that echoed through to her very soul. The voice that urged her to protect the man in her arms.

She doubted anyone had ever bothered to protect him before, never even offered that act of kindness. She was well aware the thought of protecting this man was laughable, she could barely continue on herself. But for him, she would continue on. For him, she could do anything. Even if it meant breaking her own heart, she would save him. Because this man, even if he didn't realize it, needed saving.

"We can get L.G. out, although it may hurt." He pressed

his forehead against hers. "Just don't give up on me."

After what seemed like hours, she loosened her grip. "Okay, we'll try again."

Darius trapped her lips with his. His other arm banded around her waist and held her in place as he dominated her mouth.

Just when he got her nice and frazzled, he grabbed her hand and marched her back to camp. Finley was leaning against a crate with the emerald next to him.

She held out her hand. "Whiskey."

He tossed her the flask and she took a long, slow swig.

What she needed was about four more flasks of the liquid courage before attempting to touch the emerald again, but she had to settle for what she had.

"So, what really happens if the skulls are brought together?" She looked at Darius. "I assume some sort of portal opens and all hell breaks loose?"

"She'll call her people from wherever they are in space. They'll come, take a majority of the populace and sell them as slaves all over the universe. After they leave Earth, L.G. will see to it the planet is destroyed."

"It's like the movie 'Independence Day'."

"It'll be much worse for those who are taken," Finley said.

"But it won't happen," Darius said. "Our skulls still remain hidden and protected."

"You told me to bring the skulls here."

"What did you say?" Darius turned on Finley, fists clenched at his sides.

"You texted me and ordered me to bring the skulls here because their locations were compromised."

"L.G." Darius let out a breath. "You should have called me to confirm."

"Why would I ever question you?"

They both glared at each other.

"So, let me get this straight," Mackenzie interrupted their glare-fest. "We're standing on rocky land, hours away from sunset with twelve skulls all in one place, and the Illuminati most likely on their way. Not only that, L.G. has been calling the shots from the beginning?"

"Eleven skulls," Finley corrected.

"I'm sorry, I just assumed we'd count the skull from the cave."

"What cave?" Finley shoved Darius back and looked at her in confusion.

"The Phoenician cave, up there. Did no one tell you why you're here?"

"Well, Darius insisted in using the fecking emerald before I could tell him I couldn't find the cave."

"Did you, I don't know, open your eyes?" She looked up again and couldn't miss the stark opening against the light reddish stone. "It's right there."

Both men, now at her side, stared at the same canyon wall she did.

"I see nothing, lassie."

"Neither do I."

"It's right there." They had to be crazy, not her.

She didn't know how to climb, so she couldn't show the idiots, who were apparently blind, where the cave was.

Then it dawned on her. The only difference between them and her was she was possessed by L.G. She pushed past the duo and retrieved the backpack Darius had dropped by the tent. She unzipped it and pulled out the skull.

"Hold this." She shoved the skull into Darius's hands, then pointed at the cave's entrance. "Look there."

He scanned up the wall until he saw the entrance. "Bloody brilliant."

"What?" Finley said and Darius slammed the skull into

the man's stomach.

Finley grunted, looked up and whistled. "I wouldn't have thought to use a skull to see the entrance."

"Finley, as soon as the helicopter can take off again, take the skulls back to the jet. We'll be in and out of the cave by the time helicopter returns for us."

Darius pulled Mackenzie towards the crate with the climbing gear. "And Finley, give the emerald to Markus. I won't risk the Illuminati finding it."

Without question or hesitation, Finley nodded and jogged over to Markus, who stood chewing next to an open box of protein bars on top of a crate. The helicopter pilot sat in his cockpit, doing whatever pilots did while making sure their equipment stayed in tip-top shape.

Darius looped ropes and harnesses from the crate over his shoulders and handed Mackenzie two bags with metal cinches and clips attached. "You're with me."

She looked at the sky. They had at least two hours, three tops, before the sun set.

"Fear not what came before, but what has yet to come." She mumbled under her breath. "Thirteen skulls will gather amongst the setting sun."

She shook herself, hard. "We'll only have twelve. Nothing can happen with twelve."

She jogged to catch up to Darius, who was halfway to the rock wall beneath the cave's entrance.

When they reached the wall, Darius dropped the gear, pulled a harness from the pile and held it out for her.

She frowned. "I guess now isn't the time to tell you I've only climbed once before and that was a climbing wall at an amusement park."

"It's okay." He gave her one of his bright, reassuring smiles that turned her insides to mush. "I'll instruct you as we go."

CHAPTER 39

Mackenzie huffed and wheezed as she used her weakening strength to pull herself up over the edge of the cliff. Finally safe from a two-hundred-foot fall and imminent death, she flopped onto her back and dangled her legs over the edge. She was dusty, covered in sweat and almost positive she had pulled a muscle in her groin.

Darius's face appeared above her, but unlike her, he wasn't fazed by the two-hundred-foot climb. In fact, the damnable man hummed from the exertion like he could have easily done it over and over.

She wanted to shove him over the ledge without his climbing harness and see how well he fared. But that required strength and the element of surprise, neither of which she had at the moment.

So, she gathered what meager amount of energy she had left, energy not reserved for breathing and other important bodily functions, and with a groan shoved Darius's face away. "Have I mentioned how I hate you?"

Darius laughed and dangled a plastic water bottle above her face. She reached for it, but the bottle slipped through her fingers and hit her in the shoulder.

"I swear when this is over," she said between shallow breaths. "I'm going to start working out. Often."

She took a swig of the lukewarm water and then another. When she started to chug the nearly full liter, Darius swiped the bottle out of her hands.

"You'll make yourself sick." He set the water aside and reached for the rope connected to the harness at her hips.

"How are you not dying?" She leaned back on her hands and watched him work.

"I run."

"Smart bastard."

He unclipped the rope from her harness and let it fall back over the side of the ledge where it was still connected to the clamps secured to the rock face.

He had told her they would rappel down when they were finished, and she sure as hell hoped that was as easy as it sounded, because at that moment she wasn't opposed to making this cave her new residence. Could she get pizza delivered to her when her address was an invisible hole in the side of a cliff face two hundred feet above the ground? Maybe if she had Darius's contacts...

With an amused smirk, Darius offered his hand. "Would you like to find the skull and get out of here or take a break while our enemies circle closer?"

"Question, will the bad guys be as fit as you?" She grabbed his hand and he pulled her to her feet. "If they're not, I think we're safe."

She adjusted her harness, tightened the leather half-gloves that protected her palms from rope burns and took one last look at the sky.

Darius nudged her arm with an extra flashlight, offering it to her. "Don't worry."

"I'm not putting 'ender of the world' on my resume, you hear me?"

"You won't have to." He kissed her, swift and soft.

"Well, when you put it like that." She turned away from the blue skies, fresh air and freedom for yet another possible subterranean grave.

In the shadows of the tunnel beyond, she noticed the darkened outline of a person and shoved Darius in front of her. "Shoot it!"

Darius let out a beleaguered sigh. "I'm going to have to ask you to stop throwing me into potentially life threatening situations."

"Less talking, more killing." She poked him in the back.

"I can't kill a statue."

"Mannequin apocalypse?" She glared at the back of his head. "Did you just sigh? I definitely heard a sigh."

Darius stepped aside and his flashlight illuminated the path ahead where two lifelike, stone statues dressed in Monk-like cloaks stood. Their hoods enshrouded their heads, leaving only their shadowed jaw lines exposed. Although Mackenzie couldn't see their eyes, they were so lifelike she had the unshakeable feeling she was being watched.

"Are you sure they're not alive?" She glared at him. "And don't sigh again."

Darius didn't, he grabbed her hand and pulled her towards the statues. Mackenzie tried to drag her heels, well she did drag them, but he just tugged her along as if she were a willing participant towards the statues and probable death.

"See?" He poked one of the statues with the end of his flashlight. "Not alive."

If she hadn't heard the tinking noise of metal against stone, she wouldn't have believed it. The two robed statues stood guard, one on each side of the passageway, and each held a metal broadsword, their tips buried in the ground at their feet. The metal swords, even after three thousand years of weathering and age, still held a glint as if freshly forged.

Mackenzie moved closer to one of the statues and noticed a day's growth of stubble on its square jaw line.

"Wow." She ran her hand over the statue-man's chin and the stubble tickled the pads of her fingers. "I've never seen statues this lifelike before."

Darius pulled her past the statue. "Come on, let's get this over with."

They left the two sentries to head deeper into the long, narrow passageway carved into the solid rock. What she had been expecting was something akin to the Hellfire Caves, but this place made the caves back in England look like they had been dug out by children with plastic spoons. Where the Hellfire Caves had rough, shoddy walls hacked out with almost archaic abandon, these walls were smooth and had clearly been carved with precision and care.

They continued on for a few hundred feet until they reached an archway carved into the wall on their right. Darius peered in and Mackenzie crowded next to him. It was a large square room with empty wooden pallets laid out in three neat rows of a dozen pallets each. The room reminded her of a cabin she once stayed in at camp as a child. It left very little room for privacy, but then again, the Phoenicians weren't there for comfort.

They moved on, past half a dozen more rooms similar to the first, carved into both sides of the passageway. After that were storage rooms containing various pots and ceramic vases, and other rooms with tools, ropes, ladders and weapons. There were also a few large, open rooms devoid of anything but pits in the middle, where perhaps fires had once burned and people had gathered to talk, laugh and eat.

It looked like someone had tried to make the space as livable as possible, but the ceilings were low, the air was starting to get musty and Mackenzie couldn't shake that feeling of being trapped.

The sunlight that filtered in at the entrance of the tunnel was a mere pinprick at that point. "I may be pale and avoid the sun like the plague, but I can't imagine living like this."

"They were here for a singular purpose." Darius moved on from the third large common room with a fire pit at its center.

"Then why not just camp outside?"

"Because that would draw attention. They wouldn't risk their mission because they felt a little claustrophobic."

He walked on, his focus farther down the passageway, but Mackenzie couldn't help but examine everything around her, slowing her down.

Then again, Darius wouldn't find the Phoenicians interesting. They were just a more ancient version of him. The only difference was that he was solitary in his mission.

"So..." She peered into another storage room. "What did Markus mean when he said, 'it's good to see you back on missions'?"

Darius didn't answer right away. She expected him not to answer.

When he did speak, he didn't look at her, just kept his focus ahead. "I was banned from all field operations because in the nineteen-seventies I hijacked a plane in an attempt to capture L.G. and almost exposed the Templars to the public."

Their passage was halted by a large, ornate, stone door that blocked them from continuing any farther. Detailed pictographs were carved into the stone. In the upper panel of the door, two winged griffins faced each other. Below that was a lone longship with a single mast and a dozen oars dipped into the water. Displayed on the sail was an image of a double-headed eagle, the same symbol as was on the map.

"Well, if we had any doubts as to whose cave this is..." She looked for a way to open the door. "There's no handle. Bet you wish you had grenades now."

Darius examined the door closer, less fazed by the obstacle than she was.

Mackenzie took a few steps back to look at the engraving as a whole, but as usual ended up distracted by checking out Darius instead. "So, how did you get back on skull duty?"

"L.G. set things into motion not even the Seers could predict." He ran his fingers over the seam of the door, his touch lingering over some indentations more than others.

Well, if he was going to fondle it, she would too.

She stepped up next to him and traced the carved lines of the boat. "How in the hell did you fail to catch L.G. on board a plane?"

"She jumped out."

"And you followed." She crouched and looked lower, for what, she had no idea.

"Yes, but she had an advantage. Not only was it winter, stormy and nighttime, but she jumped without a parachute. Finding her myself was impossible. The naïve part of me hoped she'd remain lost in the woods, but L.G.'s plan was more complex than I could have imagined."

"And where exactly did she land?"

"Impossible to say, but I suspect that's where Allyanora's knack as a Seer came into play. She found L.G.'s skull and put it in the warehouse."

"The same warehouse where Lauren works now?"

Darius nodded.

"Does Allyanora make a habit of storing dangerous

artifacts where they could kill her employees?" If so, Mackenzie was going to have a few words with that woman when this was over.

"The Seers do whatever it takes to gather the pieces needed for their prophecies. It's the Knights' duty to make sure whatever is set in motion doesn't end the world in the process."

"Well, that makes logical sense," she said sarcastically.

"They don't know if interfering helps or hinders the prophecy, because the future they see could already include interference on their part."

"So, you interfering now, that's different?"

"No, it's not, but they operate on the platform of the devil you know. They can also see our futures to an extent." Darius handed her his flashlight and placed his hands flat against the stone door. "The devil Allyanora knew was that L.G. would end the world. So, knowing where her skull was, was better than not knowing. I wasn't informed of that development however."

Darius adjusted his footing and shoved against the door.

"What are you doing?" Mackenzie frowned, he looked ridiculous trying to move stone that had to weigh a few tons. And yet there he was braced against the stone like a gladiator braced for the onslaught. "The Phoenicians built this place to safeguard the world and you think they left the door unlocked?"

He grunted as his footing slipped, but he kept pushing. It was comical until the sound of stone grinding against stone filled the otherwise silent hall. He inched the door back until it was cracked open enough to squeeze through.

"Then again..." Mackenzie shrugged. "Why bother locking a door when no one should be able to find it in the first place?"

She gave him back his flashlight and he slipped through

the narrow doorway.

She hesitated, half-expecting a booby trap to go off. When no sounds of agonizing pain reached her, she followed into the darkened room and walked face first into Darius's back. "Damnit, stop doing that." She rubbed her nose, squeezed around him and lifted her flashlight to illuminate the space. "Don't you think it's..."

That's when glitter and a splash of colors brought her full attention to the walls in this new section of the hallway.

Every inch was ornately etched with all sorts of scenes with images of people, boats, cattle and cargo. They were carved with a precision rivaling pictographs from ancient Egypt.

"Holy moly." The pictures, when viewed one after the other, appeared to tell the story about the journey of the people who came there. The first scene was of people and animals boarding not one ship but many. The next scene was of the ships voyaging across the vast ocean. She moved down the hall and saw a pictorial history of the people reaching the east coast of North America and then making their way across the continent to the Grand Canyon. Then she witnessed the intensive labor and huge manpower they used to carve out the caves she and Darius stood in now.

She stopped and peered around into the shadows her flashlight didn't reach. This was too easy and she couldn't ignore the feeling she was walking headlong into a trap. "Don't you think it's odd they left this unguarded?"

"Yes."

The next scene, after the building of the cave and the tunnels, depicted the Phoenician people carving statues that looked like the ones they passed at the entrance. Next to that was an open archway in the wall and blackness beyond what their flashlights could illuminate. Darius stopped her before she stepped through.

"What? Are there booby traps?"

He shrugged. "If there are, they'll strike me and not you. You can get Finley to finish this if you have to."

"Or better plan, you don't die." She peeked around him, then shoved past and walked into the room first.

It was huge, filled with symmetrical rows of large, rectangular stone chests that reached up to her waist. There were at least twenty in each row and at least twenty rows. She walked up to the nearest chest. There was a single, unreadable word, what she assumed to be Phoenician, etched across the stone lid. Even though she couldn't read it, she perceived its meaning on a bone-chilling level.

"A sarcophagus." She traced the lines of what she presumed were the letters of a name, the only remnant of whoever lived so long ago. She looked at another coffin. The word etched across its surface was different. "They're all sarcophaguses."

"Sarcophagi," Darius said.

"Really? You're going to correct my English?" She blinded him with her flashlight. He didn't flinch or look away. He just had a look on his face she wasn't sure of, except that it looked troubled. Or haunted. "How many years did these people live here and no one knew?"

"The skull isn't here." He backed out of the room and continued on down the hall.

She looked back at the sarcophagi around her and then followed after him. A few yards later another archway intersected the wall, revealing another room filled with more of the eerie stone sarcophagi.

They found three more rooms, all the same size, all containing the same thing.

"There has to be a thousand bodies here," Mackenzie said. "It's humbling, so much death in these chambers."

"Duty always comes with sacrifice."

Another ornate door blocked their path a few more yards down the passageway and Mackenzie couldn't help but look back the way they had come. "What's it like to have such dedication to a cause that you're willing to leave everything behind, journey so far from home?"

"You don't think about it much. You just focus on the hurdles you must overcome."

"Isn't it terrifying?"

"Yes."

"Don't you get lonely?"

"Yes." He looked at her then, his gaze filled with anguish and loss. She was reminded once again how close to the brink he was.

She wanted to close the distance between them and press her lips against his. To let him feel something other than death, loneliness and impending doom.

Her feet moved of their own accord. When she was close enough, Darius wrapped his fingers around her waist as if to hold her in place.

"It's a sacrifice I knowingly make." His hold tightened and his eyes turned cold. "I've learned some things are more important than myself, or my needs, and I've learned to appreciate the distractions I've been able to afford along the way."

So, she was just another distraction in what had to be a long line of distractions. Temporary, fleeting and forgettable.

She didn't want to be just any girl to him, she wanted to be important, remembered. Then again, there was a high possibility she wouldn't survive this. Maybe she was being selfish.

She moved his hand off her hip, unable to stare any longer at his haunted gaze and focused on a large carved picture on the wall behind him.

The picture depicted a table-like altar on a large dais with a man lying atop it. Behind the altar stood a cloaked figure with his hands held above the man.

The scene looked innocent enough until she noticed a red blotch smeared on the dais steps leading up to the altar.

She moved around Darius to inspect the picture more closely and realized the cloaked figure held a dagger poised over the man's chest.

Another picture followed it of the same hooded figure holding a dagger over a different person as two other hooded figures carried away the first man, who now sported a gaping chest wound.

She moved even closer to the wall and to the last scene right before the door. A different man lay on the altar with the cloaked figure holding a dagger over him, and in front of the altar was a line of men and women as if waiting for their turn to die.

CHAPTER 41

"I thought they were the good guys." Her respect for the ancient people turned to horror. "They were monsters."

Darius sounded less moved. "It could have been a rite of passage. The Aztecs did something similar as an offering to their gods."

"Rites of passage don't involve death. Those cloaked guys murdered a thousand of their own people." Every sarcophagus took on a new, darker meaning.

"Most likely not all the bodies were from the same voyage."

"Great, so it was a generational thing. Good to know. Phoenicians, grandfathers of our English alphabet and serial killers of the ancient world. I'm shocked they didn't get along with L.G., or maybe they just didn't want to compete with her."

Darius forced her to face him, filled her vision so she

couldn't look at the pictures anymore. "Stop ranting about the morality of what these people did. They don't matter, the skull does, and we need to find it."

She sniffed. "Why aren't you bothered by this?"

"Life was much harsher in the past than it is now. People went to great lengths to keep secrets, and from what's depicted on these walls, the Phoenicians were willing to make that sacrifice."

He walked up to the stone door carved with the same pictures as the one before. He didn't waste time looking for keyholes, he just pushed against the stone.

When the door cleared the frame, a gust of air rushed past them in a sigh. They stared at each other until the noise and breeze faded.

Mackenzie wasn't sure if she should run or cower. "Well, that was ominous."

"But not deadly." He eased through the narrow opening in the doorway.

Mackenzie frowned at a blue light that trickled into the hall from beyond the door.

Figured. Someone had already been there. Though why shut the doors behind them?

The stone door blocked her view of the room, so for all she knew she was walking straight into an ambush.

She stepped through the door and into a large circular room. It took one delayed second for her brain to register the hundreds of people who stood before her. She flinched backwards and pressed her body into the stone wall next to the door.

It took another second for her to realize the several hundred people were mere statues and they all faced a raised dais in the center of the gathering. The air itself seemed to come alive with a veiled sense of anticipation that was out of place in the ancient room.

"You know that feeling when you stand in the middle of a huge crowd?" She tried to keep her breath steady and reached out for Darius. "The energy of all those bodies moving, talking, existing around you all at once?"

He moved closer to her. "I do."

"Do you have that feeling right now?"

"I feel something." He squeezed her hand and pulled her behind him as they moved through the crowd of stone statues. "But it's most likely coming from whatever energy is emanating from that box."

The statues appeared to be transfixed on a blue light that radiated from a box that sat on top of a stone table on the dais.

Two cloaked stone figures, much like the ones at the entrance to the cave, stood on either side of the table. Both gripped large swords, forged metal gleaming, their tips pointed towards the ground.

The labyrinth of statues they passed may have lacked regal cloaks, but that didn't mean they were any less impressive. There were statues of men and women, none looking older than fifty, and every single statue she could see was different. Some had braids, pony tails, long hair and short. Even their weapons varied, from battle axes to bows and arrows. She saw even more statues on the other side of the dais, which did little to ease the creepy factor.

It was a veritable army standing at attention awaiting orders from their leader.

Mackenzie and Darius reached the bottom of the dais and ascended the half dozen steps to the top. When they reached the last step, she looked around as the hairs on her skin stood on end.

"If one of these statues moves, I swear to any god that's listening, I'll lose it."

"Mackenzie, focus."

She looked away from the sightless gazes and faced the only other interesting thing in the entire room, the mysterious, glowing box.

The luminous box was square and about a foot and a half on all sides. She tried not to focus too much on the table it sat on, but it was hard not to notice the dark brown stain of dried blood that was spread across the otherwise light, pristine stone. It didn't take a genius to conclude that's where all those 'sacrifices' had been made.

"Why is it glowing?" Mackenzie stepped up to the opposite side of the box across from Darius.

Darius set his flashlight aside and touched the lid. She flinched, waiting for a trap of some sort to activate.

"I should have guessed." He let out a faint laugh, though there was no humor in it. "Nothing from this world can stop L.G. from finding the skulls, so the Phoenicians made a box out of something not from this world. It's a material found in meteorites. I've only ever seen small pebbles of it and those had been made into jewelry."

"There's jewelry made out of this stuff?" Mackenzie touched it, surprised the stone wasn't hot, just warm. "I want."

"It was used in ancient Egypt by priests and priestesses to navigate the darkened temples where they performed their rituals, something archeologists call the Dendera Light Bulb. What few pieces remain are in the Knights Templar protective vaults."

"I still want a necklace."

Darius grabbed one side of the lid and Mackenzie grabbed the other and they worked together to lift and set it aside.

The familiar grin of an obsidian skull smiled up at them.

Mackenzie had hoped she'd feel something akin to relief at finding it, instead she felt a disturbing feeling of maniacal glee, an emotion that was all L.G.

Darius grabbed the skull and stuffed it into his backpack.

"If we're lucky, we can get out of here and into the helicopter before the Illuminati find us. In an hour's time, we'll have the emerald, L.G. will be gone and you'll live." He gave her a smile that warmed his eyes and softened his features.

She smiled back, unable to stop herself. But something told her L.G. wouldn't allow her to survive the hour.

Suddenly, Darius lunged for the front of her shirt, pulled her forward and shoved her head down on top of the table. The blade of a long sword swung through the empty air where her head had just been.

"What the—?"

The cloaked statue now sported a pair of very human eyes under his hood. It pulled back its blade, meant to sever heads from bodies, and raised it high in the air.

Darius pushed her away and she almost fell down the steps just as the sword came down swift and hard, clattering against the stone table. Then the other statue turned in her direction and raised its sword.

"Mackenzie." Darius pulled out his gun. "Run!"

CHAPTER 41

Mackenzie scrambled under the table as Darius fired four rounds into the two statues. She stumbled to her feet next to Darius and stopped.

"Darius." She breathed the word and patted his arm. The hundreds of sightless statues that surrounded the dais had turned their heads and were focused on them. "The mannequin apocalypse!"

Darius stiffened. "Statues."

"Same difference." She hurried down the steps with Darius close behind, ignoring the stone gazes as she headed for the door they had entered through.

While the mass of statues merely watched them escape, the two cloak-wearing, sword-wielding statues followed them. Mackenzie and Darius ran through the door and into the dark passageway, the lights from their flashlights bouncing off the walls.

Insta-Prophecy Hotline

"I think I know why everyone was killed." She fought for air between words as they ran past the rooms filled with sarcophagi. "They weren't killed to keep this place a secret, they were killed so they could forever protect it."

The stone door behind them scraped with a loud, crunching screech as the two statues pushed through. Their heavy footfalls reverberated off the walls. She didn't dare look back.

"Then why are only two trying to kill us?"

She had no idea, but was damn glad of it.

She flung herself through the second door, ramming her shoulder against the stone frame in the process. She cried out in pain but kept running.

They gained precious seconds as the two statues pushed open the second door wider so they could pass through.

The fading light of the evening sun filtering through the cave entrance came into view and she could have wept in happiness. Instead she skidded to a halt.

Darius stumbled into her, his focus on the devil they knew, which was behind them. She pointed towards their only exit. "Shoot them."

The robed statues that guarded the entrance drew their swords.

"Go!" He pushed her towards the two guardians and she trusted him enough to sprint forward.

Shots rang out from behind her and one statue jerked back. The bullets pierced his wrists and both his hands and sword fell to the ground. The other statue raised his weapon and his cowl fell back to reveal a lifelike, bearded face and eyes too human to be possible with stone.

"Duck!" Darius shouted.

The statue swung his sword towards her with the swift ease of a seasoned warrior. At the last second she dropped and slid across the stone floor. The blade sliced through the air inches above her head.

Darius shot again. Mackenzie scrambled for the lead rope that dangled over the side of the ledge, clipped it to her harness and did the bravest thing she had ever done. She jumped.

The rope went taught and the clips Darius had helped her place in the rock face held. She landed against the stone wall and she repelled as fast as her protective gloves would allow. A few seconds later a robed, weaponless statue careened past her in a free fall and disintegrated when it hit the ground below.

At least they weren't immortal stone killers.

Darius dropped over the side and rappelled down the wall after her.

"Faster." Darius said when he reached her.

She looked up and regretted it. The three remaining statues were studying the ropes anchored to the wall. Darius swore and she went faster. She only had about fifty feet to go, but it was high enough to break her neck if she fell.

Her line jerked as a statue pulled the rope from its top anchor on the wall.

"Mackenzie." Darius was beneath her now, reaching out.

She grabbed his hand just as the statue dropped her line. Her arm nearly popped out of its socket when Darius's grip stopped her fall. The rope slackened in her harness as her line dropped to the next anchor ten feet below the cave's entrance. With her free hand, she pulled the rope until her line went taught, then let go of Darius a moment before the homicidal statues released his line.

He plunged to the ground as the anchors ripped from their holds overhead.

"Darius!" She rappelled down the rest of the way as fast as she could.

The statues climbed over the edge of the cliff and

crawled down the sheer rock face on their hands and feet like Spiderman.

The second her feet touched the ground, she ripped the rope free of her harness. Darius hobbled over to her, grabbed her hand and they sprinted as best they could towards the campsite.

Mackenzie's lungs burned and her legs ached, but she couldn't slow down. When they reached the camp, it looked different. It was now encompassed by a large dome that glowed faintly in the shadows of the canyon. Darius seemed unconcerned and ran head first into it, so Mackenzie followed. A tingle of electricity swept through her as she passed through the barrier.

"Get that chopper going," Darius bellowed as they rounded the tent and ran for the helicopter just beyond it. But the helicopter was empty.

A man sprung out from behind the tent and slammed Darius to the ground.

Mackenzie skidded to a halt in the gravel, gasping for air. "Darius."

Darius lay motionless as the unknown man pushed himself to his feet.

He was a massive man, but she attacked him anyway with one thought on her mind, protect Darius. Before she could lay a blow, she was yanked backwards by her hair and a foul-smelling cloth was pressed against her nose and mouth.

Darkness fell.

CHAPTER 42

Darius came to with a rush of unspent violence. He wanted to lash out, but years of training kept him still.

He was laying on his side with his hands handcuffed behind his back. The air thrummed with an unnatural energy that had everything inside him clamoring to react.

Mackenzie.

He opened his eyes, tense and ready for a fight even though he knew he would lose. The camp was filled with flesh-and-blood people he didn't recognize. Their focus wasn't on him, but turned outward towards a translucent dome that surrounded the campsite. Outside the dome, the three remaining Phoenician guardian statues stood stationary, watching and waiting.

"What in the bloody hell are you doing?" A baritone voice caught Darius's attention.

A tall and trim man with dirty, blonde hair walked over to

a bulky, balding man who stood at the entrance to the tent. At his feet was Mackenzie, restrained like Darius and still unconscious.

"I told you to drag her over there with them," the blonde man ordered.

Darius sat up, hyperaware of the gun gripped in the balding man's hand.

"Calm yourself, laddie." Finley whispered in his ear. "She's not in harm's way yet."

That wasn't good enough.

As the balding man dragged Mackenzie towards them, Darius tried to get to his feet, but another man guarding them punched him in the gut and shoved him back to the ground.

"I said, calm down, you're going to get us killed before we can fix this." Finley studied their captors.

Darius was more concerned with Mackenzie. The balding man dragged Mackenzie over a rock the size of a horse hoof and Darius gave him the number two spot on his 'people he was going to kill' list, right below the number one spot held by L.G. Man.

"Easy, Darius." Markus leaned around Finley. "Stay your anger."

Darius understood Markus. The former Roman soldier had learned the hard way what unchecked anger could cause. It didn't make it any easier.

The bald man dropped Mackenzie in Darius's lap. The back of her head landed on his thigh, her face turned up towards him. At least there were no bruises suggesting she had been beaten into unconsciousness.

If only Mackenzie were free of L.G. and hidden away at his home in Carmel, she'd be safe.

His home. He never considered that house anything other than a prison, but if Mackenzie were there... He wished he was back in his little safe haven.

"Liam." A man with white hair called over to the bald thug.

With Darius's main concern in his lap, he studied the white-haired man. He had a paunch of a belly that put the quality of his belt to the test and wore light-colored workman shoes that looked like they had never seen a day of work. He stood next to an incomplete circle made up of eleven obsidian skulls. In a gloved hand he held out L.G.'s skull and in the other he held a leather-bound book, which he was reading.

When Liam got near, the white-haired man pointed to a box. Liam went to it, pulled out the final skull and placed it in the circle at the older man's direction. For hundreds of years Darius had fought to keep this very scene from happening. So much blood, sweat and tears had been shed. And on the days when he felt he just couldn't soldier on, it was his duty that had kept him going.

This was his worst case scenario, and it was now playing out before his eyes.

"How did this happen?" Darius felt the weight of his failure bear down on his shoulders.

"They arrived after you went into the cave," Finley said.

"They had an EMP gun, knocked out the helicopter's electronics," the pilot, Titus, added.

"L.G." Darius stared down at Mackenzie, not surprised he had once again played right into the alien's hands.

"You should have killed her at the beginning and ended this." Finley stared at Mackenzie, too, only his expression read more like a man who contemplated how easy it would be to snap her neck.

"No."

"They're a means to an end and sometimes they have to die, you know the rules," Finley said.

"Rules aren't everything."

"Rules protect everyone. If you had followed them instead of whatever vendetta you have against L.G.," Finley snarled the name, "the prophecy wouldn't be coming to pass in front of us."

"Mackenzie is —"

"Dead." Finley cut him off. "She just had the privilege of not knowing it. Which is crueler, Darius, killing her when she least expects it or letting her live long enough to realize there's no hope of survival?"

Darius watched in silence as the white-haired man ordered Liam to adjust the position of a skull.

Had he been cruel in toying with the idea he could save Mackenzie? If so, whom had he been fooling more, her or him?

She looked so peaceful in her slumber. He leaned in as close as he could get. "Mackenzie."

She clenched her eyes tighter and he whispered her name again.

"Shoot them." Mackenzie's head jerked up and slammed into Darius's forehead.

They both swore and Mackenzie fell back into his lap.

He shook his head to clear his vision and looked into her wide eyes.

"We're not dead?" She sat up, slower this time, and looked around. "Oh God."

She spotted the statues outside the see-through barrier and half-kicked, half-crab walked backwards on her elbows with her hands still cuffed behind her back.

"Mackenzie." Darius nudged her with his shoulder, but she scrambled past him and rammed up against the shin of the man guarding them.

"Where do you think you're going?"

"Can't you see we're all gonna die?" She tried to move

around him, but he grabbed her arms, dragged her back to Darius's side and dropped her on the ground.

"Conrad," the guard called out and the white-haired man looked up. "She's awake."

"One second." Conrad looked down at the book in his hand.

"How are we not dead?" Mackenzie couldn't take her eyes off the statues.

"Magic," Markus said.

Mackenzie stared at Markus like he was a ghost. "You were supposed to leave."

Then the color drained from her already pale face and Darius knew she had spotted the skulls. She whispered the last line of the prophecy, "The Phoenicians will bear witness as man makes their final stand." She looked at the statues, then at Darius.

He had never wished the use of his hands more than he did now. He wanted to pull her close and let her know everything was going to be all right, even though he didn't know how it possibly could be.

He tried soothing words instead. "This isn't your fault."

"No? Then whose fault is it?" She yanked at her handcuffs. They rattled, but didn't do much more than that. "I should've listened to the Seer on the phone."

"Please, stop making a fool of yourself." Conrad walked over to them and handed the book and L.G.'s skull to the blonde man, who now wore gloves. Conrad's eyes were cold as he watched Mackenzie like a cat watched a mouse. "I believe my men said you are called L.G. now."

"I'm not L.G., I'm Mackenzie."

"Oh?"

"Yes, you ass." She glared up at him.

"Interesting. I didn't know the host could survive." Conrad crouched in front of her and wrapped a lock of her hair around his finger. "Though your eyes do lack the telling metallic glint."

"Burn in hell, you evil-looking Santa."

Conrad grabbed her chin and held her head in place.

Darius moved to lunge at him, but firm hands held him still.

"I would like to speak to L.G. now."

"And I would like you to die, but we all can't get what we want." She tried to pull free of Conrad's grasp but failed. "We're trying to stop the world from ending, why are you trying to do the opposite?"

"Naïve girl, we want to control it. Destroying it is of no use to us." He let her go and stood. "And the key to that control are these skulls."

"Are you high?"

Conrad retrieved the skull and book and walked back towards the skull circle.

Mackenzie struggled to her feet and the blonde man drew a revolver from behind his back and aimed it at her head.

"Unlike Conrad, I'm not against torturing you." He cocked the hammer with his thumb and redirected his aim to her knee. "So, I suggest you sit down."

Mackenzie flopped onto her backside.

When he seemed satisfied, he holstered his gun and took a seat on one of the crates near the shimmering barrier that kept the Phoenician statues out. He grabbed the glowing emerald that was on top of the crate and tossed it in the air, then caught it. Again and again.

"That was brave, lassie. Stupid, but brave," Finley said under his breath.

Mackenzie watched as Conrad stepped into the circle of obsidian skulls. She let out a quiet whine when he stood in the center and L.G.'s skull in his hand started to glow.

There was nothing Darius could say that would dampen

the blow of watching the prophecy play out before them. He understood the torment of it.

He looked to Finley, Markus and Titus. They all watched in silence as L.G.'s skull brightened until it was almost blinding. Then a single beam of light shot straight up, arched in the air and hit one of the twelve obsidian skulls that made up the circle. When the energy hit that one skull, all the power reached out and connected the skulls in a circle of light, obscuring the man in the middle. The light from the center of the circle diminished, but the first skull that was hit still burned bright. And the process started again.

"It's working, Ed, just like it says." Conrad raised the book to the blonde man.

"How long?" Ed held the emerald on his knee.

"It could take ten minutes? Twenty? It says here the power has to transfer to each of the skulls before the final burst of energy can come forth."

Ed nodded and resumed tossing and catching the emerald.

"This is a nightmare." Markus shifted but made no other move.

"Is there backup?" Darius looked at Finley.

Finley shook his head. "We wanted to keep the group small so we could travel unnoticed. It's just us."

Darius tried to think, they had time. Another beam of light hit another skull, leaving ten to be activated. He examined his surroundings. There were nine Illuminati guards standing around the campsite, armed with semi-automatic rifles, hand guns and knives strapped to their belts.

"Why aren't the statues attacking us?" Darius didn't understand why they were still outside the barrier when he and Mackenzie had gotten through so easily.

"It's a magic force field," Markus said. "The Druids used them when they performed rituals. You two only passed through because the bugger who cast the spell wanted you inside. Who that person is I'm not sure, but if we can kill him, the shield will fall."

And if the shield fell, the statues would storm them and maybe cause enough chaos to assist in stopping the prophecy. If nothing else, they would be three more on their side. That's if the statues didn't kill them first.

Allyanora was right. He never should have continued this mission. He should have acted without emotion and passed the torch on. Finley wouldn't have made the same mistakes. Then again, Finley would have killed Mackenzie outright, averting the prophecy that way.

A third skull in the circle lit up. Nine left.

"You never believed the emerald would work, did you?" Mackenzie's whisper was so soft Darius almost missed it. She wasn't watching the skulls or the statues, but the emerald being tossed in the air over and over again.

"I –" He stopped himself.

Her face was like an open book, it reflected everything she felt and thought. She looked resigned, sad, and more profoundly, her hazel eyes looked dead of anything but the knowledge she was going to die.

"I hoped..." He trailed off again, unsure what to say to make it right.

"How many of L.G.'s victims have you tried to save?"

"All of them."

"How many have you saved?" She looked at him with a gaze that held no fire. She already knew the answer. "I want to hear it from you. No lies, just a straight fraking answer."

"None."

Mackenzie flinched.

"But that's b-because –" he stammered over his words as he tried to make it sound better than it was. "That's because there was nothing left to save by the time I got to them.

You're different. It's different this time. The emerald will work."

He was still confident. They were just going to have to do what they had done with the Pope. It was less than pleasant, but it had worked.

"So all your talk of a life after this..." She went silent and stared at the skulls.

Darius expected her anger, for her to curse him, yell at him for his continued omissions. He expected violence. He wanted her violence because he knew how to deal with that. He wanted her to be hurt because that meant she cared about him enough to feel betrayed.

Then it hit him. He needed to know he meant something to this woman with red hair and a penchant for getting into trouble without even trying. He needed her to feel as much for him as he felt for her.

"You lied." Her voice lacked any emotion and his heart ached.

"Yes."

She nodded. "Thank you."

"What?"

"You let me have hope, even if I was a lost cause. Thank you."

Darius didn't want her thanks, he wanted her ire, her fire. "Macken–"

She cut him off. "Can't we do something to stop the skulls? To destroy them?"

"We can't destroy them. Nothing on this planet can destroy them, you know that."

"As to stopping them, lassie," Finley cut in, "those beams of light shooting from L.G.'s skulls are pure energy. They'll kill anyone who gets too close, unless by the looks of it, you're holding L.G.'s skull."

Another skull alit with energy in the periphery of Darius's

vision. Eight skulls left, but he couldn't feel any urgency while he watched Mackenzie.

She got up on her knees and faced him. Her features were soft, but lacked the passion he had grown accustomed to.

"Hey." Ed yelled at her but was ignored. "Sit Down."

"I want you to know..." She looked into Darius's eyes, the fear in her gaze palpable. "No matter what happens next, I want you to know that I tried. I tried."

His heart started to race and a shiver of fear ran down his spine when her eyes filled with tears.

"Don't give up. Fight it," he ordered her.

She leaned closer as a tear ran down her cheek.

"What did I tell you?" Ed said even louder now.

"I know it's selfish and cruel, but I want you to know... I love you." Then she kissed him and he just sat there like a dumb ox.

She loved him.

He wanted to sweep her in his arms and laugh, he wanted to rip her clothes off and satiate both their needs. Most of all, he burned with a need to say the words back, words he had never spoken to anyone, not even to his twin brother in his long, endless life.

She broke the kiss and pressed her forehead against his. "One."

CHAPTER 43

Darius's joy turned to dread as Ed yanked Mackenzie away from him and drew his gun with a look in his eye that said he was going to use it.

"Wait," Darius said.

"Ed, I want her alive." Conrad yelled over the hum of the energy.

Mackenzie's hazel eyes glinted metallic in the setting sun just as Ed turned her towards the barrel of his gun.

"Interesting," L.G. said, unperturbed by the weapon in her face.

"Mackenzie!" Darius couldn't keep the desperation out of his voice. He couldn't lose her, not now. Not ever.

"Darius, stay yourself." Finley barked out the order.

"You." L.G. studied Ed's face. "You look familiar. Did I kill one of your ancestors?"

The muscle in Ed's jaw bulged. "No, but you nearly killed

me, or don't you remember?"

"I have lost interest in this conversation." L.G. shrugged and focused on the skulls. "I am, however, very interested in that."

"You don't remember?" Ed lowered his gun. "At the Hindenburg?"

"Wait, you are one of the men I met with." L.G. smiled. "You have aged well."

"Some of us don't grow old like the pathetic masses." He put his gun away.

L.G. looked at Darius. "You have competition it would seem."

"Shite," Finely said and Darius agreed. But immortal Illuminati henchmen were something he didn't have time to contemplate right then.

"Now, be a good lad and take these shackles off me." L.G. turned her back to Ed and lifted her handcuffed hands. "I weary of this."

"Like hell." Ed snorted.

"Do it," Conrad said. "She can't do anything now."

"I won't."

"I order you."

L.G. chuckled. "It would seem you are still taking orders like a good foot soldier."

Ed grimaced, pulled a set of keys from his back pocket and undid her cuffs. Before he let her go, he whispered something in her ear.

"We need to do something," Markus said.

"And get the emerald to Mackenzie." Darius watched L.G. rub her wrists as she observed the statues. Then she looked at the circle of skulls.

"Now, what are you doing there?" The playful tone L.G. had with Ed was gone as she confronted Conrad.

She stepped up to the circle of skulls and stood next to

Liam.

"Do I need to explain it to you? Has it been that long?" Conrad motioned with the leather-bound book at the circle of skulls that surrounded him.

She stared at him until he shifted on his feet. "Only I know how to call my people. How is it that you know?"

Conrad didn't answer and as brave as Darius thought the man was at that moment, he wanted Conrad to talk.

Without warning, L.G. grabbed Liam, yanked him forward and shoved him into the glowing ring of skulls. He let out a blood-curdling scream and then disintegrated before everyone's eyes.

"New plan, laddies." Finley shifted where he sat. "We need the statues. It's our only chance."

"If they don't kill us." Darius hoped for some sign Mackenzie was still alive.

"Regardless." Finley looked around at the Illuminati soldiers. "We need to find the man who cast the shield.

"And if it's Conrad?" Markus asked.

"Then we die."

Ed pulled out his gun and ran up to L.G., but she ripped it out of his hands.

"Now, how?" She tossed the weapon into the glowing ring of obsidian skulls and it disintegrated as well.

"The Phoenicians," Conrad blurted out before she threw Ed in the ring, too.

"Conrad." Ed snapped as he stumbled away from L.G.

"She can't stop it at this point."

"Darius, we should —" Finley started to speak but Darius shushed him.

"A Phoenician was visiting Hattusa when you gathered your skulls. He watched as you called your 'gods.'" As Conrad spoke, Ed put more distance between L.G. and him and almost stepped on Titus as he backed up. "He managed to sneak back to his people and told his uncle what had happened. His uncle thought it wise to steal the skulls."

"That does not answer my question as to how you know this," L.G. said.

"He wrote a journal detailing everything he could remember. A journal he hid when a lone woman destroyed ship after Phoenician ship looking for the skulls his uncle had stolen."

"Phoenicians." L.G. cursed the name. "So, instead of me calling my people, you would call them for me? That is... confusing."

"We want to negotiate with your people."

"What can you negotiate with?"

"We'll give you humans for your technology. A fair trade."

L.G. laughed. It wasn't a false laugh either, this one came from the gut, lit up her face and reverberated through the air. "What makes you think we will waste our time negotiating with you? Even if you wanted to, even if you tried to stop us with the paltry weapons your governments have, you would not succeed. However, the amusement you would give us for thinking you had any power whatsoever might actually spare you alone from death."

"We studied your skulls and studied the journal. If you refuse to negotiate, we now know how to manipulate the power of your skulls and use it as a weapon against your ships."

That cut off L.G.'s amusement. "You have a theory. You will fail."

"We might or we might not. The people who figured out this theory know about these things. I'd stake the safety of this planet on it."

L.G. just stood there, contemplating.

Finley whispered to Darius, "Let's hope L.G.'s people are

no longer around after three thousand years."

The one other man who knew L.G. as well as Darius had given Darius a warning a few short years before his death when Darius had voiced the same concern. "Kingdoms span tens of thousands of years outside of our planet," Darius repeated what Jonathan had told him years ago.

Darius was about to find out the truth of those words, to see if L.G.'s people would come. Or would it be someone else? Would they be worse or better? Either way, whoever came, his world wouldn't be prepared to face them. It would be like bringing mountain lions to penned sheep.

Finley and Markus whispered to each other as the skulls lit one by one until one skull remained. Suddenly, Markus shot to his feet and made a dash for Ed. Finley followed.

There were shouts and gun shots. L.G. and Ed ducked and Finley and Markus fell. Darius turned and saw Titus take on the guard as other Illuminati men rushed him. Darius jumped to his feet and ran for L.G., not sure what he would do once he reached her.

"She called me to the surface," L.G. said when he got close, her gaze riveted on the last skull yet to be lit. "I have never had that happen before. I will let her live long enough to see her planet vanish from her sight when I finally leave."

"It's happening!" Conrad yelled, oblivious to the chaos erupting outside the skull ring.

L.G.'s skull in the center brightened like before. A tendril of light reached out and connected with the final skull.

They had lost.

L.G. stumbled, her hand went to her temple. Her head shot up and the metallic glint was gone.

"Mackenzie?"

She dove head first into the circle that had incinerated Liam.

"No!"

She was engulfed in pure white energy. Her body convulsed on the ground and her foot and fist collided into two of the skulls, knocking them free of the circle and deactivating their power. They skittered across the ground, one to the feet of a cloaked statue outside the barrier and the other to a spot a dozen feet away from Darius.

Mackenzie cried out and rolled free of the circle, clutching her head.

"Darius!" Titus threw a set of handcuff keys at him and Darius caught them behind his back.

He freed his hands as the energy from the obsidian skulls began to fluctuate. He rushed to Mackenzie's side as she lay curled up on the ground.

Mackenzie let out another anguished cry, her eyes closed tight against the war that no doubt waged inside her.

She sat up suddenly and opened her eyes. They glinted in the light.

No, not Mackenzie, L.G.

"What did she do?" L.G. looked up at Darius with something akin to shock.

He knew then that Mackenzie had taken L.G. by surprise.

He looked over at the circle. The light in the center was still growing brighter and he couldn't believe Mackenzie's sacrifice had been in vain.

Then Conrad started to scream in agony.

"No." L.G. glanced around and then dashed for the skull that lay a few yards away from Darius.

Darius grabbed her arm and pulled her back. L.G. jabbed at his throat, but this time he expected the attack and blocked.

With her other hand she swung around in a wide arc, cupped her palm and boxed his ear, perforating his eardrum.

Pain shocked his system and a high-pitched ringing filled what remained of his hearing.

L.G. lashed out again and cuffed him under the eye. He grabbed her wrist, but her other hand landed a crushing blow to his throat.

Air refused to move into or out of his lungs. L.G. moved closer, using her slight size and speed against him. All he could do was defend himself and struggle to breathe.

Her movements were swift and wild. Gone was the calculated, even playful L.G., and in her place was a crazed animal. With wide-eyed panic she looked over Darius's shoulder to the dislodged skull that had rolled to a stop nearby and then glanced at the circle of energy where Conrad screamed at the top of his lungs.

Her expression was something similar to what he had seen at the antique store, but this time it was ten times stronger.

She spun around and with a strategically placed roundhouse kick brought Darius to his knees, and then ran to the skull.

Finley shouted something, but Darius couldn't hear him.

A towering man stepped in L.G.'s path and without hesitation she leveled him with a jab to his throat and a kick to his knee. Then she snapped his head to the side with a heel to his face.

She grabbed the skull and dashed back to the circle. Without touching the ring of energy, she rolled the skull into the circle, then waited, wringing her hands as she watched.

Conrad continued to scream and the perfect dome of energy the circle of skulls had created warbled and rippled.

"No. No. No," L.G. said. "Come on, even out."

Darius snuck up from behind and grabbed her. She turned around in his grasp.

"One's still missing." She yelled the words. "Tell me, where it is?"

Conrad's screams faded away, but the circle's power

didn't diminish, it continued to grow.

L.G. spun around, searching wild eyed. When she turned to the stone statues she stilled. "No."

She pulled out a semi-automatic pistol from behind her back, a weapon she must have swiped from the man she took down.

Darius cursed, in the chaos he missed the telltale bulge.

She shot him before he could grab his weapon. Her aim was precise and the bullet severed his spine. His lower body went numb and he collapsed to the ground. He was conscious, but immobile.

L.G. ran but stopped just inside the safety of the barrier.

"Pelagios." She spat the word and raised her gun at the hoodless statue that held the skull.

She fired off four rounds, but the bullets did little damage. The statue she called Pelagios didn't even react to the attack, but the other two raised their swords in preparation to fight.

Ed charged L.G. as Finley chased after him.

L.G. didn't even turn her head. She just rotated her arm and shot Ed in the shoulder, propelling him backwards to the ground. The slide locked back on the pistol, the magazine empty.

She threw it at Pelagios and sprinted forward through the barrier.

One statue sliced the gun in half mid-air, the other swung for L.G.

"No!" Darius dragged his body away from the skull circle and towards L.G., his healing ability slow in repairing the damage done to his spine.

L.G. ducked underneath the sword and lunged for the skull. The two statues raised their swords again and flanked her as Pelagios lured her further from the barrier.

"Mackenzie!" Darius's legs twitched but he still couldn't

do anything other than watch as a sword arced through the air towards the love of his life.

The fluctuating energy created by the circle grew brighter. The air hummed with unspent electricity as the light became blinding.

Darius dragged himself forward and yelled for Mackenzie again, but his words were drowned out when the center of the circle exploded outwards, hurtling him across the rocky ground.

CHAPTER 44

If this was death, Mackenzie thought, then holy crap, she made the wrong decision.

Death was supposed to be peaceful, quiet and, most importantly, painless. But she felt like someone had strapped her in an electric chair and flipped the switch. Twice.

"Mackenzie." The familiar British accent reached past the pounding in her head and snapped her out of whatever rant she was about to spiral into about how much death sucked.

Darius.

He shouldn't be here with her. He should still be on Earth, happy the world had been saved.

Against her better judgment she opened her eyes and the first thing she saw was the sun, or lack thereof, since it had already set, casting long shadows in its dimming light. Her attention drifted to Darius. His face was shielded from her, but he hugged her so tightly she took a moment to revel in the very real, very alive feeling of it.

She lived.

"What happened?" She intended to ask a different question, in fact she had many questions, but those two simple words beat out the rest.

Darius's grip tightened around her to the point she groaned in protest. He pulled back enough so she could look him in the eyes. The tragedy that was written there made her wish she really had died.

"I failed, didn't I?" Her foolish thought that she could outsmart a three-thousand-year-old alien was laughable now. She deserved the aches and pains as penance and prepared herself for the inevitable. L.G. would kill her for sure, any minute now.

She searched inside herself for that constant growing presence of the alien entity and frowned when she found nothing.

"Darius, wh—"

Darius silenced her with a bone-crunching hug, pushing the air from her lungs and warming her with its intensity. It took her a second for her poor abused senses to come online enough to put her arms around him and hug him back. She thought she would never get a chance to touch him again and if death was imminent, she wasn't going to miss it.

She just wished they were alone, in a bedroom, with a lot less clothes on. Not outside, under the setting sun, surrounded by three stone statues with those impossible human eyes.

"Darius, the statues." She tensed.

"It's okay, but we need to find the emerald." Darius stood, picked her up and cradled her whole body in his arms.

"Darius, you might want to see this," Markus called out to him.

Darius looked around the chaos of the campsite. He carried Mackenzie towards where the tent had been when Ed was playing with the emerald like it was some sort of baseball. At least she thought that's where it had been. It was hard to tell with the large tent tossed on its side, thirty feet from where it had been.

"It has to be here." Darius looked around at the rubble.

Everything in the camp had been destroyed and scattered like an F-5 tornado had roared through the place. Even the helicopter in the distance was on its side. Mackenzie tried not to look at the handful of scattered, lifeless bodies of the Illuminati men. They too looked like they had been tossed about by some unseen force, but what had killed them was obvious. Most had bullet holes in their chests and two of the bodies were missing their heads.

"What the hell happened?" She looked around at the chaos, unsure what to make of it all. Had the world ended while she was unconscious?

"You did something incredibly stupid. Again." Darius tightened his grip around her as she attempted to stand.

He carried her over to where three men were handcuffed and sitting on the ground. Titus stood guard, gun in hand and blood smeared across his forehead. She couldn't miss Ed, who sat disdainfully between his two lackeys.

Darius set Mackenzie on her feet, then grabbed Ed by the shirt and yanked him off the ground. "Where is it?"

"Where's what?" Ed tried to be defiant but failed when all he could do was squint through half-swollen-shut black eyes.

"The emerald."

Mackenzie searched inside herself again for L.G. and still found nothing. "Darius. I don't think —"

"Where the bloody hell is it?" He punched Ed's injured shoulder.

"I don't know," Ed cried out in pain.

"Darius, stop." Mackenzie tensed when the hoodless,

robed statue approached her.

Her first instinct was to run, but she held her ground. His brown eyes looked at her in a way only a human, not a stone statue, could. In one hand he held an obsidian skull and resting in the palm of his other hand was a chunk of midnight-black glass the size of a small, deformed coffee mug.

He held it out to her.

"Darius." She slapped at his arm.

Darius dropped Ed and looked at Mackenzie. "You see the emerald?"

"Damnit, man." Finley stormed up to Darius. "Stop and think for one bloody second."

Mackenzie took the offered piece of glass from the statue. It took a second for it to dawn on her she was holding what looked like a section of jaw from an obsidian skull.

The statue held up his obsidian skull and she looked from it to the piece in her hands. Then she understood what the statue was trying to tell her.

"If you think for one second, Finley, that I'll let her die –"

Mackenzie slapped her hand over Darius's mouth and held up the obsidian jaw in front of his eyes. "Look at what Finley wants you to see before you rip him a new one."

Much like she had, his face showed confusion, then uncertainty, then it was as if a light bulb switched on.

Darius took the piece of obsidian from her hand and examined it.

Mackenzie couldn't quite believe it. "She's gone."

"You sure?" Finley appraised her and she understood his concern.

She searched again and tried to find that oppressive weight of another consciousness pressing down on her soul. She tried to find it three times, afraid to believe that she might have won. When she looked for the fifth time and felt no remnant of anyone other than herself in her mind, she let out a puff of air, dazed. "She's gone."

She had done the impossible, she beat L.G. Man.

Darius dropped the skull piece and grabbed her.

"You." He kissed her. "Brilliant, stupid, violent, brilliant, you."

"Thank you?" Mackenzie let out a shocked squeak when he kissed her again. She wanted to get lost in his touch, but she couldn't, not yet. "Wait."

Darius pulled away, but the look in his eyes said she better hurry up.

"Did we stop the prophecy?"

"Aye," Finley answered. "The power collapsed in on itself before it sent out its beacon to L.G.'s people. The question, I wonder, is how you survived?"

Mackenzie reached for her left wrist and looked down. The ugly, silver cuneiform bracelet was gone. "The bracelet. I remembered Darius telling me it had protected L.G. from getting electrocuted at the antique store. So, I just hoped it would protect me long enough in the circle to do what I needed to do."

"Which was?"

Mackenzie turned to where she last remembered the skull circle, which was now nothing more than an open area of charred ground.

"Darius explained that L.G.'s possession was like a computer virus. Watching her power-up the skulls reminded me of a time when I fried the motherboard on my laptop a few years back. I was running too many high-powered programs and my computer didn't have enough processors to keep it from overheating. I saw L.G.'s skull create all that energy and then push it off on the smaller skulls. She needed them to share the burden. I thought if I could eliminate some of the skulls from the circle, maybe I could overheat L.G.'s skull long enough to stop the prophecy. I didn't expect..."

"That her own power would destroy her," Markus finished.

"Nothing on this planet could destroy the skulls." Darius hugged her close. "But L.G. wasn't from this planet."

Mackenzie still couldn't quite believe what had happened.

"I'll get the chopper up and running." Titus strode towards the overturned helicopter.

Mackenzie leaned into Darius. "He can see it's tipped over on its side, right?"

"Their helicopter," Markus kicked Ed, "is around the bend."

"So, it's over?" She eyed the statue and wondered why they weren't on a beheading spree.

"Yes, it's over." Darius kissed her temple. "We'll bring in a team to clean up this mess and determine if the cave has any more artifacts we need to be aware of."

The robed statue gave her a stiff nod as if he agreed with the statement and walked away. The two other statues joined him as they trekked back to the cliff wall and their cave above.

"I guess the mannequin apocalypse will have to wait for another day." Mackenzie smiled.

"Pardon, mannequin apocalypse?" Finley looked slightly befuddled.

Darius sighed. "Don't ask."

"You know, the one where all the mannequins of the world come to life and kill everybody." Mackenzie didn't miss Finley's eye roll before he walked off mumbling under his breath.

Mackenzie and Darius stood together for a long while. Markus took the three captives to the helicopter and Finley salvaged equipment from the rubble.

The shadows grew thicker as the last tendrils of the sun's rays disappeared over the horizon.

It was over.

Darius seemed happy enough, too. The sadness that seemed to linger over him was replaced with something... lighter. Of course, that could have been from the rush of having survived a near-death experience.

Still, she didn't feel like celebrating. Everything that tied him to her was now gone.

Darius kissed the top of her head before he turned her to face him.

"Come on, let's get you home."

She tried to put on a smile and pretend those words didn't hurt so much. It would have helped if he didn't sound so damn happy about returning her to her normal, homeless and jobless life.

CHAPTER 45

Mackenzie sat ramrod straight at the kitchen table, her gaze glued to the clock that hung on the wall.

Darius had taken her home all right, to his home. Of course, he didn't tell her he was taking her to his home until after they landed at a private airstrip in Carmel, California.

"Relax, Mackenzie." He offered her a glass of wine.

"They're late."

"They'll get here when they get here."

Mackenzie drained the glass and held it out to him. "Another."

Darius didn't pour her another. "You don't have to do this, you know. Being what I am –"

"Way too serious all the time?"

"No."

"Domineering and controlling?"

"No."

Insta-Prophecy Hotline

"Someone with a He-Man complex who must always be obeyed? Or. Darius. Gets. Angry."

"Mackenzie."

She smiled, but she felt the edge in his voice. "What you are is a Templar Knight who protects the world from the apocalypse, one prophecy at a time."

"What I do is dangerous."

"Hold on... It's dangerous? I had no idea."

"You're going to drive me insane for the rest of my days, aren't you?"

"You're figuring this out now?"

"I love you." His words warmed her heart.

They had known each other for only a few weeks and what she had decided to do was far more significant than even marriage. She was risking eternity for a chance to be with this man, who looked at her as if she were the world.

She leaned forward and kissed him. She didn't deepen it, but let the moment linger on their lips. "I love you."

The doorbell rang and Mackenzie jumped.

Darius pressed his forehead against hers. "They're here."

"Let's do this."

Her nerves returned with a vengeance as Darius opened the door.

Finley, and only Finley, stood from a coffee cup in the other. He shoved the box at Darius.

"Mackenzie." He nodded and strode into the house. "How are ye this fine afternoon?"

"Wondering where Allyanora and Bastian are."

"Couldn't make it I'm afraid, they've been delayed in London. Allyanora sent that for ye, however." He motioned to the box Darius now held.

It was hard to keep the disappointment at bay. She'd been stressed over her decision to become a Templar Knight for days, a week even, and just wanted to get it over with already.

"The Grand Master wasn't happy with our request to allow a woman into the Order." Finley gave her an appraising glance.

"And I care why?" She silently dared him to say something sexist.

"You're very lucky."

"Am I?" Oh, he was so close to a tirade.

"I wasn't talking to you, lassie, I was talking to him." Finley motioned at Darius.

"Oh, well." She wrapped her arm around Darius's waist. "I couldn't agree more. He's such a lucky bastard."

Darius muttered to himself and wandered into the living room. He pulled a knife from the sheath strapped to his ankle and sliced open the box. He pulled out a DVD and a plastic water bottle and placed them on the coffee table.

Mackenzie felt a weird sense of déjà vu.

"Shouldn't you be at the cave in the Grand Canyon?" she asked Finley as Darius put the DVD in the player and turned on the television.

"I have a team there who has the area locked down. Your friend, Lauren, is helping to catalogue all the artifacts. She's an interesting lassie."

"Have you found anything?"

"Nothing to warrant a thousand statues standing guard. We still don't know why only four gave chase when you stole their skull, but it does makes me wonder."

Judging by his pensive expression, whatever he wondered was probably something along the lines of an apocalypse.

And after she became a Templar Knight, that would be right up her alley.

"Sit." Darius motioned to the couch and Mackenzie obeyed.

He joined her and hit play on the remote, ending the

conversation and her numerous questions. She couldn't be miffed at his abruptness, he did say he had plans for them later. So did she, naked, whipped cream plans.

The screen lit up with a bright, cheery face of a woman whose black, curly hair ran wild in a messy bun atop her head.

"Cheers, everyone." Allyanora smiled from the television screen. "I'm sure Finley told you we're stuck in London. As it turns out, putting hair removal gel in the shampoo bottles of narcissistic Russian mobsters doesn't go over well with said mobsters. Go figure. Anywho, today isn't about me, it's about you, Mackenzie, and your initiation into the Order of the Knights Templar."

"You can make people Immortal from a DVD?" Mackenzie asked Darius, skeptical of the crazy-eyed stare she was getting from the Seer.

"Don't be ridiculous." Allyanora motioned towards the coffee table. "I intend to turn you immortal with that water bottle. The video is just for your benefit and wonder."

The water bottle was battered and dirty, like an entire soccer team had kicked it around for practice. "She's joking right?"

"Will gargling some eye of newt make you feel better?" Allyanora huffed. "It won't have anything to do with you becoming a Knight, but Finley can whip something up if you're unsatisfied with my finesse."

Allyanora pinned Mackenzie with a haughty stare from the TV, which was fine until Mackenzie shifted and Allyanora's gaze followed her with impossible accuracy.

"Can she see me?" Mackenzie hated to ask the question, it sounded stupid even to her.

"Of course I can't. This is a pre-recorded DVD." Allyanora tapped her temple. "Seer, remember?"

"Cool."

Allyanora shrugged. "It has its moments. Anyway, back to business. Please pick up the water bottle." She waited long enough for Mackenzie to tentatively pick it up. "Good, all you need to do now is say the oath, drink the water and BAM, you're an immortal Templar Knight."

Mackenzie frowned at the water in her hand. It seemed clean enough, but the filthy bottle had previously been opened. "Is it sanitary?"

Again, Allyanora huffed. "Have you ever climbed to Shamballa?"

"No."

"If you had, you'd understand the water bottle's condition. Moving on."

"You're forgetting something," Bastian, who sounded identical to Darius, said off camera.

"Oh, right. Darius would you be a dear and make me some tea? I'm parched."

He didn't move.

"Darius?"

"You're on TV."

"And you're a bit slow. Tea. Please." When Darius still didn't move, Allyanora admired her fingernails and mused, "I can sit here all day if needed."

"Darius, get the blasted tea." His brother's voice snapped over the speakers.

"This is preposterous." Darius motioned to Finley and they left Mackenzie alone in the living room.

"Okay," Allyanora continued after a beat of silence. "Here's the skinny. Once you drink the water, there's no going back. Do you understand?"

"Yes."

"This isn't some happily ever after I'm offering you. You will watch the normal people you care for, age and die. You'll live to see countries rise and fall, maybe even your own.

You'll witness triumphs and tragedies. You'll be like a ghost in your own world. Do you understand?"

When put that way, Mackenzie's future didn't sound so appealing. Still, she found herself nodding when she remembered Darius would be by her side.

"Good. Lastly, and this deals primarily with Darius, in the near future you'll find yourselves in Las Vegas. Don't you even think about eloping without my hubby and me in attendance. If you do, I'll not be responsible for my actions. Do you understand?"

The crazed look in the woman's eyes kept Mackenzie from scoffing off the threat as a joke. "Yes?"

"Oh, he's about to return. He's too lazy to make me tea, decided to pour me a glass of wine instead. Feel free to drink it when we're done. Now act like I just revealed something juicy and embarrassing about him and giggle." As Darius walked back into the room, Allyanora started to laugh and said, "I have so many more stories to tell you about our Darius."

Mackenzie had to give Darius credit, he didn't look the least bit fazed as he reclaimed his seat next to her and set a wine glass on the coffee table.

"All right now, Mackenzie, uncap the water bottle."

Mackenzie did as she was told. Darius rested a comforting hand on her knee.

"Repeat after me. I, state your name."

"I, Mackenzie."

"Do solemnly swear to abide by the Templar code, which in its basic principle is to prevent the fall of humanity at any cost and to protect the world from itself, if need be. Should I break the code and the laws by which we must abide, I forfeit my honor, my life and my soul."

Mackenzie repeated the words.

"Now, drink the water."

She prayed the water wouldn't give her dysentery and took a swig. The moment it hit her tongue, it sparked a thirst in her that made her chug the rest to the last drop. When she finished, she found Darius, Finley and Allyanora staring at her like they were all waiting for something to happen.

Nothing did.

"Congratulations." Allyanora broke the silence first. "It's official, you can now be stabbed repeatedly and heal shortly thereafter."

"That's it?" She looked to Darius.

"Yup," Allyanora answered for him. "The words are just a formality. They serve as a 'speak now or forever hold your peace' kind of thing."

"Huh." Mackenzie took stock of herself. Nothing seemed different. Maybe she felt a little rejuvenated, but nothing that bespoke of immortality.

"Wanna stab yourself and see if it worked?" Allyanora looked far too excited at the idea, then looked disappointed when Mackenzie scowled.

"Oh, I almost forgot. We recovered the money L.G. received for the stolen diamonds from the safe inside the house Darius blew up. It's been deposited into a Swiss bank account for you. You'll find the particulars in your email. Don't worry, the insurance company has already covered the jewelry store for the loss."

"I thought we were the good guys."

"I prefer the term, 'chaotic neutral.' Besides the insurance company is a subsidiary of the Illuminati." She mimicked her brain exploding with her hands. "Mind blown, right?"

Allyanora then reached down and lifted a small, black plastic box with a large, red button on it. "Transmission over. Your DVD will self-destruct in three, two, one."

Allyanora pressed the button and the screen went black. The DVD player popped and sizzled, and a small tendril of smoke rose out of it.

"Can she do that?" Mackenzie wasn't sure whether to be impressed or terrified.

"I think she just did." Darius sat back on the sofa, unbothered by the smoking DVD player.

"Right. I'll leave you two to it," Finley said and walked to the door.

Mackenzie heard the door open and then something drop on the wood floor a few moments later.

"By the way, I left a wee box of grenades on the floor here. Welcome to the team, lassie." Finley shut the door behind him and left.

Mackenzie smiled at Darius as he let out a beleaguered sigh. "Dear Lord, what has he done?"

She swung a leg over his lap and straddled his hips. She couldn't help but smile as she thought of the surprise she had in store for him. "What's wrong with grenades?"

"You're dangerous enough without explosives."

"Just wait until I learn how to shoot a gun."

"I shudder at the thought."

"You make it sound like I'll use you for target practice. I would never hurt you."

"Never is a long time for us."

"And don't you forget it." She reached between the sofa cushions and brushed up against the cool metal of her surprise.

It was really a long time coming.

"What are you doing?" Darius quirked a brow when she yanked her hand out and hid her surprise behind her back.

"Nothing?" Feigning innocence was not her strong suit.

He didn't believe her, but that was fine. She leaned in and kissed him. His hands trailed to her hips and squeezed.

"What are you hiding, Mackenzie?" He reached behind her and she shimmied free of his grip.

"Uh, uh. You're not calling the shots today." She pulled her hand out from behind her back and dangled a pair of his police-grade handcuffs in front of him. "It's my turn."

EPILOGUE
SOMEWHERE IN LONDON

Allyanora stood on the roof of an office building and giggled as she held the black box with the red button. She had put everything on hold for this moment when she would 'see' her soon-to-be sister-in-law finish the video.

Bastian said she was crazy to actually set tiny explosives to detonate at the press of a big red button, but she loved clichés.

Bastian wrapped his arms around her from behind. "You realize you risked getting shot at up here –"

"So worth it."

"– just to mess with my brother's wife."

"Wife-to-be." She pocketed the transmitter. "Besides, a girl's gotta have some fun, and what better way than to make Mackenzie think I can magically blow stuff up? It's so much more epic than the reality that I merely had their DVD player rigged to crackle and spew smoke." Allyanora turned around in his arms, kissed him and then froze.

The tendrils of a prophecy swept through her in a flash of light and a clap of thunder. When the vision subsided, she kissed her husband again. "Come along, love, we need to see a girl in Piccadilly Circus about an apocalyptic poker game."

This story might be done,

but the series has just begun.

Continue reading for the next prophecy in

book two of the Insta-Prophecy Series,

INSTA-PROPHECY OF THE NINTH

INSTA-PROPHECY OF THE NINTH

The Ninth will march, the North will fall.

And they won't need to build a wall.

If that happens, worse will come.

The world you know will be undone.

Five thousand strong or millions more.

What will change in days of yore?

Know the past is not in stone.

So, what future will you condone?

The exact origins of the author B.V. Kingsley are shrouded in mystery. Legend has it she was born in Southern California but grew up in the haunting mists that envelope the Pacific Northwest.

What's known for certain is that she has made it back to her native land of Southern California and often adventures to such exotic places as England, Scotland, South Africa and Central Wisconsin, and writes about many more.

Check out her website and her social media to learn more about the world of Insta-Prophecy Hotline:

> Website: www.BVKingsley.com
> Facebook: /BVKingsley
> Twitter: @BVKingsley

Made in the USA
San Bernardino, CA
12 February 2017